The Night-Watchman's Friend

MARY FITT

With an introduction by Curtis Evans

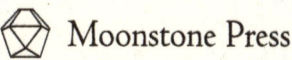 Moonstone Press

This edition published in 2023 by Moonstone Press
www.moonstonepress.co.uk

Introduction © 2023 Curtis Evans

Originally published in 1953 by Macdonald & Co, London.

The Night-Watchman's Friend © the Estate of
Kathleen Freeman, writing as Mary Fitt

The right of Kathleen Freeman to be identified as author of this work has been
asserted in accordance with the Copyright, Designs and Patents Act 1988

ISBN 978-1-899000-64-7
EISBN 978-1-899000-65-4

A CIP catalogue record for this book is available from the British Library

Text designed and typeset by Tetragon, London
Cover illustration by Jason Anscomb
Printed and bound in Great Britain by Clays Ltd, Elcograf S.p.A.

Contents

Introduction   7
About the Author   11

THE NIGHT-WATCHMAN'S FRIEND   19

INTRODUCTION

Kathleen Freeman's twenty-first Mary Fitt mystery, *The Night-Watchman's Friend*, which the author published in 1953, had its inception, rather uniquely, in a much-lauded radio play for the Welsh Home Service of the BBC, broadcast in the winter of 1951 under the title *The Case of the Night-Watchman's Friend*. In the spring of 1952, the play was picked up for broadcast by the BBC, for airing on its Light Programme. At the time the Welsh newspaper the *Cardiff Western Mail* noted proudly and patriotically that only rarely did the Light Programme take "a serial from any of the regions, so this is an honour for Wales". For his part, the radio critic at the *Manchester Guardian* praised the play as a blow against Britain's so-called "received pronunciation", that is, the posh "BBC accent" associated with the public school-educated class of southern England, which the Beeb deemed "proper" speech. The *Guardian*'s critic pointedly observed that the Welsh Region's production "stands out for its quality both of writing and production" and "gives listeners a chance to hear the voices of actors whom they do not often hear", venturing to add that the success of the high-quality broadcast "suggests that there might well be more opportunities for regional drama to be heard on the Light Programme".

In both the play and the novel versions of *The Night-Watchman's Friend*, Dr. Freeman, herself a "misfit" Midlander of modest origins by birth, who for many years had lived and taught in Wales, refers to the 1607 Bristol Channel floods, a devastating inundation which is believed to have killed more than two thousand people. Southern

Wales was especially hard hit, with Cardiff suffering most. The novel is evocatively set in this low-lying region eternally menaced by the sundering sea, in the village of St. Dyfrig-in-Lostlands in Monmouthshire, while the requisite murder takes place at a humble outlying hut by the towering sea wall occupied by two elderly men, insular "old bachelors" by the names of George Pollicott and Henry Rowles, solitary companions of some two decades' standing. "Some girl or other let him down," we are told of Pollicott, "and that made him take to solitary ways." As for Rowles, he had been "on his beam ends: ill, and pretty near starving" when "Pollicott took him in and fed him and nursed him back to health", transferring his bountiful affection and devotion to his hard-luck friend in need.

Rowles, an obviously educated man, in stark contrast with the plain Pollicott, who reveres him so, is making his will one night, naming the absent George (who works as a night-watchman on the local road repair works) as his heir, when he is set upon by two men and slain, his battered body thrown off the sea wall. The local police, with the lack of imagination typical of their fictional kind, fasten upon Pollicott as the culprit. However, a local farmer by the name of Lomax and a retired attorney by the name of Vaughan think differently about the matter—and Vaughan, like many a determined amateur sleuth before him, sets out to prove the police wrong.

The novel's Welsh setting and its prominent working-class character make *The Night-Watchman's Friend* somewhat exceptional for a classic British mystery, even one published in the ostensibly more egalitarian 1950s. However, we find out soon enough that we are on familiar "Fittful" ground, as the author develops the backstory of the mysterious Henry Rowles. Characteristically with Fitt, there is a story within the story, detailing Henry Rowles's rather posher past. It transpires that discovering who really killed him necessitates determining just who he really was.

Once again a Mary Fitt mystery won plaudits from British reviewers. (Like most of the later novels, it was not picked up for American publication.) Longtime mystery-fiction reviewer Maurice Richardson in the *London Observer* described the author's latest crime opus as a "cosy, consequential murder mystery with snug old-fashioned flavour and good Monmouthshire background with plenty of genius loci… Nice." A particularly interesting notice came from West Yorkshire's *Huddersfield Examiner and West Riding Reporter*, by a reviewer who signed her (?) name as "Ariel". Discoursing about a brace of classic (as we deem them now) British murder mysteries—Fitt's *The Night-Watchman's Friend*, Patricia Wentworth's *The Ivory Dagger*, Christopher Bush's *The Case of the Burnt Bohemian* and Andrew Garve's *The Cuckoo-Line Affair*—Ariel warmly described all of the authors as "old friends". Pride of place, however, went to Mary Fitt, "whose work I admire so greatly":

> In conception [*The Night-Watchman's Friend*] is a good old-fashioned melodrama, with a wicked mother, a lost will, a disguised aristocrat, a humble hero, and an eerie setting in a remote corner of Monmouthshire. Yet Miss Fitt makes it entirely credible, and her character drawing is as perceptive as usual. George Pollicott is a fine study, and the history of Henry Rowles… is reconstructed most cleverly. This is rather different from any other books that Miss Fitt has written, and that adds to its interest.

Another reviewer of Fitt's novel, this one with the *Kensington Post and West London Star*, reflected in his notice upon the changing mores in mystery writing at the mid-century. Opening with a fearful look at hard-boiled American author Mickey Spillane's gore-ridden latest, *The Long Wait*, the reviewer, noting that Spillane claimed

12,500,000 devoted readers in the United States and another 150,000 in the United Kingdom, chidingly wondered "whether it is the blood or the sex which attracts these customers—or perhaps it is Mr. Spillane's particularly nauseating mixture of blood AND sex that has proved so attractive."

Of Mary Fitt's new mystery, he observed:

> The mystery concerns a recluse who leaves all his wealth to a night-watchman and thus starts a train of mystery that needs all the skill of a trained legal brain to unravel.
>
> This is a nice, typically English mystery of the kind that sells well in the U.S.A. An elderly lady can read this and still have no fear of nightmares. But the brilliance of the detection does not altogether compensate for a certain lack of liveliness...
>
> Perhaps we should lay this at the door of Mr. Spillane also—that his violent fantasies have put us in no mood to enjoy the mild excitements of an English village mystery. And Miss Fitt is so much the better writer too. It seems a great shame.

These words were published on 27 March 1953. Today, seventy years later, many readers, shunning the sloppy slaughters of the modern crime novel so callously concocted by Spillane and his "cruel-school" kind, are eagerly returning to the "mild excitements" and refined stimulation of the classic English-village mystery. Long may they continue to do so!

ABOUT THE AUTHOR

One of the prominent authors of the classical detective fiction of the Golden Age and afterwards was herself a classicist: Kathleen Freeman, a British lecturer in Greek at the University College of South Wales and Monmouthshire, Cardiff (now Cardiff University) between 1919 and 1946. Primarily under the pseudonym Mary Fitt, Freeman published twenty-nine crime novels between 1936 and 1960, the last of them posthumously. Eighteen of these novels are chronicles of the criminal investigations of her series sleuth, Superintendent Mallett of Scotland Yard, while the remaining eleven of them, nine of them published under the pseudonym Mary Fitt and one apiece published under the respective names of Stuart Mary Wick and Kathleen Freeman, are stand-alone mysteries, some of which are notable precursors of the modern psychological crime novel. There is also a single collection of Superintendent Mallett "cat mystery" short stories, *The Man Who Shot Birds*.

From the publication of her lauded debut detective novel, *Three Sisters Flew Home*, Mary Fitt—like Gladys Mitchell, an author with whom in England she for many years shared the distinguished publisher Michael Joseph—was deemed a crime writer for "connoisseurs". Within a few years, Fitt's first English publisher, Ivor Nicholson & Watson, proudly dubbed her devoted following a "literary cult". In what was an unusual action for the time, Nicholson & Watson placed on the dust jacket of their edition of Fitt's *Death at Dancing Stones* (1939) accolades from such distinguished, mystery-writing Fitt fans as Margery Allingham ("A fine detective story and a most ingenious puzzle"), Freeman Wills Crofts ("I should like to offer her my congratulations") and J. J. Connington ("This is the best book by Miss Mary Fitt I have yet read").

If not a crowned "queen of crime" like Allingham, Agatha Christie, Dorothy L. Sayers and Ngaio Marsh, Kathleen Freeman in her Mary Fitt guise was, shall we say, a priestess of peccadillos. In 1950 Freeman was elected to the prestigious Detection Club, a year after her crime-writing cover was blown in the gossip column "The Londoner's Diary" in the *Evening Standard*. Over the ensuing decade several of the older Mary Fitt mysteries were reprinted in paperback by Penguin and other publishers, while new ones continued to appear, to a chorus of praise from such keen critics of the crime-fiction genre as Edmund Crispin, Anthony Berkeley Cox (who wrote as, among others, Francis Iles) and Maurice Richardson. "It is easy to run out of superlatives in writing of Mary Fitt," declared the magazine *Queen*, "who is without doubt among the first of our literary criminographers."

Admittedly, Freeman enjoyed less success as a crime writer in the United States, where only ten of her twenty-nine mystery novels were published during her lifetime. However, one of Fitt's warmest boosters was the *New York Times*'s Anthony Boucher, for two decades the perceptive dean of American crime-fiction reviewers. In 1962, three years after Fitt's death, Boucher selected the author's 1950 novel *Pity for Pamela* for inclusion in the "Collier Mystery Classics" series. In his introduction to the novel, Boucher lauded Fitt as an early and important exponent of psychological suspense in crime fiction.

Despite all the acclaim which the Mary Fitt mysteries formerly enjoyed, after Freeman's untimely death from congestive heart failure in 1959 at the age of sixty-one, the books, with very few exceptions—*Mizmaze* (Penguin, 1961), *Pity for Pamela* (Collier, 1962), *Death and the Pleasant Voices* (Dover, 1984)—fell almost entirely out of print. Therefore, this latest series of sparkling reissues from Moonstone is a welcome event indeed for lovers of vintage British mystery, of which Kathleen Freeman surely is one of the most beguiling practitioners.

*

A native Midlander, Kathleen Freeman was born at the parish of Yardley near Birmingham on 22 June 1897. The only child of Charles Henry Freeman and his wife Catherine Mawdesley, Kathleen grew up and would spend most of her adult life in Cardiff, where she moved with her parents not long after the turn of the century. Her father worked as a brewer's traveller, an occupation he had assumed possibly on account of an imperative need to support his mother and two unmarried sisters after the death of his own father, a schoolmaster and clergyman without a living who had passed away at the age of fifty-seven. This was in 1885, a dozen years before Kathleen was born, but presumably the elder Charles Freeman bequeathed a love of learning to his family, including his yet-unborn granddaughter. Catherine Mawdesley's father was James Mawdesley, of the English seaside resort town of Southport, not far from Liverpool. James had inherited his father's "spacious and handsome silk mercer's and general draper's establishment", impressively gaslit and "in no degree inferior, as to amplitude, variety and elegance of stock, to any similar establishment in the metropolis or inland towns" (in the words of an 1852 guide to Southport), yet he died at the age of thirty-five, leaving behind a widow and three young daughters.

As a teenager, Kathleen Freeman was educated at Cardiff High School, which, recalling the 1930s, the late memoirist Ron Warburton remembered as "a large attractive building with a large schoolyard in front, which had a boundary wall between it and the pavement". The girls attended classes on the ground floor, while the boys marched up to the first (respectively, the first and second floors in American terminology). "The first-floor windows were frosted so that the boys could not look down at the girls in the school playground," Warburton wryly recalled. During the years of the Great War, Freeman, who was apparently an autodidact in ancient Greek (a subject unavailable at Cardiff High School, although the boys learned Latin), attended the co-educational, "red-brick" University College of South Wales and Monmouthshire, founded three decades earlier in 1883, whence she graduated with a BA in Classics in 1918. The next year saw both her mother's untimely passing at the age of fifty-two and her own appointment as a lecturer in Greek at her alma mater. In 1922, she received her MA; a Doctor of Letters belatedly followed eighteen years later, in recognition of her scholarly articles and 1926 book *The Work and Life of Solon*, about the ancient Athenian statesman. Between 1919 and 1926 Freeman was a junior colleague at University College of her former teacher Gilbert Norwood, who happened to share her great love of detective fiction, as did another prominent classical scholar, Gilbert Murray, who not long before his death in 1957 informed Freeman that he had long been a great admirer of Mary Fitt.

Freeman's rise in the field of higher education during the first half of the twentieth century is particularly impressive given the facts, which were then deemed disabling, of her sex and modest family background as the daughter of a brewer's traveller, which precluded the possibility of a prestigious Oxbridge education. "A man will do much for a woman who is his friend, but to be suspected of being a brewer's traveller… was not pleasant," observes the mortified narrator of William Black's novel *A Princess of Thule* (1883), anxious to correct this socially damning misimpression. Evidently unashamed of her circumstances, however, Freeman evinced a lifetime ambition to reach ordinary, everyday people with her work, eschewing perpetual confinement in academe's ivory tower.

Before turning to crime writing in 1936 under the alias of Mary Fitt, Freeman published five mainstream novels and a book of short stories, beginning with *Martin Hanner: A Comedy* (1926), a well-received academic novel about a (male) classics professor who teaches at a red-brick university in northern England. After the outbreak of the Second World War, while she was still employed at the university, Freeman, drawing on her classical education, published the patriotically themed *It Has All Happened Before: What the Greeks Thought of Their Nazis* (1941).[*] She also lectured British soldiers headed to the Mediterranean theatre of war on the terrain, customs and language of Greece, a country she had not merely read about but visited in the Thirties. During the cold war, when Freeman, passed over for promotion, had retired from teaching to devote herself to writing in a world confronted with yet another totalitarian menace, she returned to her inspirational theme, publishing *Fighting Words from the Greeks for Today's Struggle* (1952). Perhaps her most highly regarded layman-oriented work from this period is *Greek City-States* (1950), in which, notes scholar Eleanor Irwin, Freeman uses her "uncanny eye for settings, as is often seen in her mysteries", to bring "the city-states to life". Freeman explicitly drew on her interests in both classicism and crime in her much-admired book *The Murder of Herodes and Other Trials from the Athenian Law Courts* (1946), which was effusively praised by the late Jacques Barzun, another distinguished academic mystery fancier, as "a superb book for the [crime] connoisseur".

---

[*] Under the heading of "Dictators", Freeman quotes Solon: "When a man has risen too high, it is not easy to check him after; now is the time to take heed of everything." Timeless words indeed!

In spite of her classical background, Kathleen Freeman derived her "Mary Fitt" pseudonym—which she also employed to publish juvenile fiction, including a series of books about an intrepid young girl named Annabella—not from ancient Greece but from Elizabethan England, Eleanor Irwin has hypothesised, for the name bears resemblance to that of Mary Fitton, the English gentlewoman and maid of honour who is a candidate for the "Dark Lady" of Shakespeare's queer-inflected sonnets. Irwin points out that Freeman's "earliest literary publications were highly personal reflections on relationships in sonnet form". The name also lends itself to a pun—"Miss Fitt"—which it is likely the author deliberately intended, given her droll wit and nonconformity.

While Kathleen Freeman's first four detective novels, which appeared in 1936 and 1937, are stand-alones, her fifth essay in the form, *Sky-Rocket* (1938), introduces her burly, pipe-smoking, green-eyed, red-moustached series police detective, Superintendent Mallett, who is somewhat reminiscent of Agatha Christie's occasional sleuth Superintendent Battle. The two men not only share similar builds but have similarly symbolic surnames.

Joined initially by acerbic police surgeon Dr. Jones and later by the imaginative Dr. Dudley "Dodo" Fitzbrown—the latter of whom, introduced in *Expected Death* (1938), soon supersedes Jones—Superintendent Mallett would dominate Mary Fitt's mystery output over the next two decades. Only after Freeman's heart condition grew perilously grave in 1954 does it seem that the author's interest in Mallett and Fitzbrown dwindled, with the pair appearing in only two of the five novels published between 1956 and 1960. Similarly diminished in her final years was Freeman's involvement with the activities of the Detection Club, into which she initially had thrown herself with considerable zeal. In the first half of the decade she had attended club dinners with her beloved life partner, Dr. Liliane Marie

Catherine Clopet, persuaded Welsh polymath Bertrand Russell, an omnivorous detective-fiction reader, to speak at one of the dinners, and wrote a BBC radio play, *A Death in the Blackout* (in which Dr. Fitzbrown appears), with the proceeds from the play going to the club.

Presumably Kathleen Freeman met Liliane Clopet at the University College of South Wales and Monmouthshire, where Clopet registered as a student in 1919. Precisely when the couple began cohabiting is unclear, but by 1929 Freeman had dedicated the first of what would be many books to Clopet ("For L.M.C.C."), and by the Thirties the pair resided at Lark's Rise, the jointly owned house—including a surgery for Clopet and her patients—that the couple had built in St. Mellons, a Cardiff suburb. In the author's biography on the back of her Penguin mystery reprints, Freeman noted that a friend had described the home where she lived as "your Italian-blue house", though she elaborated: "It is not Italian, but it is blue—sky-blue." There Freeman would pass away and Clopet would reside for many years afterwards.

Born on 13 December 1901 in Berwick-upon-Tweed in Northumberland, Liliane Clopet was one of three children of native Frenchman Aristide Bernard Clopet, a master mariner, and his English wife Charlotte Towerson, a farmer's daughter. Although Aristide became a naturalised British citizen, the Clopets maintained close connections with France. In 1942, during the Second World War, Liliane's only brother, Karl Victor Clopet—a master mariner like his father who for a dozen years had run a salvage tug in French Morocco—was smuggled by Allied forces from Casablanca to London, where he provided details of Moroccan ports, beaches and coastal defences, which were crucially important to the victory of the United States over Vichy French forces at the ensuing Battle of Port Lyautey.

Even more heroically (albeit tragically), Liliane's cousin Evelyne Clopet served with the French Resistance and was executed by the

Nazis in 1944, after British forces had parachuted her into France; at her death she was only twenty-two years old. In 1956, under another pseudonym (Caroline Cory), Kathleen Freeman published a novel set in wartime France, *Doctor Underground*, in which she drew on Evelyne's experiences. A couple of years earlier, Liliane Clopet herself had published a pseudonymous novel, *Doctor Dear*, in which she depicted a female physician's struggles with sexism among her colleagues and patients.

Kathleen Freeman, who was rather masculine-looking in both her youth and middle age (boyish in her twenties, she grew stouter over the years, wearing her hair short and donning heavy tweeds), produced no issue and at her death left her entire estate, valued at over £300,000 in today's money, to Liliane Clopet. In a letter to another correspondent she avowed: "My books are my children and I love them dearly." Admittedly, Freeman shared custody of her mysteries with that queer Miss Fitt, but surely she loved her criminally inclined offspring, too. I have no doubt that the author would be pleased to see these books back in print again after the passage of so many years. Readers of vintage mysteries, now eager to embrace the stylish and sophisticated country-house detective novels and psychological suspense tales of an earlier era, will doubtless be pleased as well.

CURTIS EVANS

The Night-Watchman's Friend

TO
LILIANE

I

The Drafting of a Will

MR. VAUGHAN'S STORY

1

My name is Vaughan.

I am a retired solicitor. This was my status when the events I am about to relate temporarily recalled me from my retirement, I trust for the last time.

Most men accept retirement as an unwelcome necessity. I chose mine. When the moment came I stepped happily from a busy practice in a small country town into the almost complete seclusion I had looked forward to for years—and I never regretted my choice, either of time or place or circumstance. Fanciful people might say that I had been guided there by an all-seeing destiny, but personally I don't think so. I don't deny that it may have been so, but neither am I prepared to believe that our petty affairs are as important in the universal scheme as such a theory would imply. I happened to be present when these strange things occurred: that is all I know. Yet I confess I am glad I was at hand to lend my small aid, and that it pleases me to think nobody else could have done so if I had not chanced—assuming it *was* chance—to be there.

2

It all began one misty October evening when I was sitting by the fire reading by lamplight. The village where I live—St. Dyfrig-in-Lostlands—is usually quiet. It lies in a very quiet part of the country, a low alluvial plain between the Bristol Channel and the hills, quite off the main route to the west; you would never think that it stretched between two large towns. Even in the daytime you hear nothing but country sounds—farm machinery, the lowing of cows; perhaps a passing train in the distance; and if you walk along the Sea Wall you'll certainly hear the bubbling of the curlew and the piping and trilling of the oyster catcher—a beautiful sound. But this was evening, and it was absolutely quiet, except for the foghorn from down Channel, which one could scarcely hear indoors.

It was so quiet that the tap on my window was as sharp and clear as if someone had thrown a pebble at it. My little dog barked, but I did not stir. I knew it was only my friend Lomax, the owner of Sluice Farm. He always announced himself this way. A moment later his rat-ta-tat sounded on the front door.

3

I heard the familiar exchanges as Mrs. Williams let Lomax in. Mrs. Williams is my housekeeper. She is a cheerful woman, fond of company herself, and convinced that anyone who spends as much time alone as I do is in need of being brightened up. Therefore she welcomed Lomax, who was my only regular visitor. I heard him say, as usual:

"Now don't you bother, Mrs. Williams. I'll show myself in," and her jolly voice replying, also as usual:

"It's no trouble at all, Mr. Lomax." Then, triumphantly flinging open the door: "A visitor to see you, Mr. Vaughan!"

Lomax walked in, bringing something of the mist in with him. He wore no overcoat; drops of moisture clung to his thick tweed jacket and his fair hair and moustache. My little dog Mac greeted him effusively and stood up on his short hind legs to get attention.

"Hullo, Mac!" said Lomax absently and kindly, snapping his fingers at Mac, who staggered backward before him, still trying to imitate a circus dog.

"Come inside!" I said. "You announced yourself when you tapped on the window." I closed my book: I was always glad to see Lomax.

Mrs. Williams was wearing her hat and coat, but she couldn't resist following Lomax into the room.

"I'm glad you called, Mr. Lomax," she said—and I knew what was coming—"it'll cheer Mr. Vaughan up. It's a nasty damp old night. Let me get you a cup of tea before you go. It won't take a minute." Mrs. Williams is convinced that the only way to keep body and soul together in this very wet corner of the country is to drink frequent cups of tea.

"No, thanks," said Lomax, "not for me." He noticed her hat and coat and asked kindly: "Off to the concert, aren't you? I've just dropped Mrs. Lomax there. The whole village seems to be going."

"Mrs. Williams can make a good strong cup of tea," I said perversely, knowing he'd prefer something even stronger, and thinking also that the good woman looked disappointed. Again Lomax said:

"No, thanks, really." He laughed: "I get enough good strong tea at home."

Mrs. Williams exclaimed: "What? On your ration?" This was only three years after the war, when we could scarcely make our two ounces of tea last out the week. Some people had ways and means of getting round that, I believe. I myself would never allow such practices: I had strictly forbidden Mrs. Williams to exceed our ration, though I fancied sometimes she looked at me a little oddly when I spoke of the importance of keeping to the law in small things as well as great. At this moment I was wishing she would go to her concert and not be inquisitive, when Lomax surprised me by saying in his slow, pleasant voice:

"Well, to tell you the truth, I do get a bit extra now and then. Old Pollicott brings it along."

"Oh yes, of course—he gets extra at his age," said Mrs. Williams, nodding and smiling. "Well then, I'll say good night, Mr. Lomax." She added, turning to me: "I'll be back about half-past ten, sir."

I said, "It's quite all right," glad to hear the last of the conversation about tea, and quite unaware that it, too, had its significance among the events of that fatal evening.

4

"Now then, Lomax," I said, "what'll you have?"

Lomax admitted that it was a damp evening. I gave him a whisky-and-soda, and took one myself. It seemed to me that this was not the usual friendly call that he made on me almost every Saturday evening: I thought he had something on his mind. But I began speaking of ordinary matters:

"Well, how are things with you?" I began. "The flood waters are down, I see."

I should explain that this piece of country I have called Lostlands is actually below sea-level—stolen from the sea, like much of Holland; in fact, the inhabitants call it Little Holland—and protected by a great Sea Wall, said to have first been built by the Romans. I don't know about that, but I do know that shortly after the death of Queen Elizabeth the Great, there was a tidal wave which overwhelmed the Wall as it then was, drowned people and flocks and herds, and caused the towers of the two grey fifteenth-century churches to take a slant which astonishes the visitors to this day. The Wall was strengthened then, but the sea is still encroaching: it has eaten up the grasslands right up to the foot of the Wall, lands that were good pasture for sheep within the lifetime of men and women I know. Nowadays even the highest tides beat helplessly against the Wall, and occasionally hurl a broken ship's timbers or a pile of seaweed over the top; on the landward side the lush grasslands intersected with "reens" as they call them here—a reen is of course a ditch dug for purposes of drainage—these clayey fields are safe enough from the sea. But they are subject to flooding wherever there is heavy rain. The floods are every farmer's chief preoccupation down here on the Lostlands.

Lomax at once responded, as I knew he would:

"Yes, they've gone down—but not before they've done a bit of damage." He leaned forward in his chair. He is the most optimistic of men, but like all farmers, especially owners, he loves a mild grumble. "The trouble is," he said, "the reens need clearing out again. It's heavy work—none heavier—clearing out all that clay that gets washed down into them, and then they get choked up with reeds and they don't drain the land. They should be done once a year—the last time they were done was by the prisoners of war—but now we haven't got the labour. The Sea Wall needs repairing, too: I'm not sure how it'll stand up to the high tides we've been having." He brooded for a minute and then recalled himself: "But I didn't come here to talk to you about my worries, Mr. Vaughan. I came along to ask you for advice—*legal* advice."

I sighed, but inwardly only. I was used to these requests, generally purveyed to me through Mrs. Williams, for all sorts of legal information *gratis*—and I still couldn't see why the inquirers should expect to get something for nothing, just because it wasn't something that could be measured with a yard-stick or weighed on the scales. Still, Lomax was different: he was a much younger man than I, but I liked his company better than that of most men, and also he had been a very good neighbour to me. So I said:

"Always ready to oblige *you*, Lomax."

At once he said what I half-expected:

"Oh, it's not for myself, Mr. Vaughan—not *this* time." Actually he had never asked me for free advice at any time; it was not his way. He went on: "It has to do with old Pollicott."

I reflected: this was the second time I had heard that name this evening.

"Pollicott?" I said. "Ah yes, I know: the old fellow who lives in that hut below the Sea Wall." I supposed I must, in return for Lomax's many kindnesses to me, include his lame dogs in the sphere of my willingness to repay. "Well," I said—and what an ordinary remark it was, to let loose such a cataract of troubles!—"What's *his* worry, eh?"

Lomax said slowly:

"It's about a will."

"A will?" I said, surprised—though in one sense nothing surprises me: I've seen too much of life and people—"I shouldn't have thought Pollicott had enough worldly goods to leave anybody. The last time I saw him he was acting as night-watchman at the road repair works down there along the lane."

"That's quite right," said Lomax eagerly, as if he were pleased that I had noticed the old fellow at all. "That's what he's doing just now. And he and his friend do a bit of fishing sometimes, so he tells me. They rub along quite comfortably," he went on, as if I had expressed some interest in Pollicott's affairs. "They've got that little shack of theirs fixed up quite nicely inside, though it was almost derelict when Pollicott first took it over"—he laughed—"about forty years ago."

But I was still thinking about the old man's desire to make a will. Sometimes these old fellows who look like tramps are better off than anyone imagines.

"Is the cottage his?" I asked. I knew the place well by sight: it lay at the foot of the Sea Wall on the landward side, about half a mile along, where the Wall begins to be at its steepest.

"No, no," said Lomax. "It belongs to *us*. It's on my land."

"Then what has he got to leave?" I said.

Lomax looked down at his hands spread out on his powerful knees.

"I forgot to tell you," he said rather awkwardly. "It's not about his own will he wants advice. It's about his friend's."

"His friend's?" This time I was genuinely surprised, and puzzled, too, as the line of *protégés* increased.

"The other fellow who lives with him," Lomax explained. "You'll probably have seen him when you've been walking along the Sea Wall."

"Yes, I think I have—in the distance," I said. "But he seems a very shy bird. He always scuttles indoors when he sees us coming." I remembered this because Mac was inclined to run barking up to strangers, and I had thought that perhaps the man I had seen hurrying to close the door of the hut didn't like dogs or was afraid of them.

"That's right," said Lomax, still apparently eager to interest me in this strange pair. "He never goes anywhere; never speaks to anyone—except Pollicott, I suppose. He's been there now for the last twenty years, and I never remember seeing him anywhere except round the hut and on the shore."

"What about work?" I said, my critical faculties sharpened by Lomax's apparent interest. "How does he earn his keep?"

"He doesn't," said Lomax, "that's the queer thing. Pollicott keeps him—always has."

"Extraordinary!" I said—and I meant it. Even my varied experience doesn't include one poor old man who keeps another, and has done so for twenty years. I sought for a plausible explanation. "Are they related?"

"Not at all," said Lomax quickly. "In fact, Pollicott would be shocked if he heard you suggest such a thing." Lomax spoke almost as if such an idea shocked him too. "Pollicott thinks this friend of his—Rowles is his name, Henry Rowles—he thinks Rowles is far above him in every respect."

At that I laughed, rather drily, I confess.

"He must do," I said, "if he's willing to keep him in idleness. I've noticed that some people regard an inability to work as a proof of superiority." I was rather pleased with this apophthegm, which struck me as remarkably true. Servants especially will never wait on any except those who obviously can't do a hand's turn for themselves. Lomax, however, was looking at me with a certain anxiety, as if he feared that I would refuse to listen any further; so I controlled my impulse of dislike for those who exploit the good nature or folly of others, and said, not without irony: "Well, so it's the friend who has the fortune."

Lomax answered quite seriously:

"He says so—and Pollicott believes him. He believes everything Rowles says."

I thought, listening to his deep and candid tone, "Yes, my friend, and you are half-convinced of the truth of this story yourself." I continued to treat it with mild ridicule.

"So Pollicott has kept him for all these years on the strength of these probably mythical expectations? Well, well! There's no limit to human gullibility."

Lomax gave me a look of real protest, as if my cynicism hurt him. I saw him searching in his mind for something that might serve to combat my sharp legal mind. At last he said:

"I don't think that's quite how it is, Mr. Vaughan."

I saw that for some reason not yet visible to me, Lomax was deeply concerned about this matter, and that, whatever I might think of it privately, I really must give him my serious attention. I felt that in another moment, if I did not, I should be causing him grave offence. I therefore made another effort to overcome my scepticism and said in matter-of-fact but still guarded tones:

"Has this man Rowles given any proof that he has any property to leave?"

Lomax considered.

"That's the difficulty," he said. "He has and he hasn't, so to speak."

I capitulated.

"Suppose you give me the details," I said, "and I'll tell you what they're worth, if anything—which I strongly doubt," I couldn't help adding.

Lomax knocked out his pipe against the chimney-piece.

5

"I don't rightly know where to begin," he said, half apologetically. "Old Pollicott told me such a rigmarole." He paused, smiled at the recollection and dismissed it. "Well, never mind about that." He went on more briskly. "The gist of it is, this Henry Rowles was on his beam-ends: ill, and pretty near starving. Pollicott took him in and fed him and nursed him back to health—and there he's been ever since." He glanced up at me to see if he had my attention, if not my sympathy.

"Go on," I said.

"In course of time," Lomax went on, "Rowles told Pollicott his story, bit by bit. It's a long story—but again, to give you the gist of it"—Lomax spoke almost hurriedly, for him—"Rowles says—and Pollicott believes him—he isn't called Henry Rowles at all. He says he's really the heir to a large fortune and a title."

The look Lomax gave me at this point was really pathetic. I made my comment as mild as I could, and a good deal milder than I felt.

"*And* a title!" I said. "Another harmless lunatic!—at least, it's to be hoped he *is* harmless."

But Lomax was launched now and not to be deterred.

"Maybe," he said doggedly. "But the point is, for some reason Rowles fled the country—or so he says—about forty years ago and went to South Africa—"

"About the same time as Pollicott settled here?"

Lomax nodded: he was engrossed in his story and did not want interruptions.

"While Rowles was in South Africa," he went on, "he called himself by what he claims is his real name—a long-winded name I don't remember—and he managed to make a little money. He put some of it by, and in the end he had a credit of some three thousand pounds at a Johannesburg bank."

"And the proof?" I said.

Lomax felt in his pocket and drew out his tobacco pouch. I could see he thought the worst was over. He was more at his ease as he continued:

"Pollicott brought me a packet of papers. They're down at the house. I didn't bring them, in case you weren't prepared to bother with the affair. I haven't really examined them myself—haven't had time—but among them I did notice there was a deposit book showing a credit of three thousand pounds odd, not in the name of Henry Rowles but in this long winded name I told you of." He pointed his pipe-stem at me. "And that's just the problem, Mr. Vaughan."

"Yes?" I said.

Lomax said, choosing his words with care:

"According to Pollicott, this man Rowles is very anxious to make a will leaving the money to Pollicott, to repay him for all he's done and all his kindness over the years."

"Very proper," I said, "though it has taken rather a long time to occur to him, surely."

"Well, yes," said Lomax, "but now, it seems, Rowles is very keen on the idea. But he doesn't quite know how to set about it, because the money's deposited in another name—his real name, so he says." Lomax hesitated as before over this statement, and gave me a dubious glance. I said nothing. He went on in firmer tones:

"Now I like old Pollicott. I've known him all my life—he came here some years before I was born—and my father liked him too. My father wasn't an easy man to deceive, and he always said Pollicott was a decent chap and a good worker, and there was nothing wrong with him except that some girl or other let him down, and that made him take to solitary ways."

"Natural enough," I said, not without reason.

"Quite so," said Lomax, pleased. "And yet he did take this Henry Rowles in and keep him all these years, a thing very few men in his position would have done. And if there's any chance of Pollicott getting a bit of money one day, well, I think he deserves it—and I'd like to see justice done." He cleared his throat defiantly.

I considered the story. The room seemed intensely quiet while Lomax waited for me to deliver an opinion, as if I were learned Counsel. I said:

"Is Rowles older than Pollicott? Pollicott can't be much under seventy himself."

"He's over seventy," said Lomax. "He's been drawing his old-age pension for some years now. The other man's about ten years younger, I should say."

"Then," I said sharply, "why has Rowles suddenly decided to make a will?"

Lomax considered this, pulling at his pipe. The room was filled with the fragrant blue fumes. I can't smoke a pipe myself—it affects my heart—but I rose and took a cigar from the box in the cabinet, and clipped it carefully, watching Lomax surreptitiously. He answered thoughtfully:

"Again, as to that I'm not sure. Pollicott wasn't at all clear on that point himself." He waved aside the smoke haze he had created, as if better to see me. "He gave me to understand," he said, "that the other old chap, this Rowles, had got very nervous and jumpy lately, and seemed to think somebody or something was threatening him. In fact"—Lomax's tone expressed the surprise he had evidently felt when he heard Pollicott's statement—"Rowles doesn't like Pollicott to leave him, especially at night—which makes it awkward, as Pollicott's job is night-watching."

"Pooh!" I said. "Persecution-mania; the whole thing hangs together: the man's suffering from delusions."

"I don't know at all," said Lomax, shaking his head. "But the result of it is, he's been badgering Pollicott so much about this will he wants to make that in the end Pollicott came along to ask my advice about it—and I said I'd ask *you*. I hope it's not too much trouble." He looked up at me with disarming confidence.

"Not at all, not at all," I said hastily. I could see myself being drawn into rather tiresome contact with these two old men, one of them apparently weak in the head, the other bordering on insanity.

The Night-Watchman's Friend 33

"Well now"—I hummed and ha'd, trying to gain time—"let me see."

Lomax's expectancy troubled me more than I cared for. I had almost forgotten what it was like to see a client's anxious eyes fixed on me while I weighed my answer. But Lomax was not a client. He was speaking for another, which made it harder to refuse one's help. An idea struck me:

"By the way, why did Rowles send Pollicott to see you? Why didn't he come himself?"

Lomax shrugged.

"He gets Pollicott to do everything for him. He never does a thing for himself—never goes anywhere or sees anyone, as I told you."

My irritation mounted again.

"All the same," I said, "if people want advice, the least thing they can do is to come and ask for it themselves. I can't give advice without knowing the facts."

"No, of course not," said Lomax.

"If this money really is his," I went on, still rather testily, "but is deposited in another name, Rowles will have to furnish proof of his identity before a transfer can be arranged. Of course, it mayn't be so easy if he has no friends or relations in the country."

"No," said Lomax again.

Suddenly my resistance collapsed. I don't really know why to this day, unless it was because of a certain obstinacy in Lomax's bearing, based on an invincible belief that I would help. Yes, I suppose that must be the explanation of my next remark, which I heard myself uttering with surprise, for I am not by nature an impulsive man.

"How would it be," I said, "if I went along to the hut and had a word with them? If I could ask Rowles a few questions I'd soon know if there were any truth in his story."

Lomax's face glowed with pleasure.

"Would you really do that, Mr. Vaughan?" he said.

I nodded brusquely, to avoid his thanks, and said:

"What time does Pollicott go to his job at night?"

"Nine o'clock, he told me," said Lomax promptly. "That is, he has to be there at nine. He gets back about half-past seven in the morning; then of course he goes to bed."

I glanced at the French clock on the mantelpiece. Its ornate hands were confirmed, as if in answer to my query, by its charming little chime. I am very fond of that clock, which I inherited from my grandmother. In fact—though it seems fanciful to say so—I have come to regard it as a sort of oracle. If its face looks forbidding I am inclined to think I am about to do something ill-advised. If it seems to smile, I always feel I have made a right decision, and I can't recall that this belief has ever been disproved—though, as I say, I am not a fanciful man, and I don't doubt there is some perfectly rational explanation.

The clock, which had just chimed half-past seven, was smiling now.

"If I walk along there," I said, "I'll probably catch him before he leaves. I'd rather he were there too, as his friend's so very nervous and shy." I glanced down to see Mac's bright eyes fixed on my face; his short tail wagging, every white hair bristling. "Mac wouldn't mind another walk along the Sea Wall, would you, old boy?" I said, knowing that with these words I completely committed myself. "You'll come with me, Lomax?"

Mac barked joyously, running to and fro.

"I'll be glad to, Mr. Vaughan," said Lomax with emphasis. He rose. "You might miss the hut. It's a dark night, and there's more than a drift of mist over the reens."

I put the fireguard up and rolled back the carpet. Mrs. Williams of course had her own key, in case I didn't get back before her.

6

It certainly was very dark, though not so misty as I had expected—not near the village, at any rate. I could hear the foghorn at regular intervals, and as we approached the churchyard my friend the barn owl was giving vent to his weird cry. The path smelt strongly of nettles, I recall, and there was also a fusty odour which Lomax assured me was goat-weed: he said that this pest was becoming a menace throughout the countryside, and I must take care to uproot every scrap of it from my garden at Old Mill House.

Then we passed through the iron gate and found ourselves walking along among the reens towards the Sea Wall. The mist grew thicker, and the foghorn seemed quite near, its sound conducted by the damp air, though it is in fact about ten miles away as the seagull flies. The familiar fragrance of seaweed, of which I never tire, came to meet me and filled my nostrils. All the time I was thinking of Pollicott, and wondering what could have induced a man to live so far away from his fellows. Lomax, as if in answer to my thought, said:

"Yes, it's a lonely spot all right. There's not another house within half a mile's radius, and the mists lie pretty heavy on the landward side of the wall. It's below sea level, you know."

"It's not a place I'd choose to live in," I said, "especially alone, though I'm fond of this bit of country, and I don't mind solitude. But what can a man like Pollicott find to occupy his thoughts?"

"Well, it was his own wish," said Lomax. He kept, I noticed, on the side of the reen, in case I should miss my footing, I suppose. One wouldn't drown if one fell in, but a bath in that muddy water covered with duckweed wouldn't be amusing. Mac, on the contrary, loved paddling about on the edge and even drinking the stagnant water. But no harm ever came to him from it.

We reached the small bridge, a single plank only, across the reen, and climbed up the diagonal path on to the Sea Wall. There was no wind at all—only swathes of mist that could be felt rather than seen in the darkness. The tide was still a long way out; on this flat shore it is remarkable how seldom one sees the tide in. The foghorn was louder now, and the smell of ozone—if it is ozone that rises from those muddy reaches sparsely grown over with marram-grass—was powerful.

We were now on the flat top of the Wall. It is about six to eight feet wide, and grass-grown, a delightful walk by day, with the Channel on the one hand, and on the other the bright green fields cut into squares by the reens, and the cows grazing, and the old church with its leaning tower, and the distant hills. But at night it is difficult to see your way. There was no danger here, because on both sides the Wall sloped away comparatively gently, and if one missed one's footing one would merely roll to the bottom, either on to the coarse sand and broken shells on the seaward side or into the long grass on the other. Lomax went ahead, occasionally calling out to me to be careful.

The Wall widened a little, and I caught up with him.

"You were saying it was by Pollicott's own wish that he came to live here?" I reminded him. "A disappointment in love, you say?"

"That's right," said Lomax. "He asked my father to let him have the old hut. He wasn't at all an unsociable sort of chap, but he was courting one of the girls on the farm and she married someone else. So he wanted to retire here and be on his own."

"He went on working?" I said.

"Yes," said Lomax. "He had no vices: never troubled the women after the first disappointment, liked a pipe and a glass of beer but was never known to be drunk. He's just the same now."

"He lived alone for twenty years?" I asked.

"Yes—doing a bit of work for us, repairing the old hut, fitting it out with furniture he'd made himself. He's good with his hands. He even made himself a guitar. You can hear him strumming on it still sometimes in the evenings."

"Well, it's a happy life, I suppose," I said, "if you can bear the loneliness."

"Oh," said Lomax, "Pollicott was never lonely. He always had plenty of visitors—passing tramps and the gypsies on the encampment down there when I was a boy. All sorts of people used to call when their beat brought them this way. I don't know if they still do. I fancy Rowles may have driven them away, especially lately, since he's got so queer."

We tramped on for a time in silence. I could hear Mac splashing about among the reeds below, and sometimes a passing train. The main line from London to Fishguard crosses the Lostlands about three miles to the north of where we were walking, yet here we seemed to be far away from every manifestation of modern civilisation, as if we had stepped several centuries back into the past.

"The Wall in its present form was built after the Great Flood of 1606, I suppose?" I said, trying to envisage the terror of the population as the huge tidal wave thundered up Channel, spreading over fields and farmyards, carrying away sheep and cattle and even men. I thought of Jane Ingelow's wonderful poem:

> "So farre, so fast the eygre drave,
> The heart had scarcely time to beat
> Before a shallow, seething wave
> Sobbed in the grasses at our feet.
> The foot had scarcely time to flee
> Before it brake against the knee
> And all the world was in the sea…"

Not that I am a man much addicted to poetry. I have a small store of well-used volumes that I like, and I like my verse to have rhythm and meaning. Otherwise it doesn't interest me.

"I've heard so," said Lomax in answer to my question. "But it's been added to a good deal since then. There's a small stretch of it further along that's quite thirty feet high, and perpendicular on the seaward side, not shelving like here. It wouldn't do to step over *that* in the dark!"

"No, indeed," I said with a shudder. I had often walked along it by day, and thought how dangerous it was, especially as at the bottom one would strike, not sand, but huge jagged boulders piled up one on another.

"But we don't go so far," said Lomax. He stopped and clicked on his torch. "Here we are: this is where we go down. Wait a minute: let me go ahead. The path may be slippery."

The beam of the torch was refracted by the mist, which was thicker there. I don't see in the dark at the best of times, but now I had to take the path on trust, putting my foot against Lomax's much larger one and allowing him to act as a brake. He steadied me with his hand on my elbow as I edged crab-wise after him. I could hear Mac splashing about in the reen ahead.

"Very dark, isn't it?" I said. I could see nothing ahead of us, and though I remembered the place well by day, I wondered if Lomax could possibly have misjudged the distance. "Are you sure the hut's here? I don't see any lights."

"They must be still using their black-out curtains," said Lomax with a laugh. He continued quite unnecessarily to urge caution. I called Mac, thinking he had gone astray, and then I heard him barking in the distance. I was very glad when we reached the bottom.

"Here we are," said Lomax, releasing me. "Now we have to cross the bridge. You'll need to be careful here too: there's only a single plank, and it's slightly less safe than the other." He helped me over, and then went ahead.

The dim shape of the hut rose up suddenly out of the mist.

"You're right," said Lomax, standing and staring. "It's in darkness. I hope I haven't brought you on a wild goose chase. But I understood from Pollicott he'd be here."

He banged loudly on the door.

7

There was no response at first. Lomax banged again more loudly. Then the door opened a little, creakingly. A tremulous voice said:

"Who's there?"

Lomax answered heartily:

"All right, Pollicott. It's me—Lomax. I've brought the legal gentleman to see you."

I shall always remember the suggestion of nervousness or faint hope with which Pollicott repeated:

"Legal gentleman?" But he opened the creaking door a little further.

Lomax shone the torch back on to his own face. At that Pollicott's tone changed.

"Oh yes, Mr. Lomax, sir!" he said. "Come inside. I'll light the lamp. Just a minute." He bustled ahead, and we heard him striking matches which at first he broke in his eagerness—or perhaps they were damp, like everything else in that place.

"All in the dark, eh?" said Lomax. "We thought you'd gone to work—or gone to bed."

Pollicott's voice, issuing from the still unlit room, again had a note of uneasiness.

"No, no, sir," he said, "we has to be careful with the oil in these times."

He was still fumbling with the matches. I had never before heard him speak, and I suppose it was because I could not yet see the man that his voice made such an impression on me. It was a soft voice, with a Welsh accent imposed on something else, I didn't know what. He had trouble with his tenses, but he never missed an aspirate; and though superficially there was a tremor in it, beneath this timidity, or gentleness, or whatever it was, there was a certain determination, a quality of not being deflected. Lomax called out:

"You don't read, then?"

"No, sir, not much these days, except the paper sometimes. I gets used to just sitting, like, me being a night-watchman." He managed at last to strike a match and light the old-fashioned oil lamp on the mantelpiece. "There, sir," he said with satisfaction as the very yellow light, enclosed by the pink glass shade, dimly lit the room. "There you are: now we can see a bit better."

I took a look round the living-room of the hut. It was furnished plainly enough; at one end was a table covered with a red cloth, and beside it a door leading into what must have been very cramped sleeping quarters. There was a stove in one corner, giving out a pleasant heat. There was also a dresser with coloured china, and there were a number of closed cupboards and a very small bookshelf high up on the wooden wall. There was only one armchair; the other chairs, solid and straightbacked, had seats of plaited withies; I judged them to be of Pollicott's own manufacture, good to look at but not very comfortable to sit on. The armchair, however, looked well-cushioned and well-used.

"You seem quite cosy here," I said to the old man, who was watching me with a certain expectancy.

"Not so bad, sir, on the whole," he answered promptly. "We keeps warm and we has enough to eat, and that's the main thing, I always say." He spoke with modest pride, and I noticed the recurrent "we". Then his face fell a little as he added: "It's a bit damp here sometimes—but I'm used to it, you see." This time he didn't say "we".

Lomax broke in decisively.

"Well, Pollicott, this is Mr. Vaughan from the Old Mill House. I've told him about your friend—about his bit of worry—and Mr. Vaughan has kindly come along to help you. Tell him what you told me—or rather, I expect he'd prefer if you just answered what he asks you." He gave me a look, and I nodded confirmation. "Mr. Vaughan'll tell you both what's best to do." He glanced at the door to the sleeping quarters and said: "Where *is* your friend, by the way?"

Pollicott shuffled his feet. After a perceptible pause he said evasively:

"He's not here."

"Not here?" Lomax said sharply. "I thought he hardly ever went out. That's what you told *me*."

Pollicott said, with that mixture of evasion and obstinacy I was soon to get to know so well:

"He don't as a rule, sir—not at night, anyway." And then, with a more candid air: "He's gone for a stroll along the Sea Wall."

Lomax said suspiciously:

"We didn't meet him."

"I expect," said Pollicott innocently, "he went the other way."

I intervened:

"Isn't that rather dangerous on such a dark night?" and Lomax came in after me with:

"The Wall's pretty high along there."

But Pollicott, looking sideways, said with that queer obstinacy of his:

"He's got the dog with him. Clipper'll look after him."

Lomax laughed.

"I shouldn't think that whippet of yours would be much good as a watch-dog," he said. "More likely to want looking after himself, I'd say."

I was getting impatient. I had come here to give advice to a couple of helpless old men, leaving my book and my fire. I hadn't expected to be kept standing about waiting while one of them took the dog for a walk. I interrupted rather impatiently, turning to Pollicott:

"Will your friend be long?"

Pollicott shuffled his feet and averted his red-rimmed eyes. He looked rather a wreck, I could see, now that my own eyes had grown used to the dim light: his grey hair was too long, and he had not shaved for a couple of days. When he answered his voice was thin and tremulous again. He said:

"I can't exactly say. He'll stay out a long while sometimes, when he's in the mood." He glanced nervously at the door that led out of the hut, but the night was as quiet as before.

I was annoyed. I said:

"Then there's no point in my waiting. It's a pity I've wasted my time coming here."

Lomax, also annoyed and disappointed, came forward and said with compunction:

"I'm sorry, Mr. Vaughan. It's my fault for bringing you."

We were about to go when Pollicott stepped forward between us and the outer door. He put out a long, thin, not too clean hand towards Lomax, though he didn't actually touch him. His voice wheezed with anxiety as he said:

"Mr. Lomax, sir!"

"Yes?" Lomax said abruptly.

"*I* could tell the gentleman about Henry, if he wouldn't mind." His tone was pleading. "You see, sir, I don't think Henry'll come back—not if he knows there's strangers here. He don't like visitors. So long as he do hear voices, he'll stay away—especially just now—" His voice trailed away.

Lomax glanced at me. I nodded. It seemed stupid to leave without knowing what they wanted, after we had come so far. And I was beginning to be curious.

"Very well, then," I said testily. "What is it exactly you want to know?"

Pollicott said hoarsely, turning to me:

"It's about Henry's will, sir." Again he glanced fearfully towards the door.

"Yes, yes, I know that," I said. "Mr. Lomax has explained that much to me. Your friend wants to make a will leaving his property to you. He says he has some money deposited in a bank in Johannesburg, but in a different name."

"Yes, sir," said Pollicott eagerly. "That's it, sir!"

"And you think he's speaking the truth?" I said. "You don't think he's imagining it?"

Pollicott retreated a step. He sounded utterly shocked.

"Oh no, sir!" he said fervently.

"Well," I said briskly, "all he has to do is to furnish this bank with evidence of his identity—that is," I explained, seeing his worried look, "he must prove to them that he is the person who deposited these monies with them. What *is* his name—the name he is now known by, I mean?"

Pollicott looked down at his boots, which were old and cracked at the toes. He said almost sullenly:

"Henry Rowles."

"And his other name," I said, "the name he was using when he lived in South Africa?"

He hesitated. I watched him with interest as he slowly raised his eyes to mine. He opened his mouth, as if about to attempt something too difficult for him. Then he said lamely:

"I don't rightly know, sir."

"You don't know?" I glanced at Lomax, who also was watching the old man, but sympathetically. Pollicott shook his head as if hoping to shake out the recalcitrant name from his memory, and said apologetically:

"Henry've told me a thousand times if he've told me once; but my memory's that bad—I just can't remember it more than five minutes together. There's a string of names—they always do have half a dozen in them grand families, I reckon. It's all written down, though, in them papers I giv' Mr. Lomax."

Lomax laughed encouragingly.

"The name certainly *is* a jaw-breaker, taken all together!"

"Well," I said, "it doesn't matter." I was anxious now to get this unsatisfactory interview over and be gone. "All your friend has to do," I explained, "is to take a sheet of paper and write on it—whatever it is he wishes. I gather he wants to leave the whole of his property to you?"

"That's right, sir," said Pollicott. His tone appeared to express no excessive eagerness, nor any surprise.

"Has he no family?" I thought it proper to ask.

"Oh yes, sir," said Pollicott, quite brightly for him. "He's got relations. He's got a brother and a sister. But"—his naïve look was followed by a more knowing, or at least, more knowledgeable one—"they don't need nothing *Henry* can give them."

I did not think it worth while to pursue this inquiry further:

I could see we were on the verge of hearing about Rowles's noble connections. I spoke rapidly and clearly.

"Then if he has finally decided what he wants to do he must write it down on a piece of paper quite simply. For instance: 'I, Henry Rowles, of such and such an address, give and bequeath all my real and personal estate to so-and-so.' Or if he wants to leave something to his relations—a keepsake to his sister, say—he must put: 'I give my gold—or silver—watch to my sister Jane Smith of such and such an address,' and so forth."

I had made it as simple as I could, but from the way the old man was staring at me I doubted if he had taken in a word. I broke off, therefore, adding:

"But I'll write down the formula and let Mr. Lomax have it. Then your friend must fill in the details and sign the draft in the presence of two independent witnesses."

Pollicott looked as startled as if I had suddenly pointed a pistol at him. He jumped and said:

"Eh?"

Lomax came to the rescue.

"Mr. Vaughan means you must get two men—or women—to watch your friend sign his name, and sign their own names under his."

Pollicott nodded.

"Remember," I warned him, "you mustn't witness it yourself if you're a beneficiary." Then, seeing the blank look coming again, I interpreted: "I mean, you mustn't be one of those who sign the will if he leaves anything to you."

Lomax admonished:

"Two *other* fellows, Pollicott, besides Rowles, you understand?"

It was then that the interruption came.

8

I had forgotten about Mac. He had tumbled into the hut with us when we entered, had rushed up to Pollicott with a wagging of the tail, and after a frenzied rush around the living-room and a thorough examination of every corner, he had lain down before the stove with his nose on his wet forepaws and apparently gone to sleep. Now he raised his sharp muzzle and growled.

A second later we heard footsteps, men's voices, and then a loud bang on the door. Mac rushed to it, barking furiously.

Pollicott was showing every sign of agitation. He stammered:

"Excuse me—just a minute, if you please, sirs."

He shuffled hurriedly to the door, opened it, and closed it after him, leaving Mac still growling and scratching the door from the inside.

Lomax and I looked at each other.

"Is that Rowles, do you think?" I said to him.

"No, I don't think so," he said. "Rowles surely wouldn't bang like that on his own door. Besides, I fancied I heard *voices*."

We could hear nothing except an indistinct murmuring.

"I think," said Lomax, "we'd better do a little eavesdropping. Will you lower the lamp and stand by it while I see what I can manage with this window?"

I took the lamp down from the mantelpiece, and setting it on the table, lowered the flame to a mere flicker. Then, at a gesture from Lomax, I called Mac away from the door. Mac knew when to obey. He came towards me, his short stub of a tail curved downwards, and in response to my pointing finger lay down again in front of the stove, but with his eyes open and every hair aquiver. Lomax, who is a big man, crossed with surprising lightness of tread to the window.

There was only one window in the living-room. It was covered, as we had guessed, with blackout material. Lomax gently drew the curtain aside, revealing an iron-framed window with three lights, and above these three smaller panes, one of which opened outwards. Very carefully and silently he pushed the iron lever a little way, and let it rest so that the staple fitted into the first hole. Then he stood aside, listening. I joined him. This is what we heard:

9

There were two other voices besides Pollicott's. Both were uneducated. One was smooth, with a strong Irish brogue—Cork, I fancied—and the other, which was rougher, I judged to be Cornish. But it was Pollicott's voice that first impinged on my ear: urgent, frightened, desperate. He was saying:

"For God's sake shut your jaw, man! I tell you I ain't got nothing for you this time. You'd better get away. There's two gentlemen inside."

"Oh," said the Irish voice, "company, eh?"

The Cornish voice said roughly:

"Look here, what are you up to?"

Lomax nudged me with his powerful elbow. He is a taller man than I, and by standing on tip-toe he could crane his neck out through the ventilator, but I gathered from his shrug as he withdrew his head that he could see nothing. We listened again.

"Leave me alone!" Pollicott was saying. "I ain't done nothing."

The Cornishman said:

"Where's Henry?"

"I dunno," said Pollicott. I could detect the sullen obstinacy in his tones. "He went for a walk."

The Cornishman appeared to be thinking of force.

"What's going on?" I heard him say. "Are you still in with us or aren't you?"

The Irishman intervened.

"Leave him alone, Jack, you fool!" he said, and then, more quietly but even more menacingly: "Who've you got in there, eh?"

"I've told you, Dan!" said Pollicott, almost crying, it seemed. "It's nothing to do with you. It's for Henry."

"I didn't know Henry mixed with anybody in these parts," sneered the one he had addressed as Dan. "I thought he was too high and mighty to know anybody but the gentry!" He called it "jintry."

"It's only Mr. Lomax," said Pollicott, "and a legal gentleman—"

"Legal gentleman?" said Dan. "Police, you mean, don't you?" There were sounds of feet scuffling on the stone threshold, as if Dan had given Pollicott a shake.

"No, no!" said Pollicott. "I ain't said nothing to nobody. But we can't do nothing more for you."

"Speak for yourself!" said the one called Jack, the Cornishman. "We can do without *you*—but Henry's useful. He knows quite a bit about our class of goods. We'd be sorry to lose Henry—wouldn't we, Dan?" He gave a laugh.

"Henry can't do nothing," said Pollicott, and now his voice was comparatively firm. "It's his nerves. He won't go out no more, not even along the shore."

Irish Dan came in again.

"Then what's he doing out walking on a night like this, I'm asking you!"

Pollicott said glumly:

"He's taken the dog for a stroll."

"Oh, he has, has he?" said Jack. "Well, I reckon he's inside here, spilling the beans to the blasted cops, see?" But his tone, though still aggressive, sounded less assured.

"I tell you," said Pollicott patiently, "he's gone for a walk along the Wall. He went because he heard them coming—not the police—Mr. Lomax and the legal gentleman. He don't want to see nobody. He's scared."

Dan spat and said:

"How d'you know *he* won't talk, a barmy sort of chap like that? He thinks he's a belted earl or something already." He spat again. "He'll be saying next he's the Pope!"

Pollicott said earnestly:

"Henry won't talk, I promise you. He don't understand enough to talk. He ain't interested." His voice grew agitated again. "Now for God's sake clear out, boys, before the gentlemen inside hear you. I'll see you again in the morning."

Jack said:

"Why not after they've gone? We could stick around."

"I have to go to my work," said Pollicott.

"*Henry* doesn't work," said Dan.

Pollicott said quite fiercely:

"It's no good you talking to Henry. You'll only scare him. He's scared stiff already."

"What about?" said Jack contemptuously.

"I dunno," said Pollicott. "He's just scared. If he hears *you* around, on top of the other two, he'll clear out altogether, I shouldn't wonder."

There was a pause. I was going to withdraw, but Lomax held me back, with a hand on my arm. I stood still.

"Okay," I heard the Cornishman say, "we'll go. But we'll be around. Give us a whistle when the coast's clear."

Pollicott said stubbornly:

"I has to leave for my job at half-past eight."

"Well then," said Jack, "we'll see you in the morning. But remember, we leave on the high tide."

Pollicott said in the same sullen tone:

"I don't get back till seven-thirty."

"That's okay," said Jack. "High water's nine-twenty tonight. That makes it nine-forty in the morning." His sudden cheerfulness sounded sinister as he repeated: "We'll be around."

The Irishman, on the other hand, sounded less happy as he interposed:

"Hadn't we better get away before daylight, Jack?"

"Oh, that don't matter," said Jack, more cheerful than ever, "so long as these chaps haven't been talking." His voice took on a laboured facetiousness as he added: "After all, we're only a couple of honest fishermen looking for dabs and winkles, eh?" He laughed.

Dan laughed too, though not quite so naturally, as he agreed:

"Sure, that's all we are!"

Lomax deftly lowered the upper pane into the closed position and drew the curtain across. Taking my cue, I crossed to the table and raised the lamp-wick. Then Lomax shouted:

"What the devil are you doing, Pollicott? Mr. Vaughan can't wait all night!"

The murmuring ceased. Pollicott's voice rose reedily:

"Coming, Mr. Lomax—coming!"

A moment later the door opened creakingly. Pollicott, pale and wild-looking, came in, and with him the mooing of the melancholy foghorn.

10

Lomax and I were sitting at the table as if we had taken our places there when Pollicott left, and had not moved. Pollicott shuffled forward. He was breathless with anxiety as he faced us.

"Very sorry to keep you waiting, sirs. Just a couple of fishermen I does business with off and on."

Lomax wisely let this pass. He looked at me. I too thought it best to get down to business immediately.

"Well, Pollicott," I said, "I don't know that there's anything more I can tell you. Get your friend to do as I say. Let him put down just what he wants done with his property in the event of his death. If he's not sure of the wording, I'll look it over before he signs it. And he should appoint an executor: that is, someone to see to the business side of it." I turned to Lomax. "I don't know if *you'd* be willing to act as executor, Lomax? I shouldn't think there'd be much trouble attached to it, but I doubt if Pollicott here could manage it alone."

Lomax nodded.

"I'll do that," he said.

"There you are, Pollicott," I said. The old man stood there looking so depressed and worried that I wanted to cheer him. "You can tell your friend that Mr. Lomax has kindly consented to be his executor. Is that all clear?"

Pollicott came forward a step.

"Thank you, sir," he said fervently. He looked away from us towards the window. "I only wish Henry was here himself. Henry'd know all about it. He understands *everything*."

It would be difficult to convey the reverence in Pollicott's tone. I could not help a small joke at his expense.

"Lucky fellow!" I said with mock solemnity.

But irony was wasted on Pollicott where his friend was concerned.

"He's had a very good eddication, sir, Henry has," he assured me, "the highest in the land."

Again I feared a harangue on the theme of Henry's lofty origins. So I stopped him hastily.

"Yes, yes," I said, "I'm sure he has." I got up. "Well, Lomax," I said, "shall we be getting along? We could walk back past your place and I could pick up those papers. I may as well have a look at them."

We moved towards the door. I called Mac, though that was hardly necessary, and wished Pollicott good night. He followed us to the door, thanking me profusely, and then got ahead of us to open it. Lomax turned to give a few more firm words of advice.

"Good night, Pollicott. Don't forget to tell your friend exactly what Mr. Vaughan's been saying. And if you want any help, come along to *me*—don't bother Mr. Vaughan."

I could now see that Pollicott, in spite of his gratitude, was longing for us to be gone. He opened the door invitingly and the mist swirled into the dimly-lit room.

"No, sir," he said to Lomax, opening the creaking door more widely and almost bowing us out. "Right, sir. Thank you, sir."

We stepped out into the dark night again, and the hut disappeared. We did not return along the Sea Wall. We took the path along one of the reens that led to Lomax's farm, but as we walked away from the Wall I could hear the lapping of the water as the tide came swiftly in over the mud flats and hissed among the marram-grass.

Lomax and I did not talk much on the way home, and for some reason we avoided discussing Pollicott's mysterious visitors. When we reached Sluice Farm I declined Lomax's invitation to enter. He went in and fetched the papers, and I walked back to the village along the road, carrying the bulky envelope and thinking about what I had heard.

I would have given much to have been present unobserved, and to have heard how Pollicott's friend received the information that they had had visitors: two pairs of visitors, in fact. But this I did not learn till later...

POLLICOTT AND HENRY

I

When Mr. Vaughan and Lomax had gone Pollicott did not close the door. He shuffled across the room to the dresser and began taking down plates, cups and saucers, and laying the table. Then from behind a curtain in one corner he took out a saucepan of broth, opened the lid of the stove, and set the saucepan carefully on the ring, stirring the broth with a long wooden spoon. Finally he took down his guitar from a hook on the panelling, and sitting down on one of the upright chairs began plucking the strings. After a few preliminary chords he broke into a tune: it was the Suffolk song called *The Foggy Foggy Dew*. He played softly, singing the words from time to time: he played no false notes, though sometimes the tune hesitated, and his voice, though wavering, was true enough.

"When I was a bachelor I lived all alone..."

As he played he smiled to himself, and his voice grew stronger:

"... And the many, many times I held her in my arms
Just to save her from the foggy, foggy dew..."

He laid his palm over the vibrating strings, and listened. A dog was whining, scratching at the door, which gradually swung further open creakingly.

Pollicott called out:

"Henry!"

"Are you there, George?" The voice was rich, cultured, and not at all elderly. "Is anybody with you?"

Pollicott said eagerly:

"They've gone. They went a little while ago. I thought you'd know from the tune." He hung up the guitar again; it jangled a little on its hook as he shuffled away to look at the broth on the stove.

2

The man who was or who called himself Henry Rowles entered. The slate-grey whippet, having slipped in ahead of Henry, had at once curled itself up on the armchair. Henry came forward, pushed the dog off with an easy gesture, and stretched himself out on the vacated cushions. He was a large man: tall, broad-shouldered though stooping, and with a large head. His nose was powerful, his eyes blue-grey, and his mouth well-shaped but petulant. His clothes were well cared for, in spite of shiny patches. His hands, which he spread out towards the stove, were white, with long flexible fingers and well-tended finger-nails. The only sign of carelessness about him was that he wore a white silk scarf round his throat instead of a collar. Beside him, Pollicott looked like an animated scarecrow.

"Good!" said Henry, lying back in the armchair, which creaked under his weight. "It's very damp and misty out tonight. It's not healthy to be out on a night like this." He coughed. "I'm afraid it will bring back my bronchitis. Couldn't you have got rid of them sooner?"

"No, Henry," said Pollicott meekly, ladling out the broth into two bowls on the table. "I couldn't do nothing about it."

"What did they want?" said Henry querulously. "I thought you said you had given the papers to Lomax. There was surely no need for them to come here."

"Will you come and have your broth, Henry," said Pollicott, "before it do get cold?"

Henry with a gesture indicated that he wished the broth to be brought to him. Pollicott fetched it, and sat down with his own bowl on a hard chair opposite.

"Mr. Lomax brought a legal gentleman," he said, "to tell you how to make a will."

Henry looked up angrily.

"I know perfectly well how to make a will! What do they take me for? I want to know the easiest and quickest way to get this money from Johannesburg. Did you explain that?" Seeing Pollicott's bewildered look, he said contemptuously: "No, I don't suppose you did. You're a perfect fool sometimes, George. I suppose you gave them the idea that I was as ignorant as yourself in these matters. Did you tell them anything about me?" He thrust forward his lower lip aggressively.

Pollicott said timidly:

"Well, no, Henry. I didn't know if you'd want me to."

Henry gave an approving nod. Encouraged, Pollicott went on eagerly:

"But Mr. Lomax has all the papers, and he says he'll give them to the legal gentleman to look through."

Henry held out the empty bowl for Pollicott to take and shook his head at the offer of bread and cheese. While Pollicott cut himself a piece of each, Henry continued talking scornfully:

"Lawyers are sharp enough when it's something they know about already or have done before. But give them something at all unusual and they're as stupid as you, George—perhaps stupider in some ways. You at least don't suffer from 'the credulity of incredulity.'"

"Eh?" said Pollicott, pausing with the bread and cheese halfway to his mouth.

Henry laughed indulgently.

"Never mind. So we're no further advanced. This man will keep my papers for a month if he's allowed, and then say nothing can be done. I know the breed!" He mused for a while, nodding at the stove and smiling bitterly to himself. Then he said sharply:

"At any rate, we needn't wait any longer to draft the will. Clear the table quickly, George, and then put the lamp back. Did you ask him which name he thought I ought to use?"

Pollicott, flustered, began clearing the table.

"I'm not sure if I did, Henry," he said. "My mind was all in a muddle, what with one thing and another. I don't rightly know *what* I said."

Henry nodded.

"I thought so. You made a complete mess of it."

Pollicott folded up the cloth, gathered up the unused knives, forks and crockery, and replaced the lamp in the centre of the table. Then he faced Henry.

"He did say as how it was *you* he really wanted to see." The words, though diffidently spoken, carried a mild reproach.

Henry said angrily:

"Why should *I* bother with these people? I asked a perfectly simple question—or rather, it *would* have been perfectly simple if you hadn't garbled it." He raised himself with some difficulty out of the armchair, and went towards the table, grumbling: "I shall have to decide for myself what's best to do." He drew up a chair and sat down. "Get me some paper and ink, and a pen—a good pen. Put the lamp *here*."

Pollicott shuffled about, fulfilling these orders. It was surprising how quickly he managed to bring Henry all he asked.

"I shall use my own name," said Henry as he waited. "That is, the name in which the money's deposited. We can think about proof of my identity later."

3

Pollicott, having turned up the lamp-wick, brought paper and a pen, and laid it on a large blotting-pad in front of his friend.

"Here you are, Henry," he said.

Henry examined the nib.

"Is this the best pen you have?" He picked up a sheet of the paper. "This is dreadful stuff. I should have told you to get some, but I really can't think of everything. It was all very well during the war, but surely there's better paper for sale now, even here. *You* should have thought of that, George; you go through the village every day."

"I could get some tomorrow," said Pollicott.

"No, no," said Henry irritably, "it must be done now. There's no time to lose"—his voice sank to an apprehensive whisper—"no time to lose." For a moment he pressed his fine white hand against his high forehead. Then he withdrew it and said firmly: "I want you to have all I possess, George. You have been good to me, to the best of your ability. No one shall ever say of me that I wasn't grateful."

Pollicott, standing at his shoulder, began a muttered protest. Henry waved it aside.

"If I had been able to establish my identity—my real position—it wouldn't be three thousand pounds I'd be leaving you, nor thirty thousand, but—" He spoke quietly and without bombast. "Well, never mind, I can't do *that* and remain alive. After my death it will be easier, I hope."

Pollicott's protest could no longer be suppressed. He spoke almost tearfully.

"I don't want nothing, Henry. I never did want nothing. You know that. You was welcome to the little I could do for you."

Henry half turned and gave Pollicott a smile of sudden sweetness.

"Thank you, George. You're a good fellow. You may be sure I shan't forget it—even beyond the tomb." He cleared his throat, drew the paper towards him, and took up the pen. "Now!" He began writing, uttering each word aloud as he wrote in a firm and elegant hand: "'I, John Henry Vincent Peter Dallingsworth Clairvaux, formerly of—'" He broke off. "No, I'd better not put that: that might cause difficulties." He continued writing: "'—formerly of Johannesburg, South Africa, otherwise known as Henry Rowles'—Rowles! What a dreadful name!—'Henry Rowles of The Hut, near St. Dyfrig's-in-Lostlands, in the County of—' What county are we in, George? Monmouth, isn't it? And is it England or Wales?"

Pollocott looked blank.

"I dunno."

Henry smiled indulgently.

"I didn't think you would. We'll leave out the county for the moment. Perhaps you have a map somewhere." He continued writing: "'—declare that I am of sound mind and that this is my last Will, there being no other Will of mine in existence.'" He laughed drily. "That's true enough. I never made one before, though I've good reason to know how they're drawn."

Pollicott, though not understanding, was smiling in general sympathy when Henry rounded on him suddenly.

"I wish you hadn't left my papers with this man Lomax!" he said irritably. "You should have brought them back immediately."

Pollicott, taken by surprise, stepped back a pace and stammered: "He asked me to."

"You shouldn't have done so without first consulting *me*."

Pollicott looked troubled, but not at what Henry was saying.

"That reminds me, Henry," he said. "Mr. Vaughan—the legal gentleman—he says something about having somebody to see to the business side of it—"

"*Ha!*" exploded Henry. "He wants his fee."

"He didn't mean for him to do it," said Pollicott. "He said for Mr. Lomax if he was willing. And Mr. Lomax, he said 'all right.'" He rubbed a finger up and down the side of his long thin nose. "I think he did call it a executioner."

Henry laughed indulgently.

"Executor, you mean—Oh, I see. Yes, George, I think we should have an executor. I doubt whether you'd be able to manage even the simplest of wills on your own. So this Lomax wants to have a finger in it, does he? Is he honest?"

Pollicott was shocked.

"It's Mr. *Lomax*, Henry," he said reverentially. "Mr. Lomax the son of old Mr. Lomax as let me have the hut when first I come to these parts." His voice took on a sing-song intonation. "Like father, like son. Old Mr. Lomax, he never charged me a penny for rent from the day I come here—and young Mr. Lomax has always done the same—"

Henry cut short these praises with a wave of the hand.

"Good, good!" he said patronisingly. "Very well, George, in view of your testimonial we will trust Lomax. What is his first name, do you know?"

"His Dad used to call him Bob," said Pollicott, still with a lilt in his voice at the thought of his benefactor, "if I remember rightly."

Henry wrote:

"I appoint Robert Lomax of—'" He looked up questioningly.

"Of the Sluice Farm," supplied Pollicott.

"'Of the Sluice Farm,'" wrote Henry, "St. Dyfrig's-in-Lostlands, in the County of Monmouth'—if it *is* Monmouth—'sole Executor of this my Will.'" He paused. "I think executors usually expect to get a legacy for their pains, but from what you say, this Lomax isn't in need of any recompense, since he hasn't charged you any rent. So we won't bother about that. Now:"

Steadily, clearly, in his large handwriting decorated with an occasional flourish, he wrote:

"'I devise and bequeath all my real and personal estate whatsoever *and wheresoever*'—note that, George: that's very important—'to George Pollicott of The Hut, near St. Dyfrig's-in-Lostlands, in the county of Monmouth, in gratitude for his devoted services to me over a period of twenty years.

"'In witness whereof I have hereunto set my hand this Ninth day of October One Thousand Nine Hundred and Forty Eight.'"

4

As he finished the last word with a flourish Pollicott startled him by calling out:

"Stop! Stop!"

Henry turned in surprise.

"What's the matter?"

"Wait a minute!" said Pollicott breathlessly. "The legal gentleman said most particular you mustn't sign it except in front of two other folk, men or women."

Henry laughed good-humouredly:

"Of course, of course! I'm perfectly aware of that. There was no need to shout: your voice goes through my head." He went on briskly: "We must get two other people. You're no good because you're the legatee. You'll have to run across to the farm and get a couple of the servants to come over immediately."

Pollicott did not move.

"I'm sorry, Henry," he said, "but I must go to work now. I'll be late already. If Mr. Jenkins comes by on his round and I'm not there, I'll get the sack. He've warned me before."

Henry said firmly:

"You're not going to work tonight."

"I must," said Pollicott. His voice was nervous, but his determination, as firm as Henry's, could be heard behind the tremor.

"But I don't wish it!" said Henry pettishly. "I've told you why. We've had all this out already."

"I must," repeated Pollicott. "I'll get the sack."

"Pooh!" said Henry. "You'll get something else to do."

"Not so easy," said Pollicott, "and not so near." He pleaded: "I ain't as young as I was, Henry, and my rheumatism's *that* bad. I can't go so far nor work so hard as I used to."

Henry pushed out his lower lip.

"There's the fishing."

"Precious little in *that*," said Pollicott.

"Well, there are those two men with the motor-boat. They bring you something."

Pollicott flushed, and his voice trembled now with sudden anger.

"I told them to keep off from now on. It's too dangerous," he said.

"Dangerous?" said Henry. He laughed scornfully. "What's dangerous about it? Are you afraid of getting your feet wet? My poor fellow, compared with the danger threatening *me* at this moment, your couple of rogues don't exist." He turned round to study Pollicott more closely. "They came here this evening, didn't they? I thought I heard them."

"They did," said Pollicott.

"Then go and get them back!" said Henry. "They'll do for our two witnesses! Go along now: they can't have gone far. Take your lantern and signal to them."

Pollicott said stubbornly:

"I don't want them here. I don't want them to come near *you*, Henry."

"Why not?" cried Henry cheerfully. "What harm can they do me? They might even serve as a body-guard, if you really are determined to go off on this wretched little job of yours. But George," he said more sharply, "you really must find some work that can be done at home. I tell you *I must not be left alone*—certainly not at night."

Pollicott wavered.

"You really want me to get them? I thought you was afraid of them. That's why I told them to keep off." He peered at Henry in anxious enquiry.

"Afraid of *them*?" Henry laughed in even richer enjoyment of his scorn. "Don't be a fool!"

Pollicott sighed, and turned away.

"All right, then. But I don't like it." He shuffled towards the door. The whippet, which had been lying curled up on the floor by the stove, rose shiveringly, stretched, and went ahead of him to the door, where it whined and scratched, eager to go with him.

"No, no," said Pollicott gently, "stay there, Clipper, old chap. Stay with the boss and take care of him."

Henry watched Pollicott's movements with disapproval, turning round in his chair.

"You can take him with you," he said sulkily. "He irritates me with his whining and scratching. Have you fed him?"

Pollicott took his lantern and opened the door.

"If I see them," he said, "I'll send them along. But I *must* go to my work."

The foghorn mooed mournfully. The lapping of the incoming tide sounded nearer in the intense stillness. The half-opened door creaked in Pollicott's hand.

"All right, go!" said Henry testily. "But do shut the door, for heaven's sake! You're making an infernal draught, and the mist is simply sweeping in." He coughed exaggeratedly.

Pollicott went out. The door was almost shut when Henry called after him:

"Tell those two fellows they must spend the night here."

Pollicott looked round the door.

"What?"

"Tell those two scoundrels," said Henry, "I want them to stay here with me till you get back tomorrow morning."

"All right," said Pollicott, "if I sees 'em."

He left.

5

Henry had forgotten Pollicott before the door had closed behind him. He turned back with lively interest to what he had written, and began re-reading it aloud with vigorous asides:

"'I, John Henry Vincent Peter Dallingsworth Clairvaux, formerly of Johannesburg, South Africa, otherwise known as Henry Rowles'—pah!—'of The Hut, near St. Dyfrig's-in-Lostlands, in the County of Monmouth'—of course it's Monmouth—'declare that I am of sound mind and that this is my last Will'—my last

Will—I think I'll put 'testament' also, though they say it's not necessary. It sounds better, somehow. Yes: 'my last Will and Testament, there being no other Will of mine in existence. I appoint Robert Lomax of the Sluice Farm, St. Dyfrig's-in-Lostlands, in the County of Monmouth, sole Executor of this my Will.'—Poor George! What a hero-worshipper he is! Even this Lomax gets a share. 'I devise and bequeath all my real and personal estate whatsoever and wheresoever'—ah, if only I could!—'to George Pollicott of The Hut, near St. Dyfrig's-in-Lostlands in the County of Monmouth, in gratitude for his devoted services to me over a period of twenty years.

"'In witness whereof I have hereunto set my hand this Ninth day of October One Thousand Nine Hundred and Forty Eight.'"

He had been writing with such absorption that he did not notice the slight creak as the door began to open, he did not hear the melancholy foghorn, nor the now nearby lapping of the tide.

"Now where are those fellows—my two witnesses?" he muttered to himself, his pen poised. "Damn! There's that draught again! George didn't latch the door properly." He turned around, to see two men in the room. "Ah, there you are!" he called out genially. "Then I can sign."

With a flourish that made his pen sputter he wrote: "J.H.V.P.D. Clairvaux, also known as Henry Rowles."

"Now, please," he said, holding out the pen over his shoulder and without looking at his visitors, "will you add your signatures just here, under mine?" Surprised at hearing no reply, he added more peremptorily: "Come along, come along! Don't be afraid! Just a formality, you know—"

And these, strangely enough, were the last words uttered by Henry Rowles, or John Henry Vincent Peter Dallingsworth Clairvaux.

II

A Grim Discovery

MR. VAUGHAN'S STORY CONTINUED

I

When I left Sluice Farm that night, carrying the envelope containing the papers Pollicott had given to Lomax, I intended to go straight home and spend an hour looking through them before I went to bed. But as I passed through the village I heard singing. It was the concert to which all the inhabitants of St. Dyfrig's-in-Lostlands had gone that evening, including Lomax's wife and my housekeeper, Mrs. Williams. Attracted by the voices, I went in.

The singing was really excellent. No one can deny that we have a remarkable amount of musical talent among us for such a small place. I was just in time to hear the end of a beautiful quartet for female voices when the chairman—who was Mrs. Lomax—announced the closing item; the whole choir, and with them the audience, gave a heart-felt rendering of *Jerusalem*.

When I got home, some five minutes before Mrs. Williams, I felt tired. Nevertheless I did not neglect my custom of making a shorthand *précis* of the conversation I had heard. This is a habit I have observed since boyhood, and I can never be too thankful to my father for having pressed it on me—somewhat against my will at the time, I'm afraid. Having made a record of most of what had been said by Lomax and Pollicott, and also by the two pretended fishermen Dan and Jack, I felt too tired to begin looking at the papers of Pollicott's friend. I decided to postpone this effort till the following morning, which was Sunday.

So placing them on my bedside table, I put out the light and was soon asleep.

2

I was awakened next morning by loud knocking on my bedroom door, and Mrs. Williams calling agitatedly:

"Mr. Vaughan, Mr. Vaughan!"

"Come in!" I said, surprised—for Mrs. Williams, though cheerful and robust, is not usually noisy or violent. But when she entered I saw at once something was wrong.

"Good heavens, Mrs. Williams, what's the matter?" I said, wide awake at once.

"Oh, Mr. Vaughan!" she gasped. "What do you think? One of those old men—you know, the ones that live in that old hut near the Sea Wall—"

My mind flew at once to Pollicott.

"Yes?" I said sharply.

"One of them's been found dead, on the rocks at the bottom of the Wall!"

"*What's* that you say?" I struggled to sit upright, while Mrs. Williams, leaning against the bed rail, recovered her breath.

"Who told you? Who is it? Pollicott?"

"It's Mr. Lomax says that one of the old men has been found dead. Not Pollicott, sir—the other—the one nobody ever seems to see."

"Go on," I said, as another fear took shape in my mind.

"Mr. Lomax says one of the men on his way to Sluice Farm found him. He was walking along the Sea Wall when he heard some dog whining."

There was a silence between us as I envisaged the scene: the man Rowles lying on the boulders at the foot of the steep and dangerous section of the Wall; the dog—a whippet, Lomax had said, I remembered—whining and keeping guard.

"It seems incredible," I said. "But—accidents happen."

Mrs. Williams rolled her eyes upwards where she presumed heaven to be. She does nothing by halves: when there is cause for sorrow, no one can be more lugubrious.

"What must be must be," she said in her chapel-going tone. Then, with a quick return to the practical: "Mr. Lomax says he'd like to see you. He'll be round in a few minutes."

3

I dressed hurriedly. By the time I got downstairs Lomax was there. He was pacing up and down my sitting-room, and his usually cheerful face was grave.

"Well, Lomax," I said, "what's this I hear?" For some reason I was nervous and even alarmed, though I told myself there was nothing to be alarmed about.

"It's a bad business, Mr. Vaughan," said Lomax without preliminary. "Henry Rowles is dead."

"A *sad* business," I said, "not a *bad* business. Anyone can miss his step in the dark."

Lomax shook his head.

"I'm afraid Pollicott's in for a spot of bother, the way things are," he said.

I pretended not to understand.

"Pollicott?" I said. "Why? What has *he* got to do with it? Accidents will happen."

"Accident?" said Lomax. "You haven't forgotten what we went to see him about last night?"

I persisted in refusing to understand.

"Eh? Oh, the will! You mean Rowles hadn't had time to make it—so poor Pollicott loses his legacy."

Lomax looked at me as if I were guilty not so much of stupidity as of levity. He said slowly:

"That's not what I mean. I don't like the look of things, Mr. Vaughan—I don't like the look of them at all—for Pollicott."

I motioned him to a chair, and he sat down, but on the edge only. He had his pipe in his hand, but he seemed to have forgotten to smoke it. He used it to emphasise his points, tapping the palm of one hand with the shining bowl.

"Tell me about it," I said in a tone as grave as his own.

"Well, for one thing," said Lomax, "he's acting in such a queer way. He's so vague—so confused. When Collins questioned him just now he seemed not to be able to make up his mind what to say." He smacked his palm with the pipe bowl. "To put it bluntly, he seemed to be telling two quite different stories. I don't know what to make of it at all. But"—he shot a quick look at me—"I do think somebody ought to be watching his interests. He's incapable of looking after himself."

Collins is our local police-sergeant, a very decent fellow, provided you're on the right side of the law, but a formidable character if you're not.

"So the police are there already?" I said. "They don't waste much time in these parts."

Lomax nodded.

"Hot on the scent, as you might say."

"H'm," I mused. "What exactly is Collins after?"

Lomax said: "He doesn't seem to think it was an accident. He's going by something the doctor pointed out to him. When I left my place just now Collins was' phoning Superintendent Fadden—and I didn't like the sound of it at all."

At that moment I had one of those strange feelings everybody has had several times in his life, that I had known about this all along. Here was I, sitting in this room, which was rather dark in the morning because it faced west, and which smelt of stale cigar-smoke. The fire was not yet laid, and Mrs. Williams had placed a small paraffin-oil burner in front of the grate full of ashes. Opposite me was Lomax, serious and preoccupied, a man I had not known until a year ago when I came here. The furniture in the room was mine and familiar to me as my own person, yet it was differently arranged from the way it had been in my previous home. There was the heavy bookcase full of law books, brought from my office. Nothing very stimulating in all this, one would say. Yet suddenly I was seized with a conviction that I had been brought here, planted in this setting, which had been arranged like a stage-scene for just this moment. The effect was like a change of focus: the room ceased to be familiar, and became full of one great question.

I glanced up at my grandmother's clock on the mantelpiece. It said a quarter to nine. And it was still smiling.

"What did happen exactly?" I said.

"Exactly?" said Lomax. "Well, Pollicott burst into the kitchen as I was having breakfast. I can only tell you what he told me—and what I heard."

I reached out to the drawer of the bureau and took out a note-pad.

4

"I don't promise to remember every word," said Lomax. "He was in a very excited state, as you can imagine, and pretty well exhausted. He'd been up all night, of course."

"At his work?"

"So he says. I got my wife to make him some tea—I didn't think it advisable to give him a drink so early—and gradually he calmed down. At first he kept talking about the dog—"

"That's the whippet, isn't it?" I said.

"That's right. He began by saying when he got back from work this morning Henry wasn't there, nor Clipper either. Then he went on for a bit about Clipper: how they called him that because he was so trim and fast, and how he was a grand dog, really, though he was more Pollicott's dog then Henry's. I don't really know what he was getting at, Mr. Vaughan—in fact, I did ask myself if he was wandering—"

"Never mind," I said. I made a shorthand note of what Pollicott had said about Clipper. "Tell me everything he said. You never know what may turn out to be important."

"Well, I'm afraid I cut him a bit short about the dog," said Lomax. "I was anxious to get on to what happened."

"Yes?"

"But I had a job to get him away from Clipper. He said he thought at first Henry—he always calls Rowles 'Henry'—he thought Henry'd taken Clipper for another walk, though Rowles never did that in the mornings. Then he went off at another tangent about Rowles—how he liked to lie in bed in the morning and wait till Pollicott got back from work and took him a cup of tea."

"That seems to fit the picture very well!" I said.

"Yes, that's what *I* was thinking. So, Pollicott said, when he got back this morning and didn't find Henry there, his second thought was, perhaps Rowles hadn't slept so well last night. I asked him if Rowles was a bad sleeper, and he said, 'I wouldn't say that, Mr. Lomax—not as a general rule. But last night he was kind-a worried.'"

I looked up.

"You remember the conversation with those two men? Pollicott said then that Rowles was scared."

"Yes, I remember that all right, Mr. Vaughan," said Lomax. "But I thought it best not to go into that for the moment. I reckoned I had all I could do to get the plain facts out of him."

"You're right. We can ask him about that later, if it becomes necessary. Well, how did he discover that Rowles was dead? Did you get a clear account of that out of him?"

"Pretty clear. He said he waited a bit, thinking Rowles might turn up. Then he began to get worried himself. He was just going out to look for him when there was a banging on the door…"

THE BODY ON THE SHORE

I

There was a banging on the hut door.

Pollicott put down the cup and saucer he was carrying to the table and called out:

"All right, Henry, easy on there. Give the door a shove. It ain't bolted." Then, when nothing happened, he called out more loudly: "Give it a shove."

The banging began again.

"All right!" grumbled Pollicott. "I'm coming!"

As he shuffled across to the door it opened, and a head appeared round it, a man's head—a stranger's.

"Anybody there?" said the visitor; in the dim light of the hut he did not at first see Pollicott. He was a young man, a farm labourer. Catching sight of Pollicott, he said: "I say, can you come along and give me a hand? There's a chap hurt—at the foot of the Sea Wall. Seems to have fallen."

Pollicott's breath came unevenly.

"Who—who is it?" he gasped.

The labourer eyed him curiously.

"How should *I* know? He's lying face down. But if somebody don't shift him the tide'll be up over him."

"I'll come—I'll come," said Pollicott. Yet he stood staring helplessly at the visitor.

"Got a plank anywhere?" said the man. "He don't look too good to me. It'll be a job to move him over them rocks."

"There's planks outside," said Pollicott. "How—how did you find him?"

"I was coming along the top of the Wall on my way to work at Sluice Farm—my name's Morgan; I work down there for Mr. Lomax—and I heard a dog whining. I looked all round and that's how I come to see him. He's lying on his face, clean under the Wall. You can't see him from above—the Wall's a good thirty feet high just there. But you could see there was something wrong. So I climbed down."

Pollicott said quaveringly:

"Is he badly hurt?"

Morgan straddled, his thumbs in his waistcoat armholes.

"To tell you the truth, mate," he said with kindly callousness, "I doubt if there's any life left in him, judging by the looks of him. Not that I moved him: I know better than that. And, anyhow, the whippet wasn't willing for me to come too close…"

Pollicott pushed past him and shut the door.

"We must get him," he said; "bring him back here."

2

They fetched a plank from behind the hut and climbed up on to the Wall. Then at Morgan's suggestion they clambered down the sloping breakwater and over the rocks to where the breakwater ceased and the Wall rose perpendicularly above heaped-up boulders. Morgan, though he was young and strong, could not keep up with Pollicott; perhaps this was because Morgan was now carrying the plank—and perhaps because he didn't want to get there first, to where that black heap lay, guarded by a slate-grey whippet.

When Clipper saw Pollicott he began barking. Clipper seldom barked. He ran a little way to meet Pollicott, and together they scrambled over the last few boulders that separated them from Henry. On the shingle, still some distance away, the small waves of the incoming tide were lapping and hissing. Oyster-catchers welcomed the tide with their high trilling, and the curlew bubbled, flying above. There was still a slight mist on the sea.

Pollicott laid his thin, unwashed hand on Clipper's sleek pointed head and said hoarsely:

"All right, Clipper, old boy! Good dog! All right, get away now." He went down on his knees beside Henry.

Morgan laid down the plank and stood watching the scene with curiosity. The old man seemed very upset, Morgan said later. He did not touch the body. At first he just called in a low voice: "Henry! Henry!" And when his friend did not answer, Pollicott looked up at Morgan in anguish and said, as if appealing for contradiction:

"God forgive me! He's dead!"

3

Morgan had been looking on with so much interest that he quite jumped when Pollicott spoke to him; the old man's red-rimmed eyes were wild, and his grey hair blew about in the breeze. Yet though Morgan hadn't been listening, the words registered: "God forgive me!" Pollicott had said.

"Eh?" said Morgan. And then, seeing that Pollicott really was waiting for an answer: "Yeah," he said, speaking offhandedly to bring the old man to his senses, "he's a gonner all right." He stepped forward a pace to look, not at the body, but at Pollicott. The dog growled.

"You know him?" said Morgan inquisitively, prepared to give the dog a kick in the teeth, but Pollicott's "Down, Clipper, old boy!" reduced the growl to a whine.

Pollicott answered:

"He's my friend. We've lived together for twenty years." Then he turned back distractedly to the body and cried out: "I should-a done as you asked me, Henry! I didn't ought to have gone!"

This was getting a bit too much for Morgan, as he explained later. He was sorry for the poor bloke, but he didn't want a loony on his hands as well as a stiff, so he picked up the plank and said to Pollicott:

"Well, it's no good talking to *him*. *He* can't do anything. If we don't get him out of the way he'll be under the water as well." He laid the plank alongside Henry. "Come on," he said, hoping to rouse the old man by a bit of action, "help me carry him. We'll get him on to the plank. You'll have to help. I can lift him—or push him—that'd be better. But I can't carry him by myself—not over all these here rocks I can't." tie pushed the plank closer to Henry and began levering the body forward, while Pollicott still knelt beside it, looking bewildered.

"A nice place to fall over!" said Morgan, trying to cheer him. "You don't think he did it deliberate, do you?"

Pollicott didn't answer. Morgan wondered if, after all, he would do better to get help. The old man was obviously dazed with the shock, and it didn't seem at all certain that he would be strong enough to lift the other end of the plank, even though Morgan took the head and shoulders. This Henry was a big man. But when Morgan had got him somehow on to the plank Pollicott scrambled to his feet, and together they set out with their burden, avoiding the boulders as best they could, stumbling occasionally but gradually making their way to the foot of the breakwater. It was a miracle, Morgan said afterwards, how they managed to reach the top. Luckily the gradient was not too steep, and they edged up sideways until they reached the top and were able to lay down the body on the grass.

4

Morgan stood up and looked round. There was not a soul in sight. Nothing was to be seen except the long stretches of mud and the still, leaden sea on the one side, and on the other the green pastures cut up into oblongs by the reens. The hut was just below them, across one of the reens. Morgan took off his cap and scratched his head. He looked at the dead man, and then at Pollicott. Pollicott and the dog were watching him expectantly. Suddenly Morgan had a great longing to get away—to be with other people, where things were normal. He said:

"The next move is, we've got to get a doctor."

Pollicott said eagerly:

"I'll go."

"No," said Morgan, "*I'll* get him. I've got to get along to my work. I'll go back to the village and ring up from the call-box. You'd best stay here and look after your friend."

He went off along the grassy top of the Sea Wall, whistling softly to himself. His thoughts could be summed up in two words: "Rum go!"

MR. VAUGHAN'S STORY CONTINUED

I didn't of course hear the whole story of the discovery until later, when Lomax and I talked to Morgan the farm-labourer. Pollicott's account was confused; he seemed overcome by a sense of guilt, Lomax said; he supposed because he had left Henry alone. When he came to where Morgan went off to get the doctor, Pollicott quite broke down. I really was quite moved myself when Lomax—who is quite a good mimic—repeated the old man's words in something of the original tones:

"So Clipper and me was left with poor Henry, Mr. Lomax. And when I looks at him, it comes over me, like, all of a sudden. I just can't bear it. I just can't forgive myself for what I've done."

"At that," Lomax continued, "I spoke to him quite roughly. I said, 'Done? Don't be a fool, man! You couldn't help it. It was an accident.' I really was rather taken aback at his way of putting it, and it occurred to me at the time that his words might be given a different meaning—if anybody chose.

"But Pollicott just shook his head and said: 'It never would-a happened if I'd've stayed with him as he asked me.'"

"Did he leave the body unguarded on the Sea Wall when he came to you?" I said.

"That's just it, Mr. Vaughan, he did. I taxed him with that. I said it was stupid of him to run away and come here, leaving Rowles lying there. But all I could get out of Pollicott was that Clipper was there with Henry. Clipper wouldn't let anyone come near Henry, he said—not if Pollicott had told him to stay. He certainly is fond of that dog, Mr. Vaughan—and the dog seems devoted to him."

"They shouldn't have moved the body," I said. "Morgan should have gone at once and fetched the police. It would have been just as quick, probably, if not quicker."

"I know," said Lomax. "I told him that too. But he said the tide was coming in fast. Actually high water isn't till nine forty-three this morning, but Pollicott seemed to have lost all count of time. Then I asked him if Morgan was going to notify the police, and he said he didn't know: he'd only mentioned the doctor.

"So I rang the Police Station to make sure, and found they'd left a few minutes before. I thought I'd better go along and find out what was happening—and take Pollicott along with me, before the police began getting any funnier ideas.

"We went back across the fields from my place to the Sea Wall. Pollicott came quite willingly—eagerly, I'd say. He seemed to think it would be all right if I was there.

"By the time we got here Dr. Morris had arrived, and Collins and P.C. Green. They'd carried Rowles's body down from the Sea Wall into the hut, and Collins was standing with Green outside the door.

"Now this is where we come to the part that worries me, Mr. Vaughan," said Lomax, "and I can give you a better account of what was said and done, because I was present and heard and saw it all, and even asked a few questions. So if you like to take notes, I think I can remember everything pretty accurately from now onward…"

THE POLICE TAKE OVER

I

Police-Sergeant Collins, standing at the door of the hut with Police-Constable Green, watched the approach of Lomax and Pollicott with the quiet expectancy of a cat watching a mouse nearing its hole. He was a tall thin man with a long thin face, and he made no attempt to disguise his belief in the continuous guilt of practically everybody. He spoke and acted as if anyone denying this assumption were wasting his time. Otherwise his manner was correct.

"Good morning, Mr. Lomax," he said. "Glad to see you've brought Pollicott along. I was just going to send a man to find him." He spoke as if Pollicott were an inanimate object. "This is a very serious matter, Mr. Lomax. This'll have to be gone into pretty thoroughly."

Lomax, pretending not to understand, said:

"What's wrong?"

"Plenty," said Collins with relish.

Lomax demurred.

"Just a nasty accident, surely. Rowles wasn't a young man. Most of us would have got pretty badly damaged if we'd fallen off just there."

"Fallen," jeered Collins, "or got pushed?" He motioned towards the door. "Will you step inside here a minute, Mr. Lomax?" He turned to Pollicott, recognising his animate existence for the first time. "And you," he said roughly.

Lomax entered. It took him a moment to adjust his vision in the dim light. Then:

"Good God!" he said. "What on earth...?"

He could hardly believe his eyes. The body of Henry Rowles was lying on the floor with a rug over it, and the whippet was still keeping guard, but silently now. Dr. Morris was there too, standing with his back to the window. But what staggered Lomax was that the whole place was in confusion. Everything seemed to be on the floor. The amount of furniture was small; but everything had been ransacked, every drawer pulled out, everything swept off the shelves; papers, books—what few there were—clothes tossed everywhere. The door leading to the sleeping-quarters was ajar; through the opening it could be seen that confusion reigned there also. The bedding had been dragged off, and a mattress, slit open, blocked the doorway.

Lomax looked again at the living-room. The table was laid for two. But at the nearer end, where the tablecloth didn't reach, he was startled to see a sheet of paper covered with writing.

Collins, looking in over his shoulder, said:

"You see, Mr. Lomax; there's plenty to explain."

Lomax half-turned irritably.

"I see the place has been ransacked. But whatever for? I doubt if these two old men had anything worth stealing."

"I don't mean the room," said Collins. He pointed accusingly at the table. "I mean *that*. Will you take a look at that piece of paper?"

"I was wondering about it," said Lomax. He stepped forward, and was aware that Pollicott was still close behind him. "Pollicott," he said in exasperation, "why on earth didn't you tell me just now that the hut had been ransacked too?"

Collins, before Pollicott could answer, interposed:

"That's another thing I want to know." Then, as Lomax stepped forward again towards the table: "Don't touch that paper, sir—don't pick it up! We don't want it moved. But you can read it where it lays. It's worth casting an eye over."

Lomax leaned over the paper and read aloud:

"'I, John Henry Vincent Peter Dallingsworth Clairvaux, formerly of Johannesburg, South Africa, otherwise known as Henry Rowles of The Hut...' H'm." He turned to Pollicott. "Your friend wrote this will after all, then, when he came back last night?"

"Yes, sir, he did that, sir," said Pollicott eagerly. "It's lying here when I comes in this morning, just as he left it for me to see."

Lomax continued reading:

"'...declare that I am of sound mind and that this is my last Will and Testament... I appoint Robert Lomax'—what's this? Oh yes, I remember, I did say I'd act—'of the Sluice Farm St. Dyfrig's-in-Lostlands... sole Executor of this my Will. I devise and bequeath all my real and personal estate whatsoever and wheresoever to George Pollicott of The Hut, near St. Dyfrig's...'" He straightened himself to look Collins in the eyes and said significantly: "What a pity he couldn't get it signed before he had his accident!"

Collins said grimly:

"Just move the piece of blotting-paper to one side, sir, and look at the bottom."

Lomax, surprised, lifted off the blotting-paper gingerly and read:

"'In witness whereof I have hereunto set my hand this Ninth day of October One Thousand Nine Hundred and Forty Eight. J.H.V.P.D. Clairvaux, also known as Henry Rowles.' And—yes—by Jove!" he exclaimed. "He's got it witnessed after all!—'Signed by the above J.H.V.P.D. Clairvaux in the presence of himself and us: John Smith, Bill Brown, both of 200 Slype Street, Liverpool.' This is astonishing!"

Collins said with unconcealed satisfaction:

"Providential, according to the date, sir, if you know what I mean." He turned swiftly to Pollicott. "Well, Pollicott, what have *you* got to say, eh?"

Lomax protested.

"You're rattling him, Collins. He's had a bit of a shock, you know. Give him time."

Collins said grimly:

"Oh, we'll give him time all right!" Again he turned to Pollicott, speaking more suavely. "Tell me, Pollicott—these two men, John Smith and Bill Brown, who signed the will—who are they?"

Pollicott looked bewildered. He gazed first at Lomax, then at Collins, and finally said:

"I dunno."

"You saw them sign, didn't you?" Collins was impatient.

Pollicott came to life with a jerk:

"No, no, sir! I was gone by then!"

"*Then?*" Collins pounced on the word. "So you do know *when* it was signed."

Lomax intervened.

"I think I can answer that for him, Collins. There's no mystery about that. I was here with Mr. Vaughan when these two men called." He spoke encouragingly to Pollicott. "You remember, Pollicott, they came when we were here. You went outside to speak to them."

Collins said incredulously:

"*You* were here last night, sir?"

"Yes, yes," said Lomax. "I'll tell you about that later." He turned back to the old man. "You remember, Pollicott?" He urged him again, still gently.

There was a pause. Pollicott's gaze shifted. Then he said falteringly:

"What men, sir?"

"Oh, come now!" said Lomax, less gently. "You can't have lost your memory to that extent. You know who I mean: the two men who came to the door, and you went out to speak to them. You stayed out there talking to them long enough."

Pollicott said slowly:

"Maybe I did."

"You certainly did," said Lomax firmly. "Mr. Vaughan and I were getting impatient. You didn't say their names, but"—he almost winked at Pollicott to give him his cue—"they were John Smith and Bill Brown, I suppose?"

Pollicott said hastily:

"Oh no, sir—no!"

"What?" said Lomax, disgusted at the old man's evasiveness. "Surely two other men didn't call as well? You don't mean to say you had two pairs of callers?"

But Pollicott would not be drawn. He said stubbornly:

"I dunno, sir. I leaves the hut to go to my work, and after that I don't see nobody except the two chaps who passes me by in the lane where I sits in my cabin, like."

"What, another two chaps?" Lomax exclaimed. "Is this another pair again?"

Pollicott answered quite solemnly:

"Only gypsies, sir."

Lomax glanced at Collins. Collins gave a scornful bark.

"Ha! You'd better think again, man: the gypsies broke camp a week ago."

Pollicott said obstinately:

"They was gypsies passed me in the lane. I see'd 'em. I see'd their ear-rings."

"In the dark?" snapped Collins.

Pollicott's reply came with unusual quickness:

"By the light of my fire."

"Sure you didn't dream it?" sneered Collins.

Pollicott's thin face grew suddenly red and his voice cracked with rage.

"They *was* gypsies, I tell you! I see'd 'em. One of 'em said 'good night' to me as he went by, and the other one asked me the time."

The old man's outburst had startled even Collins into temporary silence. Before he could think of another question, Dr. Morris called out from his stance before the window:

"Let him alone, Collins, for the present. He's all in, and no wonder."

Collins, baffled, looked at Pollicott, who was still muttering to himself angrily and inarticulately.

"All right, doctor," he said, "if *you* say so. But he'll have to come along to the station presently and make a statement. I'll have to get in touch with Superintendent Fadden."

Lomax interposed soothingly:

"By the way, Collins, don't you think I'd better have some breakfast sent down before we go any further? He'll be more use to you if he's fed. I'd suggest taking him along, but I doubt if he can stand any more. And you'll want to 'phone for an ambulance, won't you? If you care to come with me, you can put your call through from my place."

"All right," said Collins reluctantly. "Green can stay here. He'd better come inside."

2

A few minutes later they were trudging along the wet path beside the reen, across the fields towards Sluice Farm. Collins, impatient to reach a telephone, plunged on ahead. The doctor, however, would not be hurried. Lomax walked with him, wondering how he could get this rather taciturn member of a dictatorial profession to speak. After one or two false starts he said bluntly:

"What's your view, doctor?"

This did not work either. Dr. Morris walked on without replying.

"Oh, of course," went on Lomax, "I know what the police suspect. It's their job. But I just don't accept it. Pollicott may look like an old tramp, but he's a decent enough old fellow really. No, I just can't see him planning anything so devilish against a man he's always looked after like a brother." He found himself getting quite heated as he talked and argued—against a blank wall. But at last the doctor was speaking. He said coldly:

"You can't get past the facts, Lomax."

"It's the *facts* I'm concerned about," retorted Lomax. "So far, there are only suspicions—prejudices."

"Rather more than that," said Dr. Morris drily. "The man was murdered."

Lomax, startled though he was by this firm statement, did not show it.

"How?" he said sceptically. "You mean you accept Collins's suggestions—that Rowles was pushed over the Wall, and Pollicott pushed him?"

Dr. Morris's tone was unemotional.

"Worse even than that, Lomax. This man Rowles was lying face downwards. He'd been struck a heavy blow on the *back* of his skull. Actually he was dead before he was 'pushed.'"

"What?" said Lomax. He was not an excitable man, but he was excited now, and for the first time dismayed. "But surely you don't think—?" he began. Hope rose again. "You didn't see Rowles until his body was brought into the hut. You can't be sure how he was lying when he was found."

Dr. Morris remained unperturbed. He trudged along, never looking at Lomax, watching the ground before him, never varying his tone.

"There's all that damage to the face," he said, as if he were already writing his report, "though it was the blow on the head that killed him. And another thing: there were no marks on the palms of the hands. A man falling—what's the first thing he does? Puts out his hands to save himself, of course. But Rowles's hands were uninjured. In fact, they looked as if he'd never done a day's work in his life. Remarkable for a man in his position," he mused. "I noticed them particularly."

They reached the farmyard. Hens ran clucking from under their feet. Starlings were whistling on the ridge-tiles of the house. Somewhere out of sight the rattling of milk-cans could be heard. Lomax, leaving Dr. Morris to continue on his way undisturbed by the cobblestones under his small feet, hurried ahead to where Collins waited impatiently, his long neck already bent to adjust itself to the low door.

"Molly!" called out Lomax, striding into the big kitchen. "Could you send some breakfast over to poor old Pollicott? He's in a spot of bother, I'm afraid. And here's Sergeant Collins—and Dr. Morris is nearly here—"

Mrs. Lomax came forward, bright and smiling.

"Good morning, Sergeant! Of course, dear: I'll send something over at once. You go on inside—the fire's lit in the front room."

"This way, Collins," said Lomax. "Come along in, doctor. Help yourself to a drink. Here you are, Collins—in the hall. You'd better suggest to Superintendent Fadden that he meets you here. This is the shortest cut."

As he passed through the kitchen he said to his wife:

"I'm going along to see Mr. Vaughan. Look after these fellows first, will you, Molly? You'd better wait till Fadden comes, and give him a start. Then bring something for Pollicott. I daresay I'll be there before you."

Molly nodded. Reassured as always by the sight of her, Lomax hurried away. Passing through the hall, he heard Collins's incisive voice asking for Superintendent Fadden.

III

The Enquiry Begins

MR. VAUGHAN'S STORY CONTINUED

I

Lomax ended his narration, with which my shorthand had easily kept pace, though I could not record the mixtures of doubt and concern that accompanied it in his tone and gestures.

"So you see, Mr. Vaughan," he said, "things don't look too good for Pollicott. Every time he opens his mouth he comes out with something that makes matters worse. First he won't say anything about those two fellows we overheard talking to him last night; he even tries to pretend he can't remember they were there. Then he knows nothing about the signatures. Then he tells a cock-and-bull story about gypsies. It's beyond me. If only he'd tell the truth! Surely he can see the matter's too serious for lying! What has he got to hide?"

I reflected. Then I put away my notebook and pencil.

"Come along, Lomax," I said. "There's nothing else for it. I'd better come with you to the hut and have a word with him. There's certainly more in this than meets the eye, I agree."

I took my coat and hat, and we managed to slip out without the knowledge of either Mac or Mrs. Williams. It was a beautiful autumn morning; sunny, with traces of white mist still clinging to the reens. People were going to church or chapel. The church bells were pealing merrily, and on the tower the golden cockerel was gazing south-westward. We talked little as we made our way along the top of the Sea Wall.

2

When we came near to the path leading down to the hut we saw Fadden approaching from the other direction. He had evidently been inspecting the place where Rowles's body was found. We met at the junction. He gave Lomax a curt nod and me a more penetrating look as he wished us good morning.

"You're here early, Mr. Vaughan," he said.

He and I knew each other well. We had met before over various cases when I had been in practice, and I knew exactly what sort of man we had to deal with. Fadden is an able man within his limitations, which are determined by his absolute devotion to his job. He has complete integrity. Like most men who are concerned with the detection of crime, he is a little over-ready to believe that everybody else is trying to thwart justice, or at least himself. But he is not uncooperative when he is rightly handled, and he has—what most of his profession lack—a touch of imagination, which sometimes leads him to do the unexpected. He is not, however, to be treated lightly—and certainly never with weakness. I therefore announced sharply:

"It's just possible, Superintendent, I may be able to help you—in getting at the truth of this unfortunate affair."

Fadden, polite but sceptical, said:

"Well—maybe. Shall we go down?"

We climbed down—it was easy enough by daylight—crossed the reen, and entered the hut.

It was a melancholy sight. The body of Henry Rowles had been taken away, and Pollicott was sitting disconsolately in the midst of the disorder. All was as Lomax had described: the table partly laid, the drawers open, papers and books on the floor—and Henry Rowles's will lying conspicuously at one end of the table. I walked across at once to look at it. Fadden went over to Pollicott, and Lomax followed. While seeming not to listen, I heard the whole of their conversation as I bent over the will.

3

Fadden began, rather sternly:

"Well, Pollicott, there's no doubt your friend's death was not accidental. You know that?"

Pollicott's voice was tremulous.

"So they tell me, sir." With sudden vehemence he cried out: "But I didn't have nothing to do with it, sir, so help me God!"

Fadden, a little taken aback, said gruffly:

"I'm not saying you had. Nobody wants to fasten anything on to you—you realise that?" Fadden, I knew, was sensitive to any suggestion that the police did not always keep all Judge's Rules. "All the same," he went on more mildly, "I want to know a few things you and nobody else can tell me."

Lomax's voice was lowered, but it carried across to me as I polished my glasses and bent down again over Rowles's will.

"Aren't you going to warn him or something?" he remonstrated.

Fadden, again touched on his tender spot, said stiffly:

"He's not being charged with anything—yet." But his tone was less aggressive as he said to Pollicott: "When precisely did you last see Henry Rowles?"

Pollicott answered readily.

"When I leaves for my work last night, he were sitting at that table, like."

"When was that?" said Fadden. "Seven—eight—nine?"

Pollicott hesitated.

"It were a bit later than ordinary, because Henry, he don't want me to go—God forgive me!"

Fadden checked him.

"He didn't want you to go. Why not?"

"He was scared."

"What was he scared of?"

Again Pollicott hesitated—then he said slowly:

"He'd been having letters."

Fadden snapped at this, and I too pricked up my ears.

"Letters?" he said. "Who from?"

But Pollicott had gone vague again.

"I dunno."

"You never saw them?"

"Oh," said Pollicott, weighing his words, "I *see'd* 'em all right—but not so as to know what was in them."

"Didn't he tell you who wrote them?"

Pollicott answered with a certain pride:

"Henry wasn't one to talk." Then some other idea or recollection seemed to occur to him. "Leastways, he was and he wasn't. Sometimes he'd talk and talk, and other times he'd shut down like a limpet on a rock."

Fadden said with controlled impatience:

"Where are the letters now?"

The answer was as I expected.

"I dunno."

4

There was a pause. Fadden began again.

"Well—you went to your work. You're employed as a night-watchman, aren't you?"

"Yes, sir," said Pollicott. He always answered eagerly at first. "I be a night-watchman down where they're laying the new water-pipes to Cousins' Farm."

"And what time do you get there in the evening?"

"Nine o'clock, sir—leastways, that's when I did ought to be there. And as a rule I gets there in good time. But last night I reckon I was a bit later—what with Henry keeping on so."

"How much later?" said Fadden, missing his cue, in my opinion. I knew what the answer to *that* one would be:

"I dunno."

"Was Rowles expecting visitors last night?"

"No, sir," said Pollicott hesitantly, "not visitors—leastways—" His voice trailed away.

"Well?" Fadden said. He waited. But all he got from Pollicott was:

"I dunno."

5

Fadden walked across to the table. I moved away and stood with my back to the window.

"Now about this will," Fadden began. "Your friend apparently drafted it yesterday."

Lomax took a step forward.

"I really think Pollicott should be warned."

Fadden said angrily:

"I know my business, Lomax! I'm simply asking for information at present." His voice grew harsh. "If and when I decide to make a charge against *anyone*, the usual warning will be given." He turned again to Pollicott. "You were here when Rowles drafted this will, weren't you?"

"Yes, sir."

"When was that?"

"It were just after Mr. Lomax and the legal gentleman there had left," said Pollicott, "and Henry come back with Clipper."

"Oh," said Fadden, "so you were there when it was signed?"

"No, sir."

"You mean to say"—Fadden was getting annoyed again—"this will was written while you were here, and not signed until after you'd left to go to your work?"

"Must-a been," said Pollicott stolidly.

Another pause. Fadden began again.

"These names—John Smith, Bill Brown—are they the names of friends of yours?"

"No, sir," said Pollicott. "Never heard of 'em, sir."

"You're sure you don't know of *any*body who came in here after you left, and witnessed Rowles's signature?"

Pollicott's hesitation was noticeable.

"I—don't think so, sir."

Fadden motioned to me to come nearer. I crossed to the table, and he said to me in an undertone:

"Well, Mr. Vaughan, this is a queer set-up, isn't it? Do *you* make anything of it, eh?"

I turned to the table and focused my pocket magnifying glass on the bottom of the will. Then I said with deliberation:

"I should say these signatures aren't genuine." And when Fadden exclaimed in surprise, I added: "The writing's obviously faked. The signatures are in the handwriting of uneducated persons who have made a strenuous attempt at disguise. Look at 'John Smith' here: violent backward slope. And 'Bill Brown', violent forward slope."

"Let me have a look," said Fadden. I handed him the magnifying glass, and he bent himself almost into a right angle. I left him and crossed again to the window.

6

Lomax was saying in an undertone to Pollicott:

"You didn't sign that will yourself, did you? You weren't such a crazy fool?"

Pollicott whispered back:

"Oh no, sir—no indeed!"

"Why won't you tell the Superintendent," said Lomax, "about those two men who were here last night? If *they* signed the will, that lets you out, don't you see?"

Fadden evidently heard the whispering. He came back to Pollicott and said more sternly:

"What time did you get back this morning?"

Pollicott gaped at him. There was a pause before he said:

"About half-past seven, sir."

"And you found the hut as we see it now—everything scattered about?" said Fadden.

"Yes, sir, that's right, sir," said Pollicott.

"Then," said Fadden, "why didn't you go at once and summon the police?"

Another long pause. Pollicott began with many hesitations:

"I were that dazed, sir—and Henry not being here, I didn't know what to do. And then the fellow come here—and he tells me Henry's fallen off the Wall…"

7

It was a relief when we heard Mrs. Lomax's voice outside speaking to Green.

"That's all right, officer. My husband's here." Without more ado, she entered. She was carrying a tray, with tea and a covered plate of food. We all stared at her, and Fadden scowled.

"Oh, good morning, gentlemen," she said in the cheerful manner of one used to getting her own way in all circumstances. "Please forgive me if I'm disturbing you, but I've brought this poor man something to eat. You don't mind, do you, Superintendent?" Ignoring his black look, she swept towards the table. "Now come along, Mr. Pollicott, you must keep up your strength, you know. I'll pour you out a cup of tea."

Lomax hurried forward to take the tray from her, but she had already reached the table.

"Look out, Molly! Be careful of that piece of paper!" he called. He moved to snatch Rowles's will from under the descending tray, but Fadden forestalled him.

"*I'll* take charge of that," he said. "Excuse me, ma'am." He took the will, folded it and put it into his inner breast pocket. Then he turned to me. "I'll get a handwriting expert on this at once, Mr. Vaughan, especially in view of what you say."

"Yes, do," I said, "and you'll check up on that address, too, of course."

"Of course." He seemed anxious, now, to be gone.

"I think you'll find," I said, "that the signatures are *not* by the same hand."

"Maybe," said Fadden rather irritably, "maybe not. Well, I'll be getting back now. I've a lot to see to. Good morning, Mrs. Lomax. I'll leave you to your errand of mercy." He jerked his head at Lomax. "Will you kindly step outside with me for a moment?"

They went out together.

8

Mrs. Lomax cheerfully took charge.

"There, that's better!" she said. "There's more room to breathe now." She called to Pollicott, who was standing helplessly where Fadden had left him. "Come along now, Mr. Pollicott, come and eat up your bacon! That's none of your grocer's stuff—that's a special side of our own curing."

Pollicott, reassured, shuffled forward, sat down and began eating ravenously. The way he cleared up that plate of bacon, two eggs and fried potatoes was, I suppose, the quickest thing he'd ever done. When he slowed down a little Mrs. Lomax began talking again.

"My, what a mess your place is in! What wicked men there are in the world nowadays!"

Pollicott, putting down his cup, nodded at her solemnly.

"A truer word was never spoken, ma'am." His voice quavered.

"You mustn't take this too much to heart," she said. "Your friend—he's gone, poor fellow, but he wouldn't want you to grieve too much, you know."

Pollicott said earnestly:

"Henry do know I never would have hurt a hair of his head."

"I'm sure he does," said Mrs. Lomax soothingly. She looked round the room. Her eyes fell on the guitar hanging near by on the wall. "That's a fine guitar you have there. Was that his?"

"No, ma'am, that's mine," said Pollicott.

"*You* play this guitar?" cried Mrs. Lomax. "Why, that's clever of you! I tried to learn once, but I never could master it. Will you play me something—when you've had another cup of tea?"

Pollicott set down his cup and saucer; his hands trembled, and cup and saucer made a rattling sound.

"I dunno as I could play today, ma'am," he said slowly, "or ever again. I allus used to play it when Henry was out walking with the dog, to let him know it was time to come home—supper was ready, or whatever it was. And last night I played to let him know the coast was clear. I played the old tune..." His voice cracked as he said frantically: "I can't play it again, ma'am! It'd make me think at any minute I'd see Henry coming in through that door—and Clipper—" He laid his arm on the table and his head on his arm, and I was dismayed to hear several loud sobs.

Mrs. Lomax looked across at me.

"Poor man!" she said.

Pollicott's sobs had ceased. He was feebly groping in his pocket. Suddenly Mrs. Lomax stooped.

"Here—here, Mr. Pollicott!" she said. From under the table she brought out a large red silk handkerchief. "Here's your handkerchief, lying on the floor—which is no place for such a fine one. Here, dry your eyes, and I'll give you another cup of tea." She held out the handkerchief to Pollicott, and when he did not take it she placed it in his hands. "You'll soon feel better," she went on, bustling round the teapot. "There's nothing to be afraid of. Don't be frightened of the police: they're perfectly fair, you know, and if you've done nothing wrong they can't hurt you."

Pollicott did not answer, and did not appear to have heard. He was staring at the handkerchief in his hands.

"Mr. Lomax will help you," she continued, as if that were the answer to everything. She cast me an anxious look—anxious for Pollicott, not about me. "Mr. Vaughan, too—isn't that so, Mr. Vaughan?"

I said distinctly, not sure if he would even remember who I was:

"That's why I'm here, Pollicott."

But Pollicott was still staring at the red handkerchief. He said slowly:

"This ain't my handkerchief, ma'am."

"Isn't it?" said Mrs. Lomax. "It was lying here under the table. I suppose it's your friend's: it's such a grand one."

Pollicott came to life a little at that.

"Under the table, was it, ma'am?" he said wonderingly. "Yes—it must be Henry's. He liked all his things to be of the best, Henry did." His pride in Henry gave place again to wonder. "Funny, though: I never see'd that one before."

9

Lomax looked in at the door.

"Are you ready, Molly?" he said. "The Superintendent wants Pollicott to go along with him to the Police Station." He came into the room. "Nothing to be afraid of, Pollicott. They just want you to make a statement, that's all."

Pollicott had risen. He stuffed the red handkerchief into his sleeve. Lomax stepped up to him and said rapidly in a lower tone:

"But for Heaven's sake tell him the truth! Tell him about those fellows who called last night." Pollicott looked up at him, vacant and stubborn. "You *must*," Lomax insisted, "otherwise Mr. Vaughan and I'll have to tell him, and that looks so bad—as if you had something to hide—especially as Sergeant Collins knows about them already. Tell the Superintendent the whole story."

He spoke very emphatically. Pollicott's answer was acquiescent but evasive.

"All right, Mr. Lomax, sir. I'll do the best I can."

"And don't try to be smart and make anything up," admonished Lomax. "The police can always check up on everything you say."

Pollicott stood silent, looking at the floor.

"No more talk of gypsies, for instance!" said Lomax, rallying him.

But Pollicott merely muttered to himself:

"Gypsies…"

It was impossible to tell if he had given up the idea or was simply confirming it. Lomax chose not to press the matter further. He gave Pollicott a friendly pat on the back:

"Right!" he said. "Now off you go—and keep your pecker up."

Pollicott shuffled away mechanically. At the door he turned.

"What'll become of Clipper, sir," he said, "if there's no one to look after him?"

"That's all right," said Lomax kindly. "We'll take care of Clipper. Go along now. Mr. Vaughan and I'll see you later."

Pollicott went.

10

Mrs. Lomax turned with lively concern to Lomax.

"What's all this about, Bob?" she said. "They surely don't think that poor old man would do anybody any harm, let alone his friend that he's kept ever since I can remember?"

"Well, Molly," said Lomax awkwardly. "Things don't look too good for him, that's sure. Fadden doesn't say much, but a blind man can see the way his mind's working. There's Rowles found dead with his head bashed in. There's the will made only last night and in Pollicott's favour. And there are those signatures—phoney"—he shook his head—"phoney."

Mrs. Lomax said incredulously:

"They think he wrote them—Pollicott, I mean—they think he wrote them himself?"

"Fadden does," said Lomax. He looked to me for support. "Mr. Vaughan doesn't agree."

"No," I said, "I don't."

Mrs. Lomax continued with her own line of argument.

"But the hut—in such a state!—as if someone had been searching for something." She gave a quick look round the chaotic room, and I felt that for two pins she would start putting it straight.

Lomax said: "Yes, I know—but Fadden, now, he thinks this mess is a fake, to make the whole thing look like a burglary. He says you can always tell, because fakers overdo the business."

"A good point," I said, "but—"

Mrs. Lomax cut across me with lively scorn.

"Meaning Pollicott did this too? Oh, what nonsense! Why, the poor old fellow's incapable of even imagining such a thing! He's got a nature that's as sweet as—wild honey."

Neither of us smiled: the expression seemed natural on her lips. Lomax said admiringly:

"And so have you, Molly, my love!" He threw off his Fadden-induced depression. "Don't you worry: somehow, in spite of everything, I feel the same—and I know Mr. Vaughan does too." He gave me a look half-confident, half-appealing. "I'm hoping he'll decide to take up Pollicott's cause."

Mrs. Lomax came a step towards me.

"Oh, I hope you do, I hope you do!" she said. Her firm conviction found the right words. "It'd be an act of *justice* as well as charity!"

I made a non-committal gesture: but I knew I was committed.

11

Soon afterwards I left them. As I walked slowly home along the Sea Wall in the bright autumn sunshine, Mrs. Lomax's words re-echoed in my mind: "An act of justice as well as charity." I began pondering on the circumstances of the death of Henry Rowles—or whatever his name was...

The tide had now receded; the little waves at the edge were hardly visible beyond the mud flats with their oases of coarse grass not yet claimed by the all-engulfing sea. Starlings wheeled above me, sometimes visible against the pale blue sky, sometimes disappearing as the sunlight caught them at a certain angle. I saw one group that seemed to dive straight into the sea, but just as I was getting anxious they all rose up again like a swarm of bees. On the other, the landward side, I saw the heron standing immobile at the edge of one of the reens, watching for his prey...

"Henry Rowles," I thought, "what *was* the name on that newly-drafted will?"

My memory has always been good. When I was a boy I used to be able to remember a whole page of printed matter after a single reading. It is a visual memory. I can bring it into action still, if I wish. No sooner had I asked myself the question than the written page floated before me:

"I, John Henry Vincent Peter Dallingsworth Clairvaux, otherwise known as Henry Rowles... declare that I am of sound mind and that this is my last Will and Testament..."

"Clairvaux," I said to myself. "Clairvaux: that name has a familiar sound..."

12

As I came out of the church lane into the road Nurse Duncan, the district nurse, wobbled towards me on her ancient bicycle.

"Hello, Mr. Vaughan!" she called out. "Busy this morning?" She dismounted. "I saw you and Mr. Lomax off together early as I was coming back from Cousins' Farm." She came closer, leaning across her bicycle. "Sad business, this, about Pollicott's friend!"

News gets about quickly in Lostlands, and our nurse is an unfailing carrier of it.

"You were out on a case last night?" I said.

"Yes—twins." She laughed heartily. In spite of her profession she still finds the birth of twins amusing. "Two boys—would you believe it? I tell Mr. Cousins she's trying to help him: he's always grumbling he can't get labour for the farm!"

I fancied I had heard this joke before, but I smiled to oblige her, and said:

"What time were you called out?"

"Three-thirty this morning," she said promptly. "What a time! Foggy it was, too. But Mother Nature doesn't consult my convenience."

"Then you must have passed Pollicott's little cabin there by the road works, didn't you? Did you have a word with him at all?"

"Funny you should ask," said Nurse Duncan. "I did pass by his cabin, of course—it's just near the entrance gate to the farm—but I didn't see Pollicott. In fact, he wasn't there."

"He wasn't there! Perhaps he'd gone away for a few minutes—"

Nurse Duncan gave me a peculiar look.

"He hadn't *been* there," she said, "for quite a while. The cabin door was locked, and his charcoal fire was almost out. It was still warm, though."

"Oh, well," I said, "perhaps Pollicott's on duty at some other point this week. They change them round, I believe."

Nurse Duncan said meaningly:

"As a matter of fact, he *was* there earlier on. Mr. Jenkins the inspector was at Cousins's when I popped in again just now, and he was telling Mr. Cousins how Pollicott was late again last night. Mr. Jenkins was saying how he'd had to speak to him several times about it—"

"What time did Jenkins see Pollicott there?" I interrupted sharply.

"Oh, about ten, I think it was," said Nurse Duncan. "He was trying to remember exactly, so as to tell Sergeant Collins. And they were saying I ought to go along myself and tell him Pollicott wasn't there at four this morning." She thrust her round face with the pointed nose towards me. "Do *you* think I should, Mr. Vaughan?"

I said coldly:

"Certainly, if you think it important. But I shouldn't speak of it to anyone else, if I were you. People are always all too ready to jump to wrong conclusions." And before she could ask me any questions I bade her good morning and went on my way.

13

That evening after chapel Lomax called on me to tell me the latest developments. The news was all bad. Pollicott, in view of his unsatisfactory answers and the discrepancies of his answers, had now been detained in custody and was to be formally charged in the morning.

"And the worst of it is," Lomax said, "Fadden has rung up the Liverpool Police and found out that there's no such address as 200 Slype Street—and therefore, he reckons, no such men as Smith and Brown."

"And the handwriting expert?" I said.

"Report's not yet received," said Lomax. "But the post mortem confirms what Dr. Morris said this morning about the way Rowles died."

"I'm afraid my news isn't very good either," I said. I told him of the encounter with Nurse Duncan. "So you see," I concluded, "Pollicott not only has no alibi: he's *proved* to be lying about his movements last night. You remember he said he didn't get back to the hut till half-past seven this morning?"

"Yes," said Lomax, "he's said that several times to us and the police."

"And now we hear that he wasn't there at four a.m. So you see there is a gap to three and a half hours or more to be accounted for."

"He must have gone back home," suggested Lomax, "probably to see if Rowles was all right."

"Perhaps," I said. "But the police won't accept that. There's also the fact that he won't say anything about the men who called when we were there—or has he done so by now?"

"Not he," said Lomax gloomily. "He just shuts up like a clam when they're mentioned. And yet he will keep on with this story of gypsies, when everybody knows the gypsies left their encampment here a week ago. I can't think what's the matter with him. God knows what sort of a figure he'll cut before a jury."

"We must see to it," I said, "that he doesn't get so far."

We sat for a time in silence, Lomax smoking his pipe and looking very lugubrious. Meanwhile, my own thoughts were maturing. The clock on the mantelpiece gave out its pretty silvery chime and brought me out of my reverie.

"You know, Lomax," I said. "I've been thinking. I believe we—or rather the police—are on the wrong track altogether in this affair."

Lomax looked up with dawning hope.

"You've got a new slant on it?"

"You see," I went on, "they're concentrating on the killer—and everything they turn up in that direction points, frankly, to old Pollicott. But I'm pretty sure he's innocent—as innocent as—well, you yourself, Lomax." I laughed, but Lomax didn't. "Now," I said, "*I* think what we should do is to concentrate on—*the man who was killed.*"

"On Rowles?" he said. "Good gracious, why?"

"Yes," I said, "on Henry Rowles—or Clairvaux—or whoever he really was." A certain excitement mounted in me as I expounded my idea. "The outstanding feature of this case, when you come to think of it, is that we *don't* know who he really was."

"That's true," said Lomax slowly, "though I hadn't thought of it."

"What are the facts about him?" I said. "He turned up there twenty years ago from—the Lord knows where: *he* says Johannesburg. He makes a will in the name of Clairvaux, so evidently that's the name he prefers—for it was under that name he lived when he was abroad, so he says, and under that name he deposited these sums of money he was so anxious to leave to Pollicott. At least it's true that there is a deposit book among those papers you gave me, bearing the name Clairvaux. Does that name convey anything to you?"

Lomax wrinkled up his brow.

"It seems familiar somehow—but I can't say I really know."

I indulged in a certain quiet triumph as I enlightened him:

"Clairvaux, my dear fellow, is the family name of one of the oldest *and richest* families in England. I haven't a *Debrett* here, but

I've looked them up in *Whitaker's*. The present head of the family is Lord Assche of Ashenford, tenth baron, born 1891, succeeded 1908. Tomorrow, when I go into town, I shall be able to add further details, but this I do know without consulting any more books of reference: Lord Assche, among other things, holds the controlling interest in Silk and Synthetic Fabrics Limited. So you see, if Rowles was an impostor or was suffering from delusions, he was flying mighty high!"

Lomax emitted a cloud of smoke and then a low whistle.

"No wonder he thought the world owed him a living!" he said. "But you surely don't think there's anything in it?"

"Probably not," I said. "It seems highly unlikely. But still, Lomax, I'm convinced that somehow the answer to this business lies in that apparently preposterous claim of Henry Rowles. And as soon as you've gone, I'm going straight upstairs to have another look through that packet of papers you gave me yesterday."

"You think there's something in them?" Lomax took the hint and rose.

"I'm sure of it—sure, that is, that they'll give us a new line. Call in tomorrow morning and I'll tell you what I find."

14

I spent the rest of the evening examining the contents of the envelope containing Rowles's papers. When Lomax called next morning, I was waiting for him with the packet beside me on the arm of my chair. I was looking forward to going through them with him. But his tap on the window-pane wasn't as lively as usual, and when he entered even Mac's joyous welcome didn't evoke a smile.

"I see you've brought news," I said.

"Yes, bad news, Mr. Vaughan. Pollicott's been charged, I'm sorry to say."

"Perhaps it's just as well, in one way," I said. "He'll be protected to some extent against himself from now onward." This didn't seem to cheer Lomax at all, so I added: "How's he taking it?"

"Pretty badly, I'm afraid," said Lomax. "He seems to have no spirit—no interest in anything. When I went in this morning he hardly looked up. Even Fadden's a bit worried. They're keeping special watch on him in case he finds some means of doing away with himself, it seems to me."

This was indeed bad news—and yet it was to be expected. One needed little imagination to realise the effect on poor old Pollicott of prison and a charge of murder in addition to the shock he was suffering from already. Well, I had decided to believe in his innocence. Therefore I had to see what I could do to help him, and quickly. He was of the type, I thought, that might just decide to give up living, and die of despair.

Lomax, echoing my thoughts, was saying earnestly:

"You do believe in his innocence, Mr. Vaughan?"

"I certainly do," I said bravely.

"I do, too," Lomax's tone was thoughtful. "And yet I don't quite know why. If it wasn't for Molly I might begin to doubt it sometimes: things look so black against him, and he'll do nothing to help himself. He's now gone completely mulish—won't give any explanation—won't make a coherent statement of any kind."

"Probably he's wise," I said. "Probably he'll do better to wait and—reserve his defence."

"You think there *is* a defence?" said Lomax eagerly.

I considered: did I? And on what grounds? I said slowly: "I don't know yet. But if he's innocent there must be."

"Do you see any ray of hope at all?" Lomax pressed me. "What about these papers? You said you thought they might give us a new line."

"That is what I hoped." I took up the package from the arm of my chair. "Last night, after you'd gone, I went through them carefully with that end in view." I extracted the largest document and handed it across to Lomax. "Item One: take a look at that. It proves nothing, but it's interesting in itself—very."

Lomax took it. It consisted of twelve foolscap sheets covered with typescript on both sides. The paper was stiff with age, and it crackled as he laid it on the table and lifted up the top page.

"What is it?" he said. "Not *another* will?"

"It's a will all right," I said, "or rather a copy of a will, of course—but a very different sort of will from the one we were looking at yesterday. It runs, as you see, to a dozen double-sided pages."

"*This* chap evidently had something to leave!" said Lomax, regarding it with awe.

"He certainly had," I said. "If you'll look at the opening clause, you'll see why."

15

Lomax began reading aloud.

"I, Charles James Richard Eustace Dallingsworth Clairvaux—" With each name his bewilderment grew. "Good lord!" he exclaimed. "This is as bad as the other one!"

"Go on," I said. He continued.

"...eighth Baron Assche of Ashenford in the County of Hampshire..." He broke off again. "Is this the man you mentioned last night—the head of Silk and Synthetic Fabric Industries Limited?"

"He was that, among other things," I said. "I doubt if he even knew what he was worth. Everything this family touched turned to money. They inherited vast estates. They went in for money-making enterprises. They married heiresses. In short, they could never have enough."

Lomax laid down the will.

"And this is the family that Rowles claimed he belonged to?" he said incredulously.

I nodded.

"But," I said, "we needn't take his claim too seriously—not yet, anyway. This document is just a copy. Anybody can get one at Somerset House on payment of a small fee. At present, it's the fact that he made the claim at all that interests me."

"Ah!" said Lomax.

"And not only that," I went on. "There's also the fact that he bothered to carry this copy of the will around with him. For you see, Lomax"—I was enjoying my effect—"Henry Rowles was claiming that he was this man's eldest son, who *succeeded* him— mark that!—*succeeded* him when he died in 1907. In other words, Henry Rowles claimed to have been the ninth Lord Assche, no less."

"Oh, I say!" Lomax leaned back in the chair till it creaked beneath his pressure, and stared at me in utter scepticism.

"So," I went on, "the present Lord Assche, the tenth Baron, would be his half-brother! Now what do you make of that?" It was my turn to lean back and stare at him, with amused inquiry.

All Lomax could say was:

"It's crazy!"

"It's crazy," I repeated. "Yes. Anybody would jump to that conclusion." I paused for a moment, then I passed on to my next point. "What would you say if I were to tell you that the ninth Lord Assche, this testator's eldest son, *was* crazy, or was reputed to have been?" I pointed to the will. "This immense document consists of thirty-two clauses—and of those, no less than twenty-four clauses concern his eldest son—his only son by his first wife—the heir to the title. The other eight clauses suffice for him to deal with his second wife and his two children by her, the Honourable Albert and the Honourable Amelia. And why, Lomax," I asked him, "why?"

The question was rhetorical, and Lomax did not bother to think out an answer. He said:

"No idea."

"Because, my dear fellow," I said, "there was a considerable doubt in the *father's* mind regarding his elder son's sanity. Now look here."

I took back the will from Lomax and turned over the pages as I explained its provisions. Apart from lump sums and annuities and certain articles of furniture and jewellery bequeathed to his second wife and her children, the eighth Lord Assche had left everything without exception to his elder son John Henry Vincent Peter Dallingsworth Clairvaux, even—I read out the actual words—'wines and consumable stores, plate and plated articles, diamonds, pearls and other jewels.'

"A king's ransom, Lomax!" I said, looking up. "But the son and heir got this vast legacy only in the event of his remaining *of sound mind*. And the will goes on to say that if the elder son prove at any time to be of unsound mind, suitable provision is to be made for him during his lifetime, but the whole estate, apart from what is entailed, is to pass to the son by the second wife, namely the Honourable Albert Clairvaux; that is, the present Lord Assche."

Lomax looked blank.

"But what has all this to do with Henry Rowles?" he said. "I don't see."

"Neither do I," I said, "not yet. But I hope—"

The telephone bell rang in the hall.

"That's my call to the Reference Library," I said, hurrying out of the room.

16

My conversation with the Reference Librarian, a good friend of mine, was short and full of matter.

He said that he had looked up the records as I had requested, and had found that the ninth Lord Assche actually was certified insane, but was registered as having died in 1908, only a year after he had succeeded to the title. His successor was his half-brother, the Honourable Albert Clairvaux, who thus became the tenth Baron, the present Lord Assche.

I thanked him, and returned to Lomax. Inwardly I could feel the prickings of a certain excitement, though outwardly I remained calm and, I hope, judicial. I recounted this information to Lomax.

"It's certainly strange," he said.

I made no comment: there was, as yet, nothing I could say. All I could do was to ascertain the facts as far as I could, in the hope that some clue to the murder of Henry Rowles would emerge.

"Was there anything else among those papers?" said Lomax, rising.

I told him. There were letters, photographs, and the deposit-book he had already seen, showing a credit of three thousand pounds seventeen shillings and fivepence standing at the Alliance Bank, Johannesburg, in the name of Clairvaux. But I was not ready to try to fit these pieces together yet. The next thing to do, I thought, was to see Pollicott. I mentioned this to Lomax.

"I must see him," I said. "I must hear his story. I must find out what there is behind all this."

Lomax looked doubtful.

"If we can get him to talk," he said.

"We must find a way," I said firmly, and then, "*I* must find a way."

Lomax brightened.

"If anybody can, you can," he said. He moved to the door. "By the way, if you do see Pollicott will you tell him Clipper's all right?"

"Clipper?" I said, then I remembered. Clipper was the whippet.

"If you'll just tell him Clipper's with us," said Lomax. "That dog means a good deal to Pollicott, and it's about all he's got now that Rowles is gone. Tell him we'll look after it till he gets out again: it'll cheer him up, maybe."

I promised to do so.

Lomax moved to the door.

"Ah, if only that dog could talk!" he said.

17

When I reached the town there were a few formalities to complete before I could assume the position of Pollicott's legal representative. After attending to these I made my way straight to the Police Station, behind which is the gaol where Pollicott was now in custody. But first I wished to see Superintendent Fadden and make my position clear.

Fadden greeted me with guarded friendliness.

"So you're going to take up Pollicott's case, eh?" he said, after I had explained the reason for my visit. "Can't keep out of the fray!"

"I'd like to begin talking to him straight away," I said. "I fancy I shall need a good many sessions with him before I get at the truth of this extraordinary business."

"Certainly," said Fadden. "Anything I can do to make *your* job as easy as *my* job allows. But I'm afraid you've chosen a tough problem to break your retirement for. *You* can talk to *him*—but you'll be clever if you can get a word back."

"He won't talk to *you*," I said, "but he may be willing to talk to *me*."

Fadden shrugged.

"Maybe. But since he came here he's scarcely looked up, much less talked. He hasn't eaten a bite, either, so far. I'm wondering if he's thinking of trying a hunger-strike."

I sat down opposite Fadden on the other side of the table.

"I wonder if you'd mind giving me a rough idea of your case against Pollicott so far," I said, "off the record, of course. I'm just casting about for an angle of approach—not preparing a brief just yet, you know!"

Fadden's answer was as straightforward and clear as I could wish, though it contained nothing that I did not know or surmise already. He said that they believed that Pollicott had killed Rowles on the night of Saturday-Sunday between ten p.m. and seven thirty a.m.

"Can you be more precise?" I interposed.

"I could—if I liked," said Fadden, "but I'm not prepared to say more at present."

"Very well," I said. "So much for the time. What about motive? Or are you equally vague about that?"

"Not at all," said Fadden imperturbably. "His motive's obvious. It was to get hold of this legacy which Rowles had left him in the will drafted on Saturday night."

"And the means?"

"A blow on the back of the head with a blunt instrument," said Fadden promptly.

"Have you found the blunt instrument?" I said.

"Not yet," said Fadden with a trace of impatience. He continued his analysis. "Pollicott killed Rowles, probably on the Sea Wall, and then rolled the body over the Wall, no doubt in the hope that it would remain undiscovered or perhaps be carried away by the tide. He hoped the whole thing would be regarded as an accident. Rowles could easily have stepped over in the dark."

"And then?" I said.

Fadden looked surprised at the question, as if he thought he had sufficiently dealt with the affair.

"Why," he said. "Pollicott then went back to the hut and affixed two signatures to the will, under the signature of Rowles alias Clairvaux, to make it seem valid."

"You think," I said, "Clairvaux—Rowles, I mean—had already signed the will?"

"Certainly," said Fadden. He did not see where my questions were leading. "The testator's signature was that of an educated man. Pollicott couldn't have imitated *that* one."

"I agree," I said. "But I don't think Rowles would have signed the will without witnesses. I have good reason to know that he knew such a will wouldn't be valid. At any rate, I carefully explained to Pollicott—"

"Ah yes—Pollicott," said Fadden, seizing on the weak link. "But you've no reason to believe Pollicott passed that information on to Rowles. You never saw Rowles at all, I gather."

"That's true," I admitted. "But surely every *educated* person knows that elementary fact about signing a will—and Rowles, as you say yourself, must have been an educated man, whatever else he was or wasn't."

Fadden shifted his ground.

"Rowles may have signed the will under duress."

"He was a much bigger man than Pollicott," I reminded him. "However—if the signature was written under compulsion, your handwriting expert would know. What does he say about it?"

Fadden looked uncomfortable.

"Well," he havered, "he's dubious."

"Oh come!" I said mildly. "Surely any *expert* would know for certain whether a signature was written in a state of agitation—while

Rowles was being threatened—or not? And surely he can tell whether the two other signatures—that is, those purporting to be of the witnesses—are both by the same hand, or by two different hands?"

Fadden said stubbornly:

"I've told you: he's not prepared to swear. We've sent the will to another expert for examination."

I laughed, not too kindly.

"I hope that doesn't mean you're going to send it round until you find someone who agrees with *your* theory!" Not wanting to annoy him further, I passed on quickly. "Another point: has Pollicott told you about the men who called at the hut on Saturday night when Lomax and I were there? You asked him about them, I suppose?"

My tone was innocent, but there was a defensive look about Fadden as he replied:

"Well, I must admit, after Lomax mentioned it to us we did press Pollicott a little on that point—before he was charged, of course," he added hastily, "and for his own sake. But all we could get out of him was that two fishermen had called about the disposal of the morning catch, and he sent them away."

"He didn't tell you anything that passed between them?"

"No. He wouldn't have it that they were anything but casual callers."

I could see a gleam in Fadden's eye which meant that he was wondering if I knew more of this incident, but I did not at this stage wish to tell him. I therefore said jocularly:

"Not John Smith and Bill Brown?"

Fadden laughed.

"I'm afraid those gentlemen exist only in Pollicott's not very fertile imagination, Mr. Vaughan."

"And the gypsies?" I said, leading him on.

"Another fairy tale!" scoffed Fadden. "I think you know that the gypsies left that encampment over a week ago. I sent a car after them. They've now reached another camp about forty miles from here, near Gloucester. Forty miles each way is quite a step."

"They needn't necessarily *walk*," I said. "The railway line passes not more than half a mile from where Pollicott's cabin stands, near Cousins' Farm. There are plenty of goods trains going up and down."

"Moonshine, Mr. Vaughan!" said Fadden with growing impatience. "Those gypsies can account for their movements. There are only six of them, three women and three men. One of the men is down with lumbago—another is over eighty—and the other is a boy of sixteen!"

"And yet," I mused, half to myself, "Pollicott was so positive!"

Fadden's reply was meant to be conclusive.

"It was all he could think of. He's seen the gypsies around. Country people blame everything on the gypsies—give a dog a bad name—and he thought they'd do. I must say it was the only articulate thing we've got out of—" He checked himself. Fadden has been reprimanded a couple of times for his methods of extracting evidence, and he is sensitive on this point. "I mean," he amended, "*heard* from him since he was here. When he found the gypsies cut no ice with us, he just wouldn't talk any more."

I changed the subject.

"What about the ransacking of the hut? Do you say that was Pollicott's work too?"

"Of course."

"You don't see an inconsistency there?" I said.

"Eh?" said Fadden, startled.

"You said just now," I pointed out, "that Pollicott probably hoped Rowles's death would be taken for an accident. Well now—even if we ignore the fact that it's funny that Pollicott of all people, who knew the tides, should wait till *after* high water to dispose of the body that night—although he must have known that when the tide came in again it would be broad daylight—"

Fadden interrupted.

"Maybe he had no choice."

"Well, let's leave that aside for the moment, as I say. But don't you see, you are now suggesting that he tried to make it look like burglary with violence. It couldn't have been both. Pollicott would have had to choose *which* he wanted it to look like: accident, or murder by some persons unknown."

Fadden played with the pencil on his table: the difficulty had clearly not occurred to him.

"Sometimes," he said after a pause, "as you know, criminals like to make doubly sure—and then they overdo things."

"Very well," I said briskly. "We'll leave it at that for the present. Perhaps something new will turn up." I rose. "But you *will* try to get hold of those two so-called fishermen, won't you?"

I could see that Fadden was nettled by this remark. He answered abruptly:

"Of course, they're being searched for. They'll come to hand." He stood up. He is a much taller man than I, and the position gave him confidence. "But I'm willing to lay long odds their names aren't Smith and Brown!"

"I didn't say they were," I remarked quietly. On my way to the door I turned. "Oh, and one more point, Superintendent," I said, "before I see Pollicott. Did you notice if the old man had a handkerchief on him?"

Fadden, having thought he had got rid of me, was pulled up with a jerk.

"Eh?" Fadden had the habit, like many men who have to be a good deal on the defensive, of gaining time by pretending not to have heard the question. I did not answer—I never do on these occasions—and he continued: "Pollicott was searched, of course. I couldn't give you the list of items off hand." He gave me a sharp look. "Why? Do you want to see the list?"

"It doesn't matter," I said, with pretended casualness. "But you'll find that he had a rather fine big silk handkerchief."

"How do you know?"

"Oh," I said, "there's no mystery about that. I saw Mrs. Lomax pick it up off the floor of the hut and hand it to him—"

Fadden was annoyed.

"Did she, indeed?" he said. "She shouldn't have touched it."

"Oh!" I said deprecatingly. "I don't think you should blame her. She really did think it was Pollicott's." I was enjoying his irritation, and I could not help baiting him a little. "You mustn't blame yourself, either," I went on, "if you overlooked it. After all, the place *had* been turned upside down, and there were so many things on the floor. Nobody could be expected to notice a handkerchief lying under the table—even if it *did* happen to be red."

Fadden, controlling his temper, said stiffly:

"We hadn't made our examination of the premises at that time. The lady should have known better. She should have handed this handkerchief to *me*."

"But my dear Superintendent," I said with mock surprise, "it was *Pollicott* who needed it! What was more natural than that she should have picked it up and given it to him? She thought it was his—or at any rate, Rowles's." I came back a step towards him and added seriously: "But this is the point: you know, Pollicott didn't recognise it, either. It might be worth your while to take a look at it and see if you can trace the owner. It may have belonged to Rowles—and on the other hand," I added daringly, "it may not."

Fadden had had enough of this conversation. He rang the bell on his desk.

"It will be examined in due course," he said in his most official manner. As I left under the guidance of a police constable I heard Fadden giving orders on the telephone that Pollicott was to be brought along to the interviewing-room.

18

Pollicott was already there when I arrived. He sat hunched on a hard chair before the long bare table, with a warder behind him. At a signal from me the warder walked off to the further end of the room and stood under the clock, where he could see but not hear. I greeted Pollicott with a cheerfulness I was far from feeling—for I had never seen a man look more utterly dejected. He answered my "good morning," but in a voice barely audible. I sat down opposite him.

"Well now, cheer up!" I said. "I've come to help you. Don't worry: we'll get you out of this. But you must help *me*, you know."

Pollicott answered hoarsely:

"Nobody can help me, sir. They don't believe nothing I do say."

"Oh, come!" I admonished him. "You mustn't take it too seriously: that's just their way. They're used to people who tell lies. And"—I leaned towards him—"you haven't yet told the *whole* truth, have you?"

Pollicott said tremulously:

"I dussn't."

"That's just it!" I said. "They can see you're hiding something, and that makes them think you're hiding everything. Now," I spoke with emphasis, determined to break through the depression—or was it despair?—that enclosed him, "I want you to realise I believe in your innocence: otherwise I wouldn't be here. I'd given up all this sort of work for the rest of my life, I thought. But I couldn't bring myself to stand by and see you accused of something you haven't done—especially," I added in a lighter tone, "as you're making such a mess of things by yourself!"

Pollicott did not look up. At first I thought he had not heard. Several moments went by before he answered in the same dejected voice:

"It's very good of you, sir" There was another pause. Then he said, rousing himself a little: "I'll do what I can, sir—but I dunno—"

Even this amount of interest was encouraging in comparison with his previous lethargy.

"That's a good fellow!" I said. "Now, before I ask you any questions, I want to say something—about those gypsies. The police think you're making them up. But I don't. I believe you when you say you saw two men you took to be gypsies."

For the first time Pollicott looked up, and when he answered there was a new note of hope in his voice.

"That's right, sir," he said. "They *was* gypsies. I see'd 'em."

I put my questions rapidly.

"Two men, you say."

"Yes, sir," he said at once, "two on 'em."

"You said you knew they were gypsies because they wore ear-rings."

"That's right, sir."

"And they spoke to you as they went by."

"'Sright."

"Now tell me," I said. "Were these the same two men as the ones who called on you when Mr. Lomax and I were there?"

Pollicott's face, anxious and worn, had been turned towards me, and his eyes had been fixed eagerly on mine. But as soon as

I mentioned the two visitors all his old mistrust and confusion returned.

"Oh no, sir—no!" he said agitatedly.

"These were two quite different men?" I pressed him.

"Yes, sir—yes, indeed."

"Now, Pollicott," I said firmly, "we're back at the same old question: who *were* the men who called at the hut on Saturday night? You'll have to tell *me* at any rate."

Pollicott was looking down again; he did not answer.

"Come now," I said after a pause. "Tell me: don't be obstinate."

Pollicott stammered:

"I—I can't remember."

"Don't be a fool, man!" I said angrily. "Your freedom, or even your life, may depend on this."

Again I waited, but there was no reply. I decided to approach the matter in a different way. Changing to a conversational tone, I said:

"Pollicott's an unusual name, isn't it?"

He glanced up, a little reassured.

"I reckon it is, sir," he said. "I can't say as I ever heard it anywhere else—except—"

"Except in Cornwall?" I prompted him.

"That's right, sir," he said, obviously surprised and pleased. "Cornwall it is. And there ain't no other family in Cornwall neither with that name, only ours."

I could see the reminiscent look in his eye.

"You came here as a young man, didn't you?" I said.

"That's right, sir," He had momentarily forgotten his fears. "I were young and strong when I come to Mr. Lomax's farm—the old man, that is. The young feller weren't born when I first come here."

"So you're a Cornishman," I said, nodding at him as one Celt to another. He gave a little laugh.

"That I be, sir—and proud of it too—though I ain't never been back there since. How did you guess it, sir? I reckon there ain't much of the Cornishman left about me now."

"Only one thing, perhaps," I said drily, "apart from your name. It's in the blood, I suppose."

I spoke gently, but my words startled him.

"What's that, sir?"

"I think you know," I said quietly. "Something your fellow Cornishmen have always had a reputation for. And unless I'm very much mistaken, you've been carrying on the tradition." I leaned forward across the table, lowering my voice: "*Smuggling*, Pollicott. Isn't that what those men came to see you about, eh?"

19

For a moment I was afraid lest he would decide on silence. But to my relief he whispered back:

"That chap over there, sir—"

My glance followed him towards the impassive warder standing underneath the electric clock.

"He can't hear you," I said. "He has to stand there: those are his orders. But he mustn't stand where he can hear." Pollicott gave a brief nod. "What were you dealing in, eh?" I whispered, rather to reassure him than because of the warder. "Was it tea? Tobacco? Or something bigger?"

Pollicott's thin throat worked. At last, slowly and reluctantly, he said:

"I'll tell you. Them two chaps—they were Jack Dodds and Dan Moore."

"And who were they? Friends of yours? Or of Rowles?"

Pollicott was shocked.

"Oh no, sir! Henry didn't have nothing really to do with them, cheap trash like that! I done a bit of business with them from time to time—and Henry used to help. He knew a lot about val'ables, did Henry, him being used to gold and silver and jewels from a baby—and then, being in Jo'burg so long."

It was my turn to be surprised: I hadn't expected anything of these dimensions.

"You mean," I said, "these men were professional burglars?"

"Oh no, sir," said Pollicott. "They don't do the jobs themselves. They only passes the goods—both ways, if you see what I mean."

By now I was afraid I did, but I wanted to hear the story in his own words. So I said:

"Not exactly. You'd better explain."

Pollicott did so. He seemed to have no particular feelings about the matter. Jack and Dan, he said, had a boat—a rowing-boat with an auxiliary engine. They picked up stuff from ships in the Channel and parked it on the foreshore in tins sunk in the mud. Pollicott's job was to collect the goods and pass them on.

"What sort of goods?" I asked him, astonished to hear what was going on under our noses.

"Watches, mostly," said Pollicott. "Of course, they runs a bit of tea and suchlike sometimes as well."

"And these people collect these goods from you?"

"Yes, sir," said Pollicott. "They comes along at night, like, to my cabin you see, and I hands over the tins."

"You spoke of a two-way traffic," I said. "What did you mean by that?"

Pollicott spoke quite readily now.

"Well, sir, I gets stuff passed to me, and I has to plant it in the mud, and Jack and Dan collects it—diamonds and stuff, like, that's going abroad to be cut up small."

I confess that momentarily I was daunted. I had envisaged petty smuggling only, not felony on a big scale. But I reminded myself that this was not the crime of which Pollicott was accused, and therefore it did not concern me—or the police—at present.

"But Pollicott," I reproached him, "that's a dreadful trade! What on earth made you take it up? Didn't you realise what you were doing?"

Pollicott answered stubbornly:

"I done it because I has to have the money—for Henry." His earnest look showed me that he expected this to explain everything. "You see," he went on, "Henry not being able to work, and liking things nice, I kind-a couldn't help myself. I gets out of work, and Henry's took bad, and the money has to come from somewhere. I ain't never been one to beg or borrow. Then when Dan and Jack comes along and they tells me about the easy money for planting these here tins and picking 'em up again, I just says 'all right' and asks no questions."

"But you found out later, didn't you? Why did you go on with it after that?"

"Well, you see, sir," said Pollicott slowly, "it wasn't *me* found out: it was Henry. One day he finds a couple of tins through Clipper digging at 'em in the mud, and he opens one of 'em and he finds brooches and rings inside. They was the ones going out, you see, sir. The ones coming in had these here watches. But the boys never told me nothing about what was in the tins. Leastways, they says it's just a bit of baccy and tea and sugar from the ships—and they gives us some for ourselves off and on—"

"I *thought* so," I said. "You passed a bit of tea on to Mrs. Lomax sometimes, didn't you, so that they could have a nice strong cup?"

"Yes, sir," said Pollicott, "that I does, sir—and why not? Mrs. Lomax is a very good kind lady, sir, and she don't know where the stuff comes from. She thinks I gets it because of my age—"

I interrupted.

"You say it was Rowles who discovered what these tins really contained. Surely *he* must have known the risk you were running?"

"Oh yes, sir—yes indeed! When Henry do see this other stuff, he do know what it's worth. And he do tell me to stop, or I'll get him and me into trouble."

"I'm glad he had *that* much sense!" I said.

"So," went on Pollicott, "I tells Dan and Jack we ain't having no more to do with it. And they takes it bad, being scared Henry'll talk. But I tells 'em Henry don't know enough to talk, and don't care neither."

"Did they threaten you at all?" I said. I was relieved to find that Pollicott, having decided to talk, was telling me the truth about his conversation with the two callers.

"Yes, sir, they threatens me, in a manner of speaking. But I don't take it seriously so long as they don't worry Henry."

"Was Henry scared of them?" I asked quickly.

At that, Pollicott gave a scornful guffaw.

"Ho! Henry? Scared of them lubbats? No, sir, he never give 'em a thought. In fact, when I leaves him that night—" A cloud passed over his face at this; he shook his head dolefully, and I heard him mutter: "God forgive me, I never should-a!" He relapsed into a brooding silence, and I thought I should have to rouse him, when suddenly he took hold of his story again. "Henry, he asks me to get hold of them two fellers to sign this here will. And I says 'right-ho' just to please Henry, but I doesn't do nothing about it. I be late already, so I goes off and never bothers. I reckons that old will can wait till morning." He looked as if he might sink again into melancholy, so again I said quickly:

"Do you know where these men live?"

Pollicott answered indifferently:

"Not I, sir. They don't tell. This here Dan's an Irishman from Cork, *that* I knows, and Jack again, he's a Cornishman like meself—I reckon that's where he learnt the trade—but where they do live, I can't say."

"The police are looking for them, you know," I said.

Pollicott said with conviction:

"They'll never find 'em. They knows where to lie low when there's trouble around."

"Well," I said, "never mind them for the present." I leaned towards him again. "But I must say, Pollicott, between ourselves, I think you did well not to tell the police that story. It certainly would have blackened your character—and we don't want that, do we?"

The old man chuckled faintly: the idea of my being in league with him evidently gave him pleasure.

"No, sir, indeed we don't."

"Then we stick to our story that these were casual visitors who really were calling on you about the morning catch."

There was humour in the situation: here was I, a respectable lawyer, conspiring with this old rapscallion to conceal a whole series of illegal actions, while the warder—as deaf, I hoped, as he appeared—looked on. But again I reminded myself that we were now concerned solely with the major charge. Pollicott was looking momentarily quite carefree.

"Right, sir," he said. "Right you are, sir!"

I controlled the desire to smile, and composed my features to a more becoming severity, for truly there was no room for levity here.

20

"Now," I began in a more incisive tone, "you've said several times Henry Rowles didn't want you to leave him on Saturday night."

Pollicott looked depressed again.

"No—no," he said.

"He was scared of *something,* then, it seems."

"Ay, that he were, sir."

"But it wasn't these men—our two fishermen—he was scared of?"

Pollicott shook his head vigorously. "No."

"You told Superintendent Fadden," I said, "that Henry Rowles had been receiving letters which seemed to alarm him?"

"That's right, sir."

"But you don't know who sent these letters, or what they contained?"

"No, sir," said Pollicott. There was pride in his voice as he added: "Henry were very close sometimes, other times"—the reminiscent look came back into his eyes, and he half-smiled—"he'd tell me everything."

I pursued my line of inquiry.

"And his fears seemed to come directly after he began getting these letters, and not till then?"

"Yes, sir." Pollicott was roused. He began to speak, for him, quite rapidly, and there was a faint flush on his thin cheeks as he continued: "And it were after *that* he begins this here talk about a will, and about him having money in this Bank overseas—but under another name, he do say—his real name. And then he do tell me how he do want *me* to have this money. And he do show me the papers, the ones I give to Mr. Lomax and he give 'em to you."

His breath came fast. It seemed to me he was feeling the strain of this long interview. I said soothingly:

"Yes, I've still got them—and it's really about these I want to talk to you. But I think you've had enough for this morning: you look pretty well done up."

Pollicott shook his head slightly, but I could see he agreed. The time had come to let him go. But there was one thing more I wanted to do before I dismissed him back to his solitary confinement. I wanted to plant an idea in his mind which would grow in my absence, and I wanted to prevent him from falling again into complete despondency. I said:

"Now will you do what I ask? I want you to go back"—I didn't mention the word "cell"—"and eat the next meal they bring you, all of it. You *must* be well and strong if you're to do the next thing I shall ask of you, which is"—I paused for effect, and he glanced up, half-fearful, half-expectant—"to tell me a story."

21

The effect was all I could have desired. Pollicott looked astonished.

"A story, sir?" he said. "Me, sir?"

"Yes," I said, "a story—a long story. Will you do that?"

"Whatever you say, sir," the poor old fellow replied.

"Then I'll go now," I said, rising. I was not sorry to do so: I too was beginning to feel the strain. Pollicott's eyes were fixed on me sadly. "I'll come back later," I assured him, "with the Superintendent's permission. There's no time to waste if we're to get this straightened out." Suddenly a rather disagreeable point occurred to me: it seemed better to clear it up at once. "Oh, by the way," I said, "why did you leave your cabin that night? Nurse Duncan says you weren't there when she passed in the small hours?"

Pollicott said glumly:

"I went home, sir."

I came back to the table. This was worse than I had feared. "You went home? Why?"

"It came over me," he said, "something may have happened to Henry."

"What made you think that?" I said sharply.

"Well," said Pollicott, staring past me at the white-washed wall, "I were a-sitting there worrying and thinking I should-a stayed, and not daring to leave in case I loses my job—and suddenly I hears Clipper whining. He've come to fetch me. He puts his paw on my knee and he looks right up in my face"—Pollicott's words came faster and his eyes grew full of recollected fear—"and he do whine something piteous. So I don't wait no longer. I just packs up and goes."

"Where did you go?"

"Straight back to the hut, where Clipper takes me."

"And what did you find there?"

"Everything all over the place, sir," said Pollicott, "and Henry not there."

"So the hut was already ransacked when you arrived."

"That it were, sir—never see such a thing in my life."

"What did you do next? Did you look for Rowles?" Pollicott shook his head.

"Didn't Clipper take you to where Rowles was lying?" Pollicott looked up.

"He tries to, sir. He tries for a bit to get me to come with him, whining and pulling at my arm. Then he goes. But I just sits there not knowing what to do. I were that dazed, I must-a sat there all the time, till that chap come banging at the door in the morning. I guess I was too scared to move. I guess I must-a knowed"—his voice quavered—"about Henry." In another moment he would have burst into tears.

"Never mind, never mind." I reassured him hastily. "It makes no difference—except that they'll say you told another lie: an unnecessary one, too," I reflected, half to myself, "because you lost your only chance of an alibi when you let Henry keep you back from your work that evening."

Pollicott was looking at me as if stupefied.

"I don't know nothing about that, sir," he said.

"No," I said, "but the police do." And sitting down again for a moment on the edge of the chair I explained this point to him, which it was essential that he should grasp without delay.

"The police know," I said, "that Rowles was thrown over the Wall *after* high tide that night, not before, because his clothes were dry. And if you'd gone to your work in time and stayed there, you'd have been in your cabin before nine-twenty when the tide came up to the Sea Wall."

I stopped. It was clear that Pollicott could not take in anything more—or was it, I wondered, that the protection of his own interests had not really occurred to him? In any event, I must leave him for the present.

"But it doesn't matter," I said. "It's not you, it's Henry Rowles we have to think about now."

Pollicott said mournfully:

"Henry's dead and gone. We can't do nothing for Henry now."

"No," I said, a trifle sharply, "but perhaps Henry can do something for *you* for a change."

This startled him: he fixed his pale blue, rather watery eyes on my face and said in awestruck tones:

"What—what do you mean, sir? You don't think Henry could come back from the dead?" His voice rose to a high pitch: he had forgotten all about the warder. "If he did, sir, he'd soon tell 'em all I didn't have nothing to do with it!"

"He won't come back from the dead, Pollicott," I said. "Nevertheless, we can still get him to tell his story—through *you*."

"Through *me*" he said blankly.

"Yes," I said with all the emphasis I could command, "you and *only* you. That's the story I want you to tell me. You're the only one who knows the truth about Henry Rowles—or at least, what he said of himself. He talked to you sometimes, you say—told you things about himself?"

Pollicott's look softened.

"He did, sir," he said. "Off and on, I reckon Henry told me *all* about himself, from the time he were a little chap no more than *so* high." He showed me with his hand.

"Then *think*" I said, rising again. "Pull yourself together and remember *all* he told you—for somewhere in it," I assured him with growing certainty, "we shall find the answer: the answer that will hang his murderers and set you free. Think, Pollicott!" I urged him. "Try to remember!" I signed to the warder, who had been standing all this time as still as a statue under the electric clock that was jerking the minutes away. "I'll be back later today," I promised, as the warder came to life and Pollicott turned apprehensively to face him. "Don't lose heart, Pollicott! Just try to remember."

22

I went back, that day and the next day and the day after. Pollicott's words at first were slow and halting, but as I listened I began to forget the bare room and the round-shouldered old man with the roughened hands who was doing his best to re-create for me the strange story. Through it all it seemed to me that I could hear the voice of Henry Rowles himself—a voice that in life I had never heard—telling me, as he had told Pollicott, of a past that reached back half a century ago.

Was Henry Rowles an impostor, or a crazy dreamer, or indeed, as he claimed, a much injured man? It was not for me to say. I merely listened, as Pollicott, almost without my help, conjured up from his memory—dim about many things, sharp enough about all that concerned his friend—scene after scene from the life of a stranger.

The story began one night soon after Rowles first came to the hut, ill and destitute. Pollicott had nursed him assiduously and Rowles was feeling better. Suddenly, Pollicott said, Rowles let out a sigh, and began:

"I can never remember having been happy before…"

IV

A Strange Life

HENRY'S STORY

I

I can never remember having been happy before.

Here I am, George, alone with you, a complete stranger in this wretched little hut—ill, without a penny to my name—in fact, without even a name. I am forty years of age—and this is my first taste of happiness. I wonder how many men could say the same?

But then, my life has been stranger than most men's. I feel I'd like to tell you about it, my friend. You look at me so anxiously, as if you really cared whether I got better or not. I believe you do. Moreover, I *can* talk to you. You're simple, in every sense of the word: foolish—not clever—not shrewd—not like the people I've known. I dare say it could be exasperating. But at present it's just what I need. You won't ask questions. You'll believe all I tell you unquestioningly, because you've already accepted me as your superior. And you'll be quite right, George—I mean, in believing me: God knows if I'm your superior in any but the most accidental of ways—because what I shall tell you will be the truth. I'm tired of being treated like a lunatic when I speak the truth. I seem to have come to the one spot on earth where I shall be believed. It looks like destiny, doesn't it, George?

I shall value your simple faith more even than your nursing. I hope I shall be able to repay you some day. Meanwhile, I'm afraid I must tell you my story.

2

The earliest recollection I have is of a little conversation.

I had crept downstairs to listen to a tune that seemed very beautiful to me. I don't know what it was: Chopin or Schumann, I suppose. I've often wondered, often tried to recapture it. But I can't be sure whether I've ever heard it since.

Mama was playing. I went into the room, and at first I didn't think she had seen me. But she had.

When she saw me she stopped playing and said:

"Harry, come here. I want to have a little talk with you, by yourself."

Her voice, like the music, was beautiful, but it was not soft or kind. I said:

"Yes, Mama."

She looked coldly at me and said:

"No. Not 'Mama.' That's what our little talk is to be about."

I watched her, fascinated. Was this the first time we had ever been alone together? I can't, of course, remember. Nor do I know what made her speak at that moment. She said—and I flinched as if she had struck me:

"Harry, I am *not* your Mama. I'm your stepmother. I'm *Bertie's* Mama. *Your* mother died when you were born. Do you understand?"

I said stupidly enough, "No, Mama," but I understood quite enough for her purpose.

"Your mother died when you were born," she repeated with merciless clarity. "Your poor father has never forgiven you for it. The sight of you is unbearable to him. So if you *love* your father, Harry, you will keep away from him. Do you understand me?"

This time I said, not quite so stupidly:

"I think so, Mama."

"Keep away from him, Harry," she said, "even when he calls you—for he only calls you from some sense of fairness. But when he sees you the old wound reopens, and he remembers that you *killed* your Mama." Her voice remained cold as she split my heart in two. She laid her hands on the keys again—her hands were much whiter than the ivory—and said with finality: "So you *must* keep away from him, mustn't you, Harry? It's all you can do for him."

"Yes—Mama," I said. I didn't know what else to call her, and I never found out. But it didn't matter so long as I knew that the word was meaningless when *I* said it.

"That's all," she said, dismissing me. She started to play the piano again, the same lovely time, and when I still stood there she said over the music: "Now you may go, Harry. But remember..."

I remembered. Her words pursued me; I could never escape from them, even in my dreams.

3

Then there was another occasion, a long time afterwards, years afterwards it must have been, but it was so much like the first time that it might have happened the very next day, except that now my brother Bertie was as old as I had been then, so I must have been somewhere about nine. I am three years older than Bertie.

This scrap of conversation, though quite clear in itself, is associated only vaguely in my mind with a place. I can't remember if we were in the day-room or in the library or the hall—only that we were somewhere in the house, in some room where there was a heavy curtain. I think it must have been in the hall. I stepped out of my hiding-place—I was always hiding, trying to keep out of my father's way as *she* had told me to do—and I almost collided with Bertie. He shouted at me in his high-pitched voice:

"*I* know where you were hiding when Daddy couldn't find you just now. You were hiding behind that curtain!"

"I wasn't," I said.

"You were, you were!" shrieked Bertie. "I saw you!"

I tried to keep my temper: the little beast was so much smaller than I. I said:

"You can't see people if they're hiding behind curtains."

"I saw you go there!" said Bertie with glee. "And I know why you went. Mummy told me. It's because you're barmy. It makes you do all sorts of funny things. Mummy says you're barmy, but she says I mustn't say she said so."

"Barmy?" I said. The idea was new to me. I did not know where to turn to escape it.

"*Daddy* thinks so too," my brother went on. "Mummy says so."

There was no release from my growing terror except in action. I advanced slowly on Bertie, saying:

"I think I'll punch your head."

Bertie backed away.

"If you do," he said, "*I'll* say you're barmy, too!" He turned and began to run, calling out: "Barmy, barmy, barmy!" in an insolent sing-song.

I caught him, of course, and I did punch his head, though not very hard. I don't remember what happened, except that Bertie, as always, set up a terrible hullabaloo, and somebody came and rescued him. It all seemed very trifling. But my action was a mistake, as I found out in due course. Not at the time: my stepmother was too cunning for that. I didn't find it out until about two years later when my half-sister Amelia was born.

4

A few days after Amelia's birth my father sent for me and explained to me that I had now a little sister as well as my brother Bertie. He asked me if I would like to see her.

My father always spoke to me with kindness, and I had ceased by now to avoid him. I went with him gladly. When we came to the door of my stepmother's room, and he did not tell me to wait outside, I followed him. I stood near the door, while he crossed over to her where she lay in the huge bed, propped up with pillows. There was a smell of eau-de-cologne, I remember; I have never been able to endure it since. At the side of the bed was a contraption all lace and blue bows, which I realised was my sister's cot, with the baby somewhere in its depths. I looked on curiously as my father—he was a tall man, grey-haired and grey-moustached for as long as I remember—my father leaned over the bed and touched my stepmother's smooth white forehead with his lips. *Her* hair was as black as night—blue-black, in fact, like the night sky. I don't know if it ever went grey. He said quite gaily:

"Well, my dear, I've brought someone along to see a very important person."

My stepmother laughed, and raising herself on one elbow, looked down at the cot.

"She *is* a very important person," she said. "And she knows it." She laughed again. "Have you noticed the little frown?—so disdainful! It's *your* frown, Charles."

My father bent to look into the cot. He said indulgently:

"She's to resemble you from top to toe. Those are my orders." He laughed too: he had quite forgotten me. My stepmother, who had not yet noticed me, said:

"I'm so happy—because *you* are."

"First a boy—then a girl," said my father dotingly. "What a witch you are to bring things about just as I want them!"

He stooped over her again. His figure blocked her view, but she must have suddenly remembered what he had said on entering the room. She asked uneasily:

"Who's my visitor, dear?"

My father turned with a gesture that summoned me to come near.

"Let him speak for himself," he said. "Harry, come here and say 'how do you do?' to Mama. She may let you kiss Amelia."

The effect on my stepmother was dramatic.

"No, Charles, no!" she said angrily. "Harry is not to come in here. Please send him away at once."

My father was shocked, truly shocked, perhaps for the first and only time by her. His impulse was to spare *me*. He said quickly:

"Hush, Caroline! Of course I'll send him away." Then he remembered that she mustn't be allowed to agitate herself—that perhaps she was not in control of her feelings. He came towards me and said with hurried kindness: "Harry, Mama isn't feeling very well. Run off like a good boy, and later on you shall see your new little sister."

He opened the door and pushed me out gently. I was less shocked than he was—in fact, I wasn't shocked at all. I was used to going off by myself: there was nothing new in any of it. But this time I didn't run off immediately. There was a heavy curtain over the door on the inside; I turned the knob and stood behind the curtain. I was curious to hear what she would say.

She realised she had gone too far in front of my father. She was saying:

"I was silly, Charles. Forgive me. But"—and her voice took on the tone of an anguished mother—"it terrifies me to see Harry anywhere near the children. He's so *vicious*." She hurried on, covering up the hatefulness of the word. "I didn't mean to tell you, but—well, it's understandable, I suppose, that a child should be jealous when there's a new baby."

My father said coldly:

"You said 'vicious,' Caroline. That's not my impression of Harry."

She resolved, evidently, to burn her boats. Having gone so far, she couldn't withdraw, I suppose, in the face of his obvious displeasure. She said eagerly:

"Don't you remember the time he attacked Bertie?—and for no reason. And there have been other times I've kept from you. Perhaps it's not the boy's fault. I often wonder."

There was no answer from my father. I knew just how he looked as he stood there, though I couldn't see him: tall, upright, distressed, anxious to be just, yet angry at the thought that he had been for so long deceived.

"Oh, Charles," she breathed, "it terrifies me!"

My father said sternly:

"*What* have you wondered? *What* has been kept from me? *What* terrifies you?"

She said falteringly—and at her words, and her tone, I turned cold with fear.

"Charles—can't you see? Are you indeed the only person who can't see—that Harry isn't—*normal?*"

I didn't stay to hear my father's reply. I ran—ran—ran as they wanted me to, away into a world of my own, a world of complete loneliness, for ever.

5

And yet, you know, George, in spite of all my stepmother must have said, my father went on being very kind to me—so kind that I always felt uneasy, as if he were watching me—as indeed he was. My days were carefully planned: so much work, so much recreation, nothing to cause me any strain. I was allowed to go riding with a groom—until one day my horse bolted and threw me. I broke my leg—just here, George, the tibia, I think you call it. Of course, this was considered my fault: I had done something wicked to the horse to make him bolt, and I must not be allowed to ride again, at any rate for a long time. When my leg healed I had to walk instead, with my tutor. To this day, George, I hate walking.

Yes, and that was another thing: my father made such a distinction between me and my brother Bertie. When Bertie was nine he was sent away to school. I, though I was three years older, was kept at home, to study under a tutor, like a girl with a governess. I was not allowed to have any friends.

My little sister Amelia began to attract my attention, *faute de mieux*, as she got older and began to toddle about. I was never allowed to be with her alone. I used to see her with her nurse in the park. I would have liked to play with her, and perhaps be the big brother to her—I was so lonely, George, so terribly lonely! There were no other children in the place now that Bertie was at school, except the children at the lodges, who ran away when they saw me coming...

One day, when my tutor had gone to get a book from the library, I looked out of the schoolroom window and saw my little sister alone on the terrace. Her nurse was nowhere in sight. I ran quickly down the stairs. It was a bright spring morning, and Amelia was dressed in white. She had glossy brown ringlets which hung down temptingly. When I came up to her she was gathering gravel together in her hands and throwing it at one of the white peacocks on the balustrade. I shouted to her:

"Amelia!" And then, as I came up: "Amelia, you shouldn't do that. You might hurt him."

The peacock, as if to endorse what I was saying, gave a loud scream and strutted away.

"There you are, you see!" I said." He's offended."

"I don't care!" said Amelia, pouting.

"His feelings are hurt," I assured her. "Look how he's walking away! He'll tell all his friends, and they'll come and carry you off, and *you*'ll be turned into a white peacock, and then what'll happen? Do you know?"

Amelia was dubious but interested. She let the gravel fall:

"No-o," she said. "Tell me."

"They'll all collect round you," I said, "and peck at you and pull your curls—like this." I took hold of one of her ringlets and gave it a gentle tug. "You wouldn't like that, would you?"

Amelia gave a screech of laughter.

"I wouldn't mind a bit!" she said. "It didn't hurt at all, you silly boy!"

"That's because I did it very gently," I said, "so as not to hurt you. But that peacock, now—he'd do it hard, and his wife would do it harder—like this!"

Again I gave one of her ringlets a very light pull. Again Amelia screeched with laughter. She was enjoying the game.

"I'd give her a great big kick—like this!" she said, running to me and kicking me as hard as she could on the shin. She was only about four, and her white kid boots made no impression on me, though I pretended to give a yelp of pain. Amelia, pleased, was preparing to renew the attack, but it seemed to me, cautious as I had learned to be always, that she was getting too excited. I therefore thought it advisable to divert her.

"I say, Amelia," I said, "how would you like a ride?" I stooped down on all fours, and let her climb on to my back. "That's right!" I said. "Now hang on tight round my neck and we'll go for a trot."

I began to trot along the terrace. Amelia was no easy burden. She bounced up and down, laughing and shouting "Gee up, gee up!" and her small hands nearly throttled me.

"Will you take me for a ride on a real horse one day?" she said, when we reached one end of the terrace and I had stopped to get my breath.

"If you like," I said. "But you'll have a pony of your own quite soon."

"I want to go on a big horse, like Mummy and Daddy," declared Amelia. "Can I come with you?"

"They won't let you," I said bitterly. "And anyway"—I dropped my grievance, not wanting to lose her interest—"if you had a big horse you might fall off like me and break your leg. *I* broke my leg just here"—I showed her the place—"where you kicked me just now."

Amelia was indifferent to my troubles.

"*You* must *make* them," she said.

"*I* can't make them do anything," I said gloomily.

"Oh, you *are* a silly boy!" cried Amelia. "I can make anybody do anything!" Her arms tightened round my throat again and her white boots drummed against my ribs. "Gee up, gee up!" she shrieked, and we were off again, back along the length of the terrace at a gallop.

I had got my second wind. The fun of the game seized me.

"Hang on, hang on!" I shouted. "This is a point-to-point." I leapt an imaginary fence, yelling: "Oop-we-go! That was a near thing!"

Amelia was screaming with glee:

"Faster, faster!"

I had forgotten all about my tutor and my sister's nurse. I wasn't aware of them until their excited voices broke through my own excitement. They came running up, the nurse leading. She began to scold.

"Put her down this instant, Master Harry!" I let Amelia slither off my back, and the silly nurse flopped on to her knees beside Amelia saying: "Oh, my little precious, are you hurt?"

Amelia was screaming, but with temper.

"Leave me alone, Nannie! Let me go!" She struggled to get back to me. "Harry! Harry!"

My tutor came up. He said severely:

"What's the meaning of all this? Harry, what are you doing out here?"

The nurse turned on him spitefully.

"I was only gone a minute—and what do I see but young Master Harry pulling Miss Amelia's hair, the little love!" Her hysteria mounted. "Oh, what a nasty, vicious boy! Everybody says so—and then to frighten the poor little darling out of her wits!" She rounded on me. "What your dear mother would say, I *don't* know."

My tutor—he was not at all a bad fellow, I remember, though rather a stick—he had taken in the situation by now, and said to her coldly:

"Calm yourself, nurse. Miss Amelia isn't hurt. There's no harm done."

All this time Amelia was screaming her head off. She never could stand being thwarted for a moment. I said glumly:

"We were only playing."

But the nurse didn't listen. She just went on saying:

"What her ladyship will say when I tell her—"

My tutor cut her short.

"You will do well," he said, "to say nothing about this, nurse, to her ladyship or anybody else. *I* shall speak to his lordship."

The nurse said, "Come along, Miss Amelia," and took her by the hand. Amelia pulled her hand away.

"I don't want to!" she said.

The nurse picked her up and carried her off. Amelia kicked and struggled. All the way to the house she screamed with rage and called: "Harry, Harry!" The peacock, who had come back, screamed too. That was the end of my rapport with my sister Amelia.

6

I don't know whether they did speak to my father about this incident. Nothing more was ever said about it to *me*. I found *that* more sinister than if I had been beaten. But the supervision seemed closer than ever.

I was again allowed to ride, with a groom. But I still had no companions even, much less friends. When my brother Bertie came home for the holidays he treated me frankly as if I were an imbecile. And I began to *feel* imbecile—for I knew nothing of the things he spoke of.

The years passed. Bertie was at Eton. When he reached my age he would be going to Oxford. *I*, at nineteen, was still under a tutor—not the one who had taken my part against the nurse, but an old man whose thoughts were all of books—who had long forgotten what it was to be young... So it went on until one day they came to tell me my father was seriously ill and wished to see me.

7

My stepmother met me at the door. She said:

"Be careful not to overtire your father, Harry. You mustn't stay more than a minute or two."

My father called out weakly and irritably from the bed:

"Let him come in, Caroline. I wish to see him alone."

She left me. I approached the bed timidly. Nobody had told me he was so ill. He looked, at sixty-five, completely white; his hair and moustache, his face and hands. I had never seen him like tins before. In fact, I had seen very little of him over the years: he was so often away in London, attending to his political and business concerns, and sometimes taking my stepmother for long trips abroad. He called out:

"Come here, Harry. Come close to me. There's no need to be afraid."

"I'm not afraid, Father," I said, and I added in a lower voice: "I was never afraid—of *you*." But I said it half to myself, and I don't suppose he heard.

"I wanted to have a little talk with you," he said. Then he laughed feebly. "Not that I think I'm going to die! I'm getting better, they tell me. But still—you're a man now. In two years you'll be of age."

"Yes, Father," I said. I wondered if this was the first time he had realised it.

"This is a wicked world, Harry," he went on musingly, "a cruel world. I have tried to protect you from it—until you were ready. I don't know if I've done rightly. I hope so—I hope so."

"Yes, Father," I said, to let him know that I was listening, not because I agreed.

"You will be the heir to a great estate, my boy," he said, "and great business interests. I trust the burden will not be too heavy. But

I have decided to entrust it to you—the fruits of the courage and enterprise and the *intelligence*"—he emphasised the word—"of your forebears. It's a great responsibility. But if you have courage—"

Elation was rising in me at his words. I said earnestly:

"I have, if *you* trust me, Father."

He was moved. He stretched out his hand, his white thin hand, and laid it on my arm.

"You'll see," he said, "I *have* trusted you—one day. But—Harry—" Agitation filled him; his next words swept away our momentary understanding. "If the burden should prove *too* heavy, remember you have those about you who will help you. Your mother—"

"My stepmother," I corrected him quietly.

"Yes—your stepmother," he said, "but also your friend."

I said nothing. He went on, removing himself to an infinite distance from me:

"When I am gone I want you to regard her as in *my* place. I want you to take her advice in everything. She has thought always and only for your good."

I looked down at him, no longer in admiration and love, but with a pitying wonder that he could be so blind.

"Was it she," I said, "who advised you not to send me to school or to the university?"

He caught the reproach in my tone, and said in a deprecatory tone quite unusual to him:

"We didn't wish to overstrain you, Harry. There were"—he hesitated, seeking the least obnoxious words—"there were signs that your mind was more delicately poised than your brother's. And if all goes well"—he smiled up at me propitiatingly and not without pride—"you will have a bigger part than he to play in the world."

I stood thinking. It seemed to me that by a strange reversal of our *rôles*, I had my rather formidable father at my mercy. He was ill—he was weak. He might die. I did not want to worry him. But I had to get out of him the knowledge that only he could give me, lest it should be too late.

"One thing, Father," I said, and stopped.

"Yes, my boy?" he said kindly.

"My mother—my real mother," I blurted out. "Is it true she died when I was born?"

My father turned his face away from me on the pillow. He was silent for so long that I thought he was not going to answer. At last he said—and his voice sounded much older and more tremulous:

"No—no, Harry; not quite that. She—died soon afterwards. You are bound to hear it one day. She—put an end to her own life. It has been the greatest sorrow of *my* life. *That* was why we always thought it best to take especial care of *you*." He looked up at me and smiled at me in a way I shall never forget: with relief, with sweetness, with *trust*. "Now you understand, I hope—and you see that all has always been done for the best."

I had to struggle with the desire to cry.

"Yes, Father," I said, deeply moved, "I understand."

Our *rôles* were reversed again.

"Don't let it prey on your mind," he said, his voice stronger and almost cheerful. "*That* fear is over now. I have the best reports of you from your tutor—and I can see for myself, dear boy. Go now," he said, patting my hand. "I think I hear your—your—" He could not say "mother," and he would not say "stepmother." He compromised. "I think I hear Lady Assche calling. Goodbye. I hope I shall soon be about again, and then we'll see more of each other. I must begin and explain to you something of our affairs."

I left quickly. I could see he was exhausted. I lay awake most of that night praying that he might recover. But he did not recover. He died early next morning, of heart failure following on pneumonia. I did not see him again.

8

After the funeral the will was read. It was immensely long, but Mr. James Dotherington, who was one of the partners in our family's firm of solicitors, was there to read it, and he didn't spare us a single word. He kept addressing my stepmother, asking for permission to read or to explain this clause and that—there were thirty-two in all—and then he would turn to me on second thoughts, like this:

"With your ladyship's—your lordship's—permission, I shall now read the will of the late Lord Assche, eighth Baron Assche of Ashenford in the County of Hampshire. It is dated January 13th, 1907..."

And so on, with little coughs and bows in the direction first of my stepmother and then of myself. It was a very trying experience for us all, especially when it became known that my father had not after all disinherited me in so far as he could have done so, but had treated me as his eldest son and heir in every respect—with only one proviso, which Dotherington proceeded to explain—though it was clear enough already.

"In effect," Dotherington said, turning with his little bows to my stepmother and myself, "your ladyship—your lordship—will have understood that the Honourable Henry Clairvaux, who now succeeds his father as ninth Baron, succeeds also at the age of twenty-one to the whole estate with the exception of the legacies heretofore mentioned, *unless* at any time he be proved to be of unsound mind, and be certified as such by two qualified medical practitioners. I hope I have now made everything clear." This time, he turned first to me: "Your lordship?"

I could scarcely bring out the words. I managed to murmur:

"Quite clear, thank you."

Dotherington then turned to my stepmother with:

"Your ladyship?"

She had no difficulty in articulating, and she did not conceal her chagrin.

"*Quite* clear," she said, with bitter emphasis, and then, pityingly: "Poor Charles! What can he have been thinking of, to entrust these great interests to an"—I suppose she meant to say "imbecile," but she checked herself, and substituted—"to an inexperienced boy of nineteen?"

Dotherington was used to these displays by disappointed legatees. He said to her quite gently:

"Your ladyship will recall that according to the terms of the will the present Lord Assche is not required to enter upon the full responsibility entailed by his late father's business interests until he attains his majority."

My stepmother said musingly:

"Yes, I understand." She turned to me and added significantly: "You will have a great deal to do, Harry, in the next two years, to fit yourself for this tremendous task."

I gave her, as Dotherington had done, a little bow, and looking her full in the eyes I said:

"Yes, ma'am."

She was aware of my irony, and that I had seen through her all these years. She drew herself up superbly and said:

"But don't be afraid. We shall all do our best to help you." She called my brother, who was red in the face with disappointment and rage. "Come, Bertie." She swept out of the room, and he stumped after her, ignoring me.

I sat down at the table with my head in my hands. When Dotherington approached me, and wanted to begin more explanations, I waved him away.

9

I don't know what happened to me during the next six months. It's true I sank into a kind of stupor. For one thing, I felt that I had lost my only friend—my father—and I didn't know where to turn. I was overwhelmed, too, by the magnitude of the responsibilities facing me, and the knowledge of my utter incapacity—thanks to the way I'd been brought up.

I couldn't deal even with ordinary society, much less with my father's huge business interests. People called with condolences: I didn't know how to receive them. People came to me for orders and instructions: I didn't know what to say. I didn't understand the well-meant efforts of my trustees, my father's colleagues, his private secretary even, to help me. I had no idea of the meaning of the simplest business terms: I didn't know how to find out for myself, and yet I was too proud or too shy to ask.

The secretary, a man called Bloggs, was my chief *bête noire*. He was a tall, thin, dark young man who took himself with intense seriousness, and me with no seriousness at all. He respected me as my father's heir, but he had nothing but contempt for me as a person. He was used to deferring to my father; he couldn't reconcile himself to working for *me*. He was extremely good at his job—facts and figures—and quite hopeless at everything outside it. I found him exasperating: his voice, his clothes, his correct manner that barely concealed his poor opinion of me. He irritated me so much that

I could not bring myself to listen to him. One day my irritation came to a head.

I had forced myself to spend a part of every morning in my father's study, attempting to cope with some aspect of his many business concerns. Sometimes, when I was left alone, a faint glimmering of understanding and even of interest began to dawn in my mind. But, just as I would be beginning to see my way a little, the unspeakable Bloggs would enter with a sheaf of papers and pester me with his demands for my attention or my signature. On this particular morning I had a headache and was sitting gazing before me, doing nothing, when Bloggs came in and laid a Company report before me.

"Will your lordship kindly look through this report?" he said. He had a way of standing behind me and leaning over my shoulder, a thing I detested. His smooth black hair smelt of some disgusting pomade. I moved aside to avoid him while he talked on, pointing with a pencil: "You will see at the end a statement showing classification of investments based on market values for quoted holdings and in book values for unquoted holdings as at the thirty-first of December 1906..." He ran on like this in his unintelligible jargon for some time, until I said:

"All right, Bloggs—presently."

He went on, unheeding:

"And here is a letter from Sir Stanley Sparkbrooke." He laid the letter before me. "He is Acting Chairman of the Board of Directors. He wants to know if you will visit him next weekend to discuss matters concerning the next financial committee meeting."

A recollection of Sir Stanley Sparkbrooke, his wife, and their three daughters, loomed before me larger than life-size—and they were large enough in reality. I took fright.

"Oh no, Bloggs," I protested, "I couldn't do that. I shouldn't understand a word he said."

Bloggs said with prim disapproval:

"I should be glad to go through the report with your lordship item by item if your lordship wishes."

I said wearily:

"What's the good? I can't cope with that all at once. I don't have to do anything about it till I'm twenty-one, anyway."

Bloggs was so shocked at this piece of childish petulance that his correct manner nearly failed him—but not quite. He said, tight-lipped:

"If your lordship will excuse me—the sooner your lordship begins, the sooner he will be able to acquire some understanding of these matters. Now"—he drew up a chair beside me and turned the pages of the report—"shall we take the Balance Sheet to begin with? On this side you have the Company's capital: seven-and-a-half per cent Cumulative Preference Stock, seven-and-a-half per cent Cumulative Preference Shares, Ordinary Stock, Ordinary Shares..."

I ceased to listen almost immediately. I felt suffocated: outraged by the presence of this creature so close beside me, polluting the air with his scent, filling my ears with the sound of his odious voice.

"Capital Reserve," I heard through a mist of wrath, "Revenue Reserve... Unappropriated Profits... three-and-a-half per cent three-and-a-half year Unsecured Loan Stock... four per cent Unsecured Loan Stock... Subsidiary Companies... Liabilities... Provision... Capital Expenditure..."

It seemed to me that with every fresh term his voice got louder and his speech faster. At last I could stand it no longer. I sprang up, overturning my chair, and shouted:

"Oh, for God's sake, stop! Leave me alone!"

Bloggs gave me one look and fled from the room. His face was as white as the Company report. He gave in his notice and left the same day.

10

As time passed I was conscious of being watched—with curiosity, with hope or fear, by everybody who came near me. And there was my stepmother, always at hand to make me aware that I had said or done the wrong thing—to countermand my orders—to show me up as an ignorant fool.

Her manner towards me had changed since my father's death and the reading of the will. She was no longer harsh, nor even cold; she had the appearance, even, of pitying me, and trying to help me. And I was not in the mood to reject even the pretence of kindness. I really was on the verge of a nervous breakdown—when she came to me one day with a new suggestion.

I was sitting in my father's study, oppressed with a pile of papers. There was no secretary to help me now; no one had been appointed to take the place of the insufferable Bloggs, and I had not roused myself sufficiently to see to it. My stepmother came up behind me and laid her white, cool hand on my forehead, and said in her kindest, sweetest tones:

"Poor Harry! It's all too much for you, isn't it?"

I answered violently, to prevent myself from breaking down: "How can I be expected to deal with all this when I've no idea what it's about? I don't understand the jargon. I don't understand the explanations, even. What *can* I know when I've hardly ever left this house and garden?"

I made a rough gesture with my arm and knocked papers and paper-weight on to the floor. My stepmother did not flinch.

"Harry, Harry!" she murmured. "It was cruel of your father to place this heavy burden on your shoulders." Her hand now rested on my shoulder as she talked. "I told him so—but he wouldn't listen. You mustn't blame him. He meant it for your good."

"He shouldn't have kept me in the dark about it all so long," I said. "He shouldn't have kept me apart. He should have let me go to school and mix with other boys—like Bertie—"

Her hand tightened on my shoulder.

"He wanted to spare you," she said. "He was thinking of—" She stopped.

"Yes," I said. "I know. My mother. She killed herself. She was—crazy."

"Not crazy, Harry dear," my stepmother said in that lovely crystal-clear voice of hers. "That's an ugly word. Where do you pick up such crude expressions? From the servants, I suppose. No, the verdict was that she took her life 'while the balance of her mind was disturbed.' And that's what we've always feared for *you*, Harry." She leaned down and said softly: "That's what I'm afraid of *now*."

I swung round to face her.

"You think I'm mad?" I said.

She put out a hand to repudiate so crude an idea.

"No, no, not mad!" she said. "Don't say such a thing! Don't even think it! But—your mind is a delicate, sensitive thing. And if the balance is disturbed—by a burden too heavy for it—" Her dark blue eyes, usually scornful, pleaded—no: appeared to plead—with me: "Harry, for your own sake, will you listen to me? You owe it to your dear father and the trust he reposed in you to look after yourself for the next two years."

I said dully:

"What do you want me to do?"

Her look brightened: I can see it still.

"Will you agree to go away from here," she said, "to a place I know of in Cumberland—a beautiful place—where you'll be looked after by two very clever men—doctors—specialists in mental and nervous conditions—friends of mine? It's all perfectly voluntary."

"What can they do?" I said, half-captivated by her sudden concern, yet unable to believe in any possible aid.

"They can give your mind the treatment it needs," she said. "Just the right amount of rest—just the right amount of exercise, like a limb that has been overstrained. You can forget all this dreadful nightmare of papers and business: just live a carefree life, healthy, in the open air, riding, fishing—shooting, if you wish. You'd like to shoot, wouldn't you?"

"I'd like to live a normal life," I said with subdued bitterness.

She ignored the implied reproach.

"And you'll have your own man to look after you," she said, "and your own horses to ride. And after a few months you'll come back here perfectly rested and ready to take over everything. It will seem easy then."

Her voice, so persuasive when she chose, awakened in me a flicker of hope.

"You think so—really?" I said.

"I'm sure of it," she said. "When you come back you can make a new start with your mind fresh and clear. But—for the present it's absolutely necessary that you should get away from here with all its unhappy associations—its atmosphere of failure…"

I don't know how much longer she talked, or what she said, finally to win my consent. I was too worn out to resist her—and perhaps I allowed myself to believe that she really wished for my welfare. She was a very beautiful woman, the most beautiful I ever saw, George, and she knew how to get her own way.

So I left for this remote place in Cumberland, kept by those two very clever doctors—those friends of hers. It was, after all, quite voluntary on my part. Quite!

One thing did surprise me a little: the man who accompanied me was not my old friend Dick, the groom, but a man I did not know. I was told that Dick was unwilling to leave his family, and that this new man—my stepmother's choice—would act as my personal servant and companion.

His name was Sebastian Rowles.

11

After a few weeks I settled down fairly well at the private mental home in Cumberland. I did, for the first time, lead a normal healthy life of outdoor exercise and freedom from oppressive cares. I did not much like the two doctors, but I saw little of them. I had my own quarters, with Sebastian Rowles to supervise my maintenance and attend to my requirements, and the doctors paid me a routine visit once a week, when they put me through certain rather childish mental exercises, asking me numbers of stupid questions to which I gave random and often flippant answers. One of the doctors was old, one young, but they were both solemn, pompous, lacking in any knowledge of human nature and entirely devoid of humour. It was a temptation, therefore, to have some mild fun at their expense. I laughed to think they took down everything I said and would use it for their statistics.

I had no contact with any of the other inmates. My only companion was Rowles. He was a young man, only four or five years older than myself, but much more mature: quiet and controlled, respectful but not excessively so. He had been a gentleman's servant before, and so his speech and manners were quite good. He looked after me efficiently and did not irritate me by talking about himself, so that I soon took him for granted. If I had to have an attendant, Rowles seemed as good as any.

Several months went by. I felt completely restored to health, physical and mental, and I began to think of my return. One day we were out riding together on the moor. We had reined in after a gallop. I was elated by the speed and the sparkling moorland air. I said:

"By Jove, Rowles, that was good! This air is really marvellous. I didn't know what mountain air could do to me. I feel a new man." I laughed. "Do you think I'm improving?"

Rowles affected to misunderstand me. He looked down between his horse's ears and said:

"Your lordship was always a first-class horseman, I understand."

"I don't mean that!" I said impatiently. "I mean—am I improving in health? I'm supposed to be suffering from a nervous breakdown, you know."

Rowles said without expression:

"Your lordship is looking fine."

For once his lack of any human warmth irritated me. This was unreasonable, because if he had been familiar I would have resented it, but my isolation made me long for some demonstration of interest, even from him. I said:

"Oh, do stop addressing me in the third person, Rowles! Look here: tell me honestly, what are you *really* supposed to be doing here with me? Aren't you something more than my personal servant? Weren't you really appointed as—my keeper?"

Rowles looked embarrassed.

"Well—" he drawled in his deep voice, the voice of an older man.

"Do *you* think I'm crazy, Rowles?" I pressed him. "My stepmother does, I know, and I suppose my brother does, and perhaps even my little sister. But what about you? You've been with me now for three months, every day and all day. *You* ought to know if there's anything wrong with me, if anybody does. Never mind 'your lordship.' Tell me the truth, as man to man."

After a pause Rowles looked up. He said in a different voice, frank and, I thought, with a touch of sympathy:

"You're as sane as I am, sir."

I was fervently grateful.

"You think so?" I said, as if he had been an oracle. "Oh, thank God! You'd know if I weren't, wouldn't you? You've seen something of the world?"

Rowles gave a laugh.

"I *have* that," he said.

"Then if I'm all right," I said, "what am I doing here? I can leave today if I wish. My being here is quite voluntary, you know."

Rowles said nothing.

"Let's ride back at once," I said, carried away by the thought of change, "and pack up and get the night train down. I don't really *like* this place, in spite of the air. I don't like those two doctors. The old one is quite sinister—and the young one is completely under his thumb. If I were really in their power I'd be afraid of them. Come on, Rowles. Let's tell them we're off—if not tonight, tomorrow at the latest."

Rowles said tonelessly:

"I'm afraid, sir, that's not possible."

"Why not?" I said, my temper rising at the thought of an obstacle.

"Because," he said slowly, "well, you remember the tests they put you through a couple of weeks ago?"

"Yes," I said scornfully. "What of it? A lot of rot!"

"They decided," said Rowles, "on the result of them, you were insane. You can't leave without permission. You'd be sent back."

I was aghast.

"You mean," I said, "those two scoundrels have certified me as insane? But—it's monstrous! You say yourself I'm as sane as you are! They can't do it!" A horrible doubt assailed me. "Or can they? I'm so hopelessly ignorant! I don't know what are my legal rights at all. If I wrote to my lawyers—"

Rowles said grimly:

"They'd be more likely to listen to Lady Assche than to you." The full horror of my position broke on me, temporarily unnerving me.

"My God," I said, "what am I to do?"

There was a long pause. Our horses cropped the grass. The day was as brilliant as ever, but for me the light had gone out of it. Then Rowles's deep voice penetrated through the confusion in my mind.

"I know what I'd do," he said, "if I were in your lordship's place."

I snatched at the straw of hope.

"Yes?" I said eagerly.

"I'd clear out quickly," he said, "before something worse happened to me." He drew his horse closer to mine, until he was beside me. "You'd best make a bolt first, otherwise you may find yourself falling out of a window—or getting drowned in the lake—or having an accident with a gun."

"But how can I?" I said despairingly. "You just said I couldn't leave now. They'd send me back—and it would be bound to be worse—much, much worse. They might lock me up or something." I beat my forehead with my fist. "If only I knew what to do!"

Rowles said slowly:

"I could help you, if you liked."

I stared at him in an anguish of expectation mixed with incredulity.

"*You* could?" I said. "How? I'll give you anything—anything—if you'll help me to get away."

Rowles said thoughtfully:

"It'd be pretty awkward for me—I'd get into serious trouble. I'd lose my job—and her ladyship would see to it that I didn't get another very easily."

"I'll make it worth your while," I promised him. My allowance had been paid regularly, and I had used hardly any of it since I had been here, though I had cashed some of the cheques, as Rowles was aware, because he had been to the bank for me. I reminded him of this. But he said firmly:

"No, sir, no. You'll need money for the journey. Give me what you can spare, if you must give me anything."

I promised him a hundred pounds, and said he could have my diamond cuff links and one or two other articles as well. They were worth quite a lot, I believe.

"I must keep the rest for myself, I suppose," I said, "in case I need money later on. What do you suggest I should do?" He pulled at his upper lip.

"Your lordship has a separate suite of rooms here," he said.

"Yes, thank God!" I said. "I'd go mad—really mad—if I hadn't."

"They rely on *me* to look after you," Rowles went on. "Apart from the weekly visit of the doctors, you hardly see anyone except me—and you can easily avoid being seen by anyone else at all."

"That's true," I said.

"I have a brother," said Rowles. "He's younger than me: about your age, though he's more sturdily built. Still, in the distance it wouldn't be noticed."

"Go on," I said. I had only the dimmest notion of where this was leading.

"He too happens to be called Henry," said Rowles with deliberation. "And he happens to be a sailor—of sorts. He's just signed on as steward on a new ship—a cargo boat going to Durban."

I began to understand. I listened carefully as Rowles developed his plan.

"I could get him here," he said, "the day after the doctors have paid you their weekly visit. We could go out riding, early one morning. You'd be muffled up to the eyes because of the cold. Somewhere up here on the moor—in the old quarry, say—you and my brother Hal could change places. He'd give you his papers—and you'd catch the next train south. He'd stay here a few days, until the ship sailed. After that—well, it'd be up to you."

"It sounds possible," I said doubtfully, "but—it would mean giving up everything. How could I ever get back my rights?"

"That's easy enough," said Rowles, "once you're out of the country. You can't do anything here: they'd stop you. But if you get to South Africa you could get a couple of doctors over there to say you're sane. By that time it'll have been found out that my brother isn't you—and I'll have got the sack. You'll lie low till you've been proved all right. Then you can apply to the lawyers to get the certificate cancelled over here."

I was still doubtful.

"You're sure it'll work?" I said. "My escape, I mean?"

"Of course," said Rowles, suddenly cheerful. "And I'm glad to be able to help your lordship. If, some day, you come into your own—"

"I won't forget," I assured him. But I was wondering, d'you know, if I would ever want to come back, once I got away.

12

It all passed off smoothly, just as Sebastian Rowles had said. One misty morning in March we rode out early, muffled up to the ears, and at the old quarry on the moor we met his brother Henry Rowles—Hal, as he called him.

Hal Rowles was as unlike Sebastian as he well could be. There was a facial resemblance; but Hal was a short, thick-set, uncouth young fellow who seemed barely able to articulate, and when he did open his mouth, even the couple of words he uttered were grunted in some vile cockneyish accent the like of which I had never heard. Sebastian, on the other hand, was perfectly at home in this unusual situation.

"Here you are, sir," he said, when we had dismounted. "This is my brother Henry." He called to the fellow, who was standing, hands in pockets, looking on surlily. "Come here, Hal, and meet his lordship."

Hal came forward reluctantly, scowling at me as if I were the strange beast, not he. I said, "How do you do?" and he grunted some surly reply to the effect that *he* was okay. I stared at him in dismay.

"But I say, Rowles," I protested, "he isn't at all like me! He's several inches shorter, for one thing—and he's much broader."

"Don't worry, your lordship," said Sebastian soothingly. "I'll keep him out of sight till you get right away. We'll go out shooting. Hal'll be glad to get hold of a gun, even if it *is* only for rabbits—won't you, Hal?"

Hal again gave a surly grunt of acquiescence, which sounded like "Don't mind."

"Well," I said, still somewhat daunted at the sight of my substitute, "I shall have to take a risk. Only for heaven's sake don't let them find out until it's too late for them to get their hands on me again!"

Sebastian reassured me. Hal stood there dumbly, his large hands hanging, and I thought he looked rather like an anthropoid ape. He seemed to take no interest in the proceedings. Sebastian said:

"Give his lordship your papers, Hal."

Hal felt in his breast pocket and handed over an envelope. I gave Sebastian a wallet containing one hundred and fifty pounds in five-pound notes, and a purse containing the jewellery I had mentioned.

"I take it you and your brother can settle things between you?" I said.

Sebastian put his arm round his brother's shoulders.

"We'll settle everything as it should be, your lordship can rest assured," he said with a laugh.

I said goodbye, shaking hands with them both, and thanking Sebastian Rowles for all he had done.

"I shan't forget," I said.

Then I set off down the hill through the mist to the station. And that, George, was how I came to begin my long journey as Henry Rowles. I was happy to get away at last, thankful to escape—from the nightmare of circumstance that had surrounded me.

I little thought, as the ship sailed out of Southampton, I shouldn't see England again for twenty years.

MR. VAUGHAN'S STORY CONTINUED

Pollicott came to the end of his story.

"Well, Mr. Vaughan, sir," he said, "that was what Henry did tell me, as near as I remembers—and I do remember 'most all he did say, and how he looked as he did say it." His voice gathered strength. "And I knows for sure he were speaking the truth. If you'd-a heer'd him, you'd-a said the same."

He gazed at me so earnestly with his red-rimmed eyes, as if searching my face for any scepticism, that I hastened to reassure him.

"I'm sure I would have, Pollicott," I said. "It's all very interesting—very interesting indeed." Out of the many questions that crowded into my mind, I chose the most important: "Now tell me," I said. "I want you to try hard to remember—did he ever explain to you how it was that he was supposed to be dead?"

Pollicott, looking bewildered, said:

"Beg pardon, sir?"

I explained.

"You see, Pollicott, in the books where such things are recorded it says that the ninth Lord Assche—that's your Henry, if he was speaking the truth—"

Pollicott started at these words, and his eyes flashed.

"He *were* speaking the truth, sir," he said indignantly, "same as I am. But"—he sank back into depression—"nobody don't believe *me* neither."

"Quite so, quite so," I said hastily. I still sometimes failed to realise that the most ordinary legal caution was liable to offend Pollicott when it was applied to Henry. "Well, as I was saying: your Henry—the ninth Lord Assche—is recorded as having *died insane* in the year 1908: that's nearly a year after the death of his father, the eighth lord—and, in fact, it seems to be about the time he said he ran away from this institution, whatever it was. What happened, do you know? Did they think he had died abroad, or what?"

"No, sir," said Pollicott with decision. "They didn't think no such thing." He brooded for a few moments. Then he said: "I'd best tell you, sir, what Henry tell'd me one night—a good time after he came to the hut, I'd say it was. We was a-sitting indoors, and there was a gale blowing, and the spring tides was a-dashing over the Wall—they don't do no more than 'kiss the foot,' as the country folk round here do say, as a general rule. Well, it was a-blowing great guns outside, but we was snug and cosy—I do remember as if it was yesterday—and Henry, he suddenly give a sort of chuckle, like, and he says to me: 'George, do you realise this is the thirtieth anniversary of my death?'"

HENRY'S STORY CONTINUED, TEN YEARS LATER

I

George, do you realise this is the thirtieth anniversary of my death? Oh, don't look so scared! I'm not a ghost, I assure you, and I assure you it's all perfectly natural. Let me explain: this is just the kind of night for such a story, when the wind's blowing and the waves are trying to get at us from the other side of the Wall and wash us and our petty little lives with all their worries away.

According to the books, George, I died on the twenty-first of March, 1908—and my half-brother Bertie, now the tenth Lord Assche, succeeded me. Would you be interested to know exactly *how* I died? Yes, I'm sure you would, in spite of your ridiculous superstition that it brings bad luck to talk that way.

Bad luck, George? The only bad luck would be if this roof blew off. Do you think the threat of bad luck can frighten *me* any more? You know, George, you're a splendid listener—but what you entirely lack is curiosity. Anyone would think you'd be interested to know how it is that I, who am sitting here before you in the flesh, should be recorded as having died exactly thirty years ago!

You're not? Well, well! Never mind, it's worth recounting. They say one's words go on for eternity, echoing throughout the universe—and as I've never told this story to anyone before, I'd like to think there'll be a record of it somewhere in space if I tell it to you, George.

And yet—I don't really know for certain *what* happened. How could I? I wasn't there. I was in Durban when I heard the sequel, after a horrible voyage over which I will draw a veil. I had actually found employment there as a commercial traveller, selling typewriters, believe it or not: they were comparatively rare at that time, and I had obtained this post quite easily on the strength of my superior manner. Isn't it strange, George, to what uses the world puts such advantages, if they *are* advantages? However, that's not the point.

I was sitting in a café having lunch one day when the man opposite me, who knew me slightly, passed me a newspaper. It was a copy of the London *Times*.

"Any connection of yours?" he said, pointing to a paragraph. I should explain that I had reverted to the use of my own name, Henry Clairvaux, as soon as I came ashore.

I took the paper and began reading. I have the cutting still, George, among my papers here. I shall read it to you—and I leave you to imagine my feelings. It says:

"At the inquest held yesterday at Penrith on John Henry Vincent Peter Dallingsworth Clairvaux, ninth Baron Assche of Ashenford, a verdict of Death by Misadventure was returned.

"Lord Assche, who was twenty years of age and succeeded to the title on the death of his father ten months ago, had entered a private institution for voluntary mental treatment and had since been certified as insane. He was, however, allowed a certain amount of liberty, being permitted for reasons of health to ride out with his personal attendant, a trusted servant of the family named Sebastian Rowles.

"Rowles stated that on the morning of the twenty-first he accompanied his master on their daily ride across the moor, when Lord Assche expressed a desire to dismount and shoot at some rabbits. Rowles, at his urgent insistence, gave him the gun. As Lord Assche dismounted the gun went off in his face and he was killed instantaneously.

"The Coroner expressed a doubt as to the wisdom of allowing Lord Assche to handle a shot-gun, in view of the state of his health; but it was stated by Dr. Bowers, head of the Gable Private Mental Home where Lord Assche had been receiving treatment, that it had been thought best to allow Lord Assche to live as normal a life as possible and to indulge in the recreations usual to his class and age.

"As stated above, a verdict of Death by Misadventure was recorded, the Coroner expressing his and the jury's sympathy with the family of the deceased."

2

Well now, George, what do you make of that, eh? Did I understand you to say that "that there Seb Rowles done him in?" His own brother too! How you jump to conclusions, my friend! We have no proof that Sebastian Rowles did him in, as you so pungently express it. But—it certainly might be surmised by the uncharitable.

I ask myself, George, supposing for a moment you are correct—what have we here? Have we the killing of two birds—or rabbits—with one shot? Was Henry Rowles—the real Henry Rowles—as inconvenient to his brother as Harry Clairvaux was to his stepmother?

Well, we shall never know. But at that moment I came to a decision not to return. For I knew my life wouldn't be safe, George, if

I came back. While I was alive, you see, there was always a chance that I might find a way of proving that I was not insane. Great interests were involved. The prize was too great, the danger too serious. Harry Clairvaux was supposed to be dead, and Bertie was wearing his shoes. If ever it was discovered that it was not Harry but a substitute who had died—well, you see what it would have meant to all concerned.

And how many were concerned, exactly?

I didn't know. I don't know to this day.

That's what made me stay away, for twenty long years. If I'd been wise I'd have stayed away till the end of my days.

MR. VAUGHAN'S STORY CONTINUED

I

I now had almost as much of Henry's story as Pollicott could remember. I could now leave him, I thought—go away and try to fit the pieces together. But just as I was gathering up my papers it struck me that Pollicott was staring at me with great intentness, as if he had something more to say. So I stopped and asked him:

"Before I go, Pollicott, is there anything else you'd like to tell me? Speak out if there is. Now's the time, you know!"

Pollicott said:

"There *is* just one thing, Mr. Vaughan, sir—but it were only the other day, like."

"All the better!" I said. "The importance of the past is that it's leading us, we hope, to an interpretation of the present."

My words passed over Pollicott's head. He was already deep in another scene.

"Henry'd been going through all his papers," he said. "He had 'em spread out all over the table, and he were reading 'em in the light of the lamp, tearing up some and putting some in that big envelope I give to Mr. Lomax. There were photos, too. After a bit he give a sort of a chuckle, like, and he looks at me over the top of what he was reading, and he says: You know, George,' he says, 'if I was to tell 'em to dig up the body of this here Lord Somebody, there's certain folk'd get a big surprise.' And I says: 'I reckon they might, Henry...' Then he hands me a photo, and he says: 'You see this here photo? That's the real Henry Rowles. It was with his papers, the ones he handed to me that morning up on the moor. He wasn't much like me, was he?'

"I looks at the photograph, which was a bit faded and yellow-like. I can't make it out very well, but I can see it's a dark, thick-set chap, no more like Henry than I am, nor ever could-a been. So I gives it him back and I says: 'No, Henry, I can't say as he was. But how did they come to bury him in your place, like? You'd-a thought they'd-a knowed.' And Henry, he looks at me very wise, and he says:

"'That's why it had to be a shot-gun accident: it kind-a blew his head off, you see. So if they wanted to, they *could* pretend it was me. And I reckon there weren't anybody wanted to argue about it. I reckon it suited 'em all too well—especially my stepmother, George,' he says, 'especially my stepmother. But what I asks myself,' he says, 'is—did she know, George? Did she know? I wonder.'

"And he do look so sad, Mr. Vaughan, sir, and his eyes do fill with tears, like as I never did see Henry before in all the years we was together. And then he do give himself a sort of shake, and he smiles at me and says quite bright again: 'And I wonder sometimes what became of that there Seb Rowles.'"

2

Pollicott watched me while I took in this new bit of information At last I said:

"When did this conversation take place, Pollicott? Recently, you say?"

"I reckon it'd be about a couple of months ago," he said.

"Strange," I said, "because, you know, it was just about two months ago that the Dowager Lady Assche died, aged eighty-three—that is, Henry's stepmother, if such she was."

"Is that so, sir?" said Pollicott, polite but not curious. "Henry didn't say nothing about that to *me*. But I notices he were getting much closer like, latterly. And he'd taken to writing letters. I must-a posted half a dozen on' em, one time and another."

"Did you notice the names and addresses on any of them?" I said.

"Well, sir," said Pollicott, "I didn't pay much heed at the time, like—not wanting to pry into Henry's affairs if he don't want to tell me hisself. So I scarcely looks at the addresses. But I can't help seeing one of 'em is addressed to this here Lord—Right Honourable he do call him—because Henry says to me at the time, he says, 'That'll give him a turn, George. That's my half-brother, Bertie, who thinks I've been shut up in the family vault these last forty years…'"

"Did you notice any of the other names?" I said, repressing my eagerness in order not to deflect him. "Any more letters to this lord?—Lord Assche, it would be, no doubt."

"I dunno, sir," said Pollicott. "I didn't pay much heed. But there was one other I do remember, because Henry he do show it to me, and he says, 'This should be worth three thousand pounds to you some day, George.'"

"And the address?" I said.

"It was to this here bank in Jo'burg," said Pollicott.

I began to see—a little way, at any rate. But I did not tell Pollicott what I was thinking. I waited for a few moments, and then I said:

"Did he ever tell you what made him come home again after all?"

3

Pollicott thought for a while before answering this question. He was now sitting slumped in his chair, and I was aware that he was nearing the end of his strength on this occasion. He passed a thin hand over his face and said:

"No, sir, he never did tell me—not exactly. But I reckon from what he says to me from time to time, he thought to make hisself known to his family—this here brother of his he calls Bertie, who's a lord. I reckon he do want to get in touch with 'em, and then something do happen that puts him off the notion, like—makes him think he'd do best to lie low again."

"Something frightened him, you think?" I said.

"I guess so, sir," said Pollicott. "Looking back on it all, it do seem to me he were scared from the start. That's how he came to land on my doorstep, as you might say. He were scared to show hisself. He'd been looking for work and couldn't get none, maybe, and he couldn't get at his money he'd left behind. He lands up here in a sort of a delerrium: lost his way, he had, on one of them dark foggy nights, like the night he—he come to his end. He says then in his ravings: 'They're after me—they're after me again! I didn't ought to have come back!'"

Pollicott's face was grey as he stared beyond me into the past.

"Yes, sir," he said, "Henry did say many things in his fever that didn't mean nothing to me at the time; but I've often thought of them since, and especially since I've been locked up here with nothing else to do but remember—remember—"

I said gently:

"Can you tell *me* any of the things he said in his delirium? It might help us, you know."

Pollicott said:

"I do remember very well what he do say: he says the same things over and over again—"

"*What* things?"

"He says: 'They're after me! I shouldn't have come back! They'll never give up! There's too much to lose! *She'll* never give up, if she finds out I'm alive!' Then sometimes he gets proper wild, as if there was someone at the door, and he sits up in his bunk and shouts: 'Don't let 'em in! Don't let 'em in! Don't say I'm here!' And he says to me: 'I'm not mad—I'm not mad, I tell you! I can prove it. Get me two doctors—two real doctors, not them two scoundrels! *She* chose 'em! *She* paid 'em! And that man Rowles!'

"He'd go on and on like that until he were quite done up, and sometimes he'd call *me* 'Rowles' and he'd say: 'Don't keep calling me "your lordship"!' Other times he'd groan and say: 'Oh, God, why did I ever come back? I'd forgotten what it was like not to be free!'

"So I soothes him down, Mr. Vaughan, sir, and I tell him no one shan't come in, he's safe enough with me and always will be. I thinks he just has the heeby-jeebies, like, but I can see he ain't no ordinary person, and it's a honour to me that he has come to *my* little hut in his deep trouble.

"So I nurses him and brings him back to health—and one day when he do come to hisself again he do begin and tell me his story, just as I tell it to you, about how he never do remember being happy afore…

"And so he were with me ever since, and I were proud and happy to have him. You'd only to speak to Henry, sir, to know he was a real gentleman. And I do wish—I do wish with all my heart," he said, his voice breaking, "he were here now for me to look after." He wrung his hands: "And to think they do say I done him any harm!"

I stood up and spoke to him gently.

"Don't worry, Pollicott. *I* know you didn't. And soon, I hope, we'll be able to prove it to everybody."

He raised his eyes to me and seemed to strain himself in a last effort to listen as I said:

"Now listen: you won't be seeing me for some little while—several days, perhaps. Will you be patient and trust me? I shall be acting in your interests all the time. So make up your mind to wait as cheerfully as you can till I come back. Don't answer any questions. And no more fasting, remember! I want you to be in good form when I get back, not a skeleton!"

I could not get a smile from the old man. He said dully:

"Just as you do say, sir."

"That's a good fellow!" I said, but I was by no means sure that he would be able to hold out for long. I hoped that when next I saw him I should be bringing better news; for I believed that I could now see a little further into this dark jungle of intrigue, and I knew exactly what next I meant to do.

V

Investigation: First Steps

MR. VAUGHAN'S STORY CONTINUED

I

After considering Pollicott's story I had come to the conclusion that my investigations must pursue lines suggested by his friend Henry's strange claim. I spent another few hours going through the dead man's papers and making a summary of the chief events as given me by Pollicott. In the light of Pollicott's account, several of the items in the envelope took on a new significance. Having weighed these carefully, therefore, I wrote two letters, one to Lord Assche of Ashenford to ask for the favour of an interview, the other to a firm of Portsmouth solicitors called Bodger and Danton, saying that I would call there on Tuesday of the following week in the afternoon.

I took the letters into the town and posted them at the General Post Office, to make sure that they would arrive the next morning. From now onward I meant to spare myself nothing in an effort to collect the evidence—if it could be obtained—that would set Pollicott free. I was convinced that speed was essential: the old man, if left too long, would abandon himself again to despair, I felt sure.

Next morning, therefore, without telling anyone, even Lomax, of my intention, I caught the early-morning train north, reaching my destination in the early evening. I had arranged to spend the night at a hotel overlooking Lake Windermere.

The Lake District is not at its best, in my opinion, in autumn. A poet might think differently, perhaps, but I am not enamoured of mountain-tops swathed in mist, yellow leaves falling, and water, water everywhere. I prefer the Lakes in springtime—and I prefer my own soft landscape with its reens and the grey-stone churches at all seasons. I spent rather a gloomy evening in the deserted hotel, meditating on the strange story of Harry Clairvaux, longing to get my business done and travel south again.

Next morning, after making a telephone call, I hired a car and drove out to the Gable Private Mental Hospital where the ninth Lord Assche—or someone reputed to be the ninth Lord Assche—had met his death in a shooting accident.

2

The morning was dull, with a fine drizzle blotting out the view. The car turned in at an ancient-looking gateway with a smart newly-painted white board saying "Gable Private Hospital," and followed a curving drive between elms. The building—or rather buildings, for there were several—stood at the base of a mountain, the top of which was of course concealed in drifting cloud. The centre of the conglomeration was a large country house, obviously the original structure, on to which had been added at various times various modern-looking wings, white and many-windowed. I climbed up the steps of the handsome porch and rang the bell.

The nurse who took my name and asked me to follow her said that Dr. Breadlebane could see me in a moment. But as she led me along bare corridors I suspected that the "moment" would prove to be half an hour in a very hygienic and uninteresting waiting-room. I was therefore rather relieved when we were stopped in the corridor by a tall, fair young man wearing bifocal glasses, who addressed me:

"Oh, good morning! Are you Mr. Vaughan?"

I said I was.

"I'm Dr. Hutchings," he said. "Dr. Breadlebane's assistant. Dr. Breadlebane sent me along to meet you. He's engaged for the moment. He wondered if you'd care to look round." He dismissed the nurse and took charge of me.

"This place is much larger than I expected," I said as I walked along yet more corridors at his side. "I had understood that it was just a country house, adapted for the accommodation of a few special—very special—patients."

Dr. Hutchings laughed diffidently.

"Oh yes," he said, "I believe it was, originally. It has changed hands since then, you know."

"Really?" I said.

"Oh, definitely!" said Dr. Hutchings. "It's really quite difficult to *find* the old house in the middle of all the new buildings. It must have been a funny little show to start with. This, by the way, is the occupational therapy wing." He opened a door, and I was at once greeted with the sounds of wheels whirring. "That's the potting-room," he said.

I glanced in. Half a dozen patients were busy shaping various objects in clay on their potter's wheels.

"Oh, I see!" I said. "You mean where pottery is made. Strange to think of the potter's wheel, once so important to mankind, being preserved for occupational therapy!"

"Yes, isn't it?" said Dr. Hutchings vaguely. "The patients love it—and some of them are very good at it, too." He released the door, which swung back silently, cutting off all noise, and we began walking again. "You'd be surprised," he continued, "how very clever they are at what they like doing. Music, for instance: it's quite a thing here. We have enough talent among the patients to make quite a useful little orchestra."

As he spoke I could hear faint sounds of orchestral music. He opened another door, and the delicious sounds of "*Die Forelle*" greeted me. The quintet were too absorbed in their playing to be aware of us.

"They're very expert," I said. "They must have had a good deal of practice together. I take it some of them stay a long time."

"Oh yes," said Dr. Hutchings. "Some of them are here for the rest of their lives. They're so happy they don't *want* to leave."

"All voluntary?" I said, watching the 'cellist as with head bowed she sawed away.

"Of course," said Dr. Hutchings. "We don't keep them here once they've been certified."

He released the door. "The Trout" faded. We walked on.

"Remarkable!" I mused. "You're very strong on occupational therapy here, I see."

"Oh yes, definitely!"

"What about outdoor exercise—games and sport and so on?"

"The patients spend as much time as possible out of doors," he assured me. "There's an excellent football team—rugger excites them too much, unfortunately—and some of them play golf. We like them to live as normal a life as they can."

"You do?" I said. "You're keeping up the old tradition."

"Oh yes, definitely!" he said once more, but his mind was now on conducting me to my interview with his chief, the proper time having elapsed. "Well, shall we go along? Dr. Breadlebane will probably be free by now." We turned and walked back through the corridors to the old house again.

3

Dr. Breadlebane was a stoutish man in the early fifties, I should say. His study was large and well-carpeted. The furniture was old, highly-polished mahogany, and the lofty walls were lined with bound volumes of psychiatric journals and books on mental disease. He sat behind a very large flat desk, and rose to greet me.

"Ah, Mr. Vaughan!" he said. "Come in. Come this way, sir. Take a chair." He gave me a chair facing the long windows, and reseated himself behind the desk. "Now what can I do for you?" His very friendly manner revealed that he regarded me as a potential bringer of patients: I had mentioned my profession over the telephone.

"This is a very interesting place you've got here, doctor," I said, staring out at the dank green lawn with its drifts of sodden leaves and its rustic seat in one corner beneath the dripping trees.

"Ah, yes," said Dr. Breadlebane. "We do our best, you know—and that's quite a lot, in these times."

"So I see." He waited for me to come to the point. After a pause, I said:

"Actually, I've come to you for information—historical information."

His manner was less cordial as he answered:

"Happy to do anything I can."

"I understand," I began, "from your assistant that this—er—institution is no longer in the hands of the original owners."

"That is so," he said. "The place was sold to a small group interested in modern psychology, shortly before the war."

"But," I said, withdrawing my gaze from the dismal garden and concentrating it on him, "I presume the records of the original establishment are still in existence?"

Dr. Breadlebane returned my gaze unflinchingly and said blandly:

"Before we go any further, may I ask in whose interests these enquiries are being made? I gather you are a solicitor—"

"A retired solicitor," I said. "Or rather, I have come out of my retirement to make this enquiry."

"—Because, of course," he continued, "our records are strictly confidential. You will appreciate that. Our *clientele*—like that of our predecessors here—has always been drawn exclusively from persons of a certain rank and standing—"

I could not help murmuring:

"A sort of psychopathic Eton."

Dr. Breadlebane was taken aback. At first he thought he hadn't heard aright.

"I beg your pardon?" he said. Then, when it dawned on him that I had made a joke, perhaps in rather bad taste, he gave a forced laugh. "Oh, of course!" he said, and hurried on with the remainder of his sentence. "And we owe it to our patients' families to maintain strict secrecy about our inmates and their affairs."

"Naturally," I said, enjoying keeping him in suspense. "But I hardly think there could be any indiscretion in enquiring about a patient who is recorded as having died"—I paused for effect—"forty years ago. I refer to—the ninth Lord Assche."

Dr. Breadlebane's relief was comic, and expressed itself in an immediate return to effusiveness.

"The ninth Lord Assche! Yes, yes, of course! A very sad case. It was long before my time—I mean, I was still at school—but I've heard it spoken of. I'm told it's the only fatal accident—if it *was* accident—that has ever occurred in this place."

"Is that so?" I said without implication. But he seemed to detect in my tone some knowledge which I did not possess, for he added rather hurriedly:

"Except, of course, for a young man who unfortunately fell out of a window—yes. And—let me see—I believe there was also an attempted drowning in the lake. But I know about these by hearsay only."

"You said just now," I went on, "'if it *was* accident.' May I ask what that implies? Has any doubt ever been expressed about it? The verdict, I recall, was 'Death by Misadventure.'"

"Yes, of course," said Dr. Breadlebane in reverent tones. "There would be a natural wish to spare the feelings of the family, if any doubt were possible."

"You mean," I said, "the alternative verdict would have been suicide?"

He bowed his head.

"There always *is* a strong presumption of suicide when the person is certified as insane."

"Doesn't it strike you as odd, doctor," I said quietly, "that this young man, a certified lunatic as you say, should have been allowed to handle a gun at all?"

"Well—er—" Dr. Breadlebane was a little put out at so direct a question; then, remembering that it did not concern him, he recovered himself. "Not knowing all the circumstances, I must refrain from passing judgment. But of course *we* shouldn't allow it *ourselves*." He brightened at the thought. "Things have changed considerably since then. The science of psychiatry didn't exist in those days. One can only think that they underestimated the seriousness of the young Lord Assche's condition."

"Where are the original owners now?" I asked.

"I really couldn't say," he replied coldly. "One of them has since died, I believe, and the other—the junior partner—left this country when the house was sold. There *was*, in fact, a certain feeling against the Home in the neighbourhood at that time over the death of the patient who fell out of a window. Yes..."

"Was his death also recorded as misadventure?" I inquired.

"I believe so," said Dr. Breadlebane. There was a touch of irritation in his voice as he added: "But the matter is really no concern of mine. May I ask if there is anything further I can do for you? Otherwise, if you'll excuse me, I must be starting out on my round." He laughed with false heartiness, longing to "Two miles of corridor, you know! Not quite as bad as Florence Nightingale's, but still, quite a step—quite a step!" He half-rose.

I remained seated, and said firmly:

"I'm sorry to delay you. But there *is* one further thing you can do for me. Can you tell me—or rather, find out for me—who identified the remains of this unfortunate young man?"

"Well, really, Mr. Vaughan!" he expostulated. "The two doctors then in charge, I presume. And wasn't there a personal attendant? It used to be the custom for patients to bring at least one servant to look after them. We don't allow that now, of course."

"But surely," I said, "some member of the family also came? Not that there was much to identify: the head was blown off, I believe."

Dr. Breadlebane, with a sigh, gave up the struggle.

"The only thing I can do," he said, "is to ask my colleague to look up the records for you. Unfortunately the records are very incomplete. Would there perhaps be something at the Coroner's office? That's your province, not mine, I'm afraid. Or"—a new way of disposing of me occurred to him—"perhaps Matron would know. She's a local woman, and her aunt was here in the days of Dr. Bowers and Dr. McGurky."

He pressed the buzzer on his desk. A nurse entered.

"Ask Matron to come here a minute, please, nurse," he said.

While we waited I thought it more courteous to explain my own interest in the matter.

"My client," I said, "is an old night-watchman named Pollicott. He is accused of murder, and these enquiries of mine are directed solely towards establishing his innocence."

Dr. Breadlebane was profoundly uninterested in Pollicott's fate.

"Is that so?" he said. "Well, you've certainly come a long way." He suppressed a yawn. "I read about the murder. Yes... Somewhere down south, wasn't it?"

A tap on the door relieved me of the need to answer and him of the obligation to listen.

"Ah, here's Matron!" he said.

4

The matron entered; she was a rosy-cheeked woman with a manner more affable than most of her kind.

Dr. Breadlebane introduced us.

"Matron, this is Mr. Vaughan. He is a *solicitor*," he said, emphasising the word significantly. "He is making some *enquiries* about a death that took place here about forty years ago in the days of Dr. Bowers and Dr. McGurky. We were wondering if you could help us."

The matron greeted me and said:

"By all means, doctor, if I can. But I'm afraid my memory doesn't go back *quite* so far." She laughed girlishly.

"Of course not," I intervened gallantly. "But—I wonder if you have since heard anything about the case in question. It's the case of the young Lord Assche—the ninth Lord Assche, who was killed in an accident with a shot-gun while out riding with his attendant, a man called Sebastian Rowles."

"Lord Assche?" the matron looked eager. "Oh yes, I can tell you about *that*! It was much talked about at the time. Everybody said he must have shot himself—but it was covered up, they said, for the sake of the family. My aunt said there might have been quite a fuss about it—but the family didn't follow it up, so it was all allowed to die down." She spoke of the family as of divine beings above the law.

"Your aunt would know the young man, I suppose?" I said.

"Oh yes, she often saw him," said the matron, "though he kept pretty closely to his rooms. He had a suite of rooms with a servant to look after him. But she said she met him once or twice going out or coming in, and he looked quite normal and spoke quite normally, though he seemed nervous—uncertain in his manner for someone in *his* position."

She had now seated herself opposite me, and was awaiting my further questions with interest. This was a stroke of luck for me: a garrulous woman with a direct link with the past. I could afford to ignore Breadlebane.

"The funeral took place in Hampshire, I believe," I told her, "at Lord Assche's home. Did anybody come north at the time of his death, I wonder—to identify the remains, for instance? But I suppose you wouldn't remember, even if you had been told."

"Oh, but I do!" cried the matron. "I remember perfectly well my aunt telling me. My aunt's still alive, and she still talks of it, though I don't think she could tell you anything I don't know by heart. She's quite deaf, and she says the same things over and over again, you see."

Dr. Breadlebane broke in impatiently.

"Mr. Vaughan is in rather a hurry, Matron. If you would just tell him what he wants to know—"

"*What* was it you asked?" said the matron to me. "Oh yes, I remember. You asked if anybody came north at the time. Well,

I *do* remember as it happens." She ran on with growing sentimentality: "It made a great impression on my aunt, to think of the poor lady coming herself. But she had no one—no one in the world, she having lost her husband only a few months before, and being left with two young children—"

Dr. Breadlebane, exasperated at her flow of words, again interrupted.

"*Who*, Matron? Who *was* this lady?"

I said quietly:

"I think I know, doctor." I turned to my informant. "Thank you very much, Matron. What you say is of the greatest help." But the matron had no intention of being cut off so soon.

"It was the poor fellow's mother," she began.

"Stepmother," I said in an undertone.

She overheard me, and it touched off a new train of thought.

"Oh yes, of course," she said. "I remember: his *mother* went out of her mind, and she committed suicide—though not here," she hastened to add, with a glance at Dr. Breadlebane, who was leaning back in his chair, his eyes closed—"at home. That's why they thought the young man must have killed himself, too," she explained, turning back to me.

"Did your aunt tell you anything about the second Lady Assche—his stepmother?" I said. "Do you remember?"

"Yes, of course I remember," said the matron. "I remember *exactly* what my aunt said about her. She was much younger than her husband—and a most beautiful woman. She bore it all with the greatest courage, though it must have been terrible for her." She rattled on. "Everybody was so sorry for her: such a dreadful thing to have to do, especially for a lady, but it seems hardly anybody could have told *who* it was, what with his head being blown off. Naturally, everything was done to spare her as far as possible…"

I stood up.

"Well, thank you, Matron," I said again. "I mustn't keep you any longer from your work."

Dr. Breadlebane came to life.

"I hope you have everything you want," he said, holding out his large white hand across the table.

"Yes," I said, "I think so. But—one comment does occur to me." It amused me to see the look of alarm that instantly returned behind his conventional smile. "I wonder if anybody thought to look at the dead young man's *hands*."

Then I went away quickly.

5

I got back from Cumberland late that night. I had no time to confer with Lomax except for a brief phone call, in which I explained where I had been and where I was going next. The visit had taken two valuable days, but I was quite satisfied with the results. I had established that there had been no proper identification of the remains, and though there was still no proof that Henry's story was true, I had not come across proof to the contrary either.

Of the two letters I had posted on the evening before journeying north, only one had been answered, and the answer, curiously enough, came from the less likely quarter: from Lord Assche's secretary saying that his lordship would see me on the day and at the time I asked. The day was the following one, on Monday, and the time was at half-past two in the afternoon. Next morning, therefore, I set out on my second journey, to Lord Assche's place in Hampshire.

6

I need not describe the magnificence of Ashenford. Photographs of the great house with its formal gardens, lakes and terraces, are to be seen in every guide-book and frequently also in our illustrated periodicals. It is one of the few English mansions which is kept up in the original style, its owners having had the sense not to rely on land for their revenue, but to engage first in purchasing colonial property and then in commerce. As I approached in a taxi, through the well-kept village and then through Lord Assche's park and grounds, I was heartily glad that his ancestors had shown such foresight and had thus preserved so much beauty to be a model to their fellow-countrymen, though that had not been their intention.

I was shown at once into Lord Assche's study. He received me quite pleasantly, though his manner was a little abrupt. I did not commit the error of being the same: my own manner was, I hoped, a tribute to his importance and my indebtedness.

"I am extremely obliged to your lordship," I began, "for agreeing to see me. I shall not take up much of your time. But my business concerns a man named Pollicott, accused of a murder which I'm convinced he hasn't committed."

"Yes, I read about it," said Lord Assche. He was a handsome man, grey-haired and grey-moustached, probably modelled on his father. "An old night-watchman, wasn't he?"

"Yes," I said, "an old night-watchman who had been keeping Henry Rowles—the murdered man—for the last twenty years, entirely without recompense, I believe."

Lord Assche was unimpressed.

"Really?" he said. "This fellow Rowles must have been a pretty plausible scoundrel." He leaned forward across his beautiful oak desk and fixed his bright blue eyes on me. "You realise," he said, "Rowles actually had the impertinence to approach *me?*"

"So I gather," I said, perhaps rather drily. "It was about the letter that Rowles wrote to you that I ventured to approach you."

"It's no use asking *me* about it," said Lord Assche bluntly. "The whole thing's in the hands of my lawyers: a very tiresome affair."

"Very tiresome," I murmured, "for quite a number of people."

"Well, I hope *my* name can be kept out of it," he said. "It really is no concern of mine." He stood up. "You'd better go along and see Dotherington. He'll tell you anything you want to know. He's in Lincoln's Inn Fields. Pewsey will look you up a train."

I stood firm.

"I wonder," I said, "if your lordship would spare me a few moments longer? There are matters in this affair of which you alone can speak with authority."

Lord Assche spoke with harsh impatience.

"My good sir, you really can't expect me to waste my time bothering about a rascal—a fellow who lived by his wits—who happened to have chosen to use the name of my late brother at some time or other—though not in this country, I believe: he had more sense than that. It's a common practice with persons emigrating to the Dominions. I'm not surprised that the fellow met with a violent end. I can't think that it's a great loss to society." His grey moustache twitched with annoyance, and his colour had risen. It was necessary to think quickly if I did not wish to be uncompromisingly dismissed.

"You know," I said quietly, "that he had in his possession a copy of your late father's will—the will of the eighth Lord Assche?"

"No, I didn't know it," he rapped out. "But I can quite believe it. It's easy to obtain a copy of a will."

"Not unless you can show sufficient cause," I began. He interrupted me irritably.

"He could have stolen it from my late brother's effects."

"You think so?" I said.

"Certainly! My brother died in an institution for the insane. Any servant in the place might have gone through his papers and taken anything he fancied."

"Possibly," I said. "But then there was also a bank book in the name of Henry Clairvaux, showing a deposit of three thousand pounds to his credit at the Alliance Bank of Johannesburg."

"A complete imposture," said Lord Assche scornfully. "My brother died forty years ago, as I told you. His death was due to an accident with a gun. A verdict of Death by Misadventure was returned, he being certified as insane at the time. There was no mystery about it. The funeral took place here. It was attended by many members of the family. I myself was travelling abroad at the time—I was only seventeen—and so it had fallen on my poor mother to make the journey north to identify my brother's remains." I noticed faint signs of a relaxation in his manner as he spoke of his mother. "I believe," he said, "one of my uncles accompanied her—but I forget the details."

"It must have been a very trying experience for her," I said, taking advantage of his momentary revelation of feeling.

He drew himself up.

"My mother was a very remarkable woman," he said, "a very courageous woman. She did not shrink from whatever she conceived to be her duty, both to my brother—my half-brother, that is: he was not her son—and to my father, who had died less than a year before. My father, as you have doubtless gathered from his will, was well aware of poor Harry's weakness of intellect, and had made full provision in the event of his becoming a lunatic incapable of managing his own affairs."

His anger had evaporated. He was becoming interested in spite of himself. I ventured on a further step.

"And of course," I said, "the late Lord Assche—your half-brother—was accompanied by a personal servant, a man named Sebastian Rowles."

"That is so," said his lordship. He sat down. "And there, I think, you will find the solution of the problem: where did this man Henry Rowles, as he called himself, get hold of this copy of my father's will and the other documents that were discovered in his possession."

I bowed, in deference to his superior perspicacity.

"I shall be glad," I said, "to learn of any solution."

"Well," he said, waving to me to sit down. "It won't have escaped your notice that the murdered man has the same surname as my brother's servant?"

"No," I said modestly, "I had noticed that."

"Well now: when I received this letter in which the writer made the preposterous claim that he was my half-brother Harry—"

"That was what he claimed?" I said as if astonished.

"It was," said Lord Assche. "There were no limits to his presumption. The letter—the original letter—is now in the hands of my lawyers. But the gist of it was this: he said that though he was supposed to have died forty years ago as the result of a shot-gun accident, he had actually escaped from the mental institution and had left the country, taking a position as a ship's steward. He said he had lived for twenty years in South Africa, using what he had the impudence to call his own name, and had then returned to this country with the idea of getting in touch with his family"—his lordship made a sound not unlike a cat spitting, something like "pah!"—"with *us*, that is to say."

"Dear me!" I said, as he paused.

A new idea had struck him.

"Let me see," he said, "the original, as I said, is now with Dotherington, but I had several copies made at the time. It might be of interest for you to hear what was actually said." He spoke like a master to a small boy, though he was ten years my junior.

"It would indeed," I said.

He rang a bell.

"A tissue of lies," he continued, his manner now quite friendly, though condescending. "Extraordinary what ingenuity these fellows display with a view to living without work."

The butler entered. Lord Assche said:

"Pewsey, ask Mr. Richardson to let me have a copy of the letter from the man Henry Rowles." As the door closed his lordship turned to me with a look of amused contempt: "I must say I'm surprised that a man of your experience should take such a story seriously for a moment. The world's full of impostors."

"True," I said. "But we have to explore all avenues in the interests of our clients."

The secretary came in, bringing the copy of the letter.

"Ah, here we are!" said Lord Assche, taking it, and dismissing Richardson. "Now this is what the fellow says."

I would have liked to be allowed to look at the letter for myself, but since Lord Assche was evidently determined to read it out to me, I sat in my chair and concentrated my attention.

"I won't read you the whole of it," he said. "You know about the preliminaries. After the fabrication about his escape and so on, he goes on:

"...'It is not with the slightest wish to embarrass you or to prove myself a nuisance in any way that I now approach you after an interval of forty years. It is because I feel myself to be growing old, and I am aware that I could not look after myself, should

> anything happen to cut off my present very meagre source of
> maintenance. I have reason to believe, too, that this *may* be
> cut off in the near future. I have been making enquiries about
> the money I deposited in a Johannesburg bank under my own
> name; but my ignorance of business is such that I am not sure
> how to set about recovering what is legally mine. Yet I feel
> I ought to do something to recompense the old man who has
> looked after me since I returned to this country twenty years
> ago. If, therefore, out of your abundance, which should have
> been mine, you will pay me a small annuity, I promise neither
> to visit you nor to trouble you with letters or any other sort of
> communication.'"

Lord Assche looked across at me to see if I had taken in the enormity of the communication so far.

"After this piece of impudent begging," he said, "he proceeds to something very like a threat." He continued reading with growing indignation:

> "... 'If, however, you do not choose to pay any attention to this
> very modest demand, then I must tell you that I have it in my
> power to cause you a considerable amount of trouble. When
> I say that the body buried in my name in the family vault is not
> mine, but that of a certain *Henry Rowles*—the *real* Henry Rowles,
> brother of my old servant Sebastian Rowles—*I can prove it*.
>
> "'In that case, you may well ask, why didn't I do so before?
> *Because I knew I should be circumvented:* treated as an escaped
> lunatic and promptly arrested—perhaps even done to death.
> At any rate, I could have got no one to take me seriously while
> your mother was still alive. She would have been too much for
> me, as always. But now that she has gone, it is different. Please

do not force me, Bertie, to take strong measures to recover this infinitesimal share of my due. Give me the little that will content me and that you will never notice having given; and then let us cease to exist for each other, now as before.

"'YOUR half-brother,
"'HARRY CLAIRVAUX

"'P.S. Please address your reply to Henry Rowles, the name which I have been obliged to assume in this country.'"

Lord Asschë threw down the letter.

"Well!" he said. "What do you think of that? It's a masterpiece of fiction, isn't it?"

I made a non-committal sound.

"May I ask," I said, "what steps your lordship took about it?" He gave a contemptuous laugh.

"My good sir, I haven't time to answer all the begging letters I receive from rogues and madmen. I told my secretary to make a few copies of it. I sent the original to my solicitors, and one of the copies to Rowles."

"Sebastian Rowles is still alive?" I said.

"Certainly," said Lord Asschë. "He retired from our service when my mother died two months ago. An excellent butler—held the position for forty years—since my brother's death in fact. My mother thought highly of him. She left him a small legacy, and he has gone down to live with his married daughter in Portsmouth."

"So you sent him a copy of this letter?" I said.

"I did," said Lord Asschë. "I thought he had a right to know what was being alleged by this fellow who was now using the name of Rowles's brother Henry."

I said deferentially:

"Your lordship suggested just now that you might be able to offer a solution of the problem of this man's identity?" Lord Assche looked gratified.

"Not exactly that," he said. "But I think I can explain how he happened to have a copy of my father's will in his possession, and also this deposit book you speak of, made out in my brother's name."

"I should be deeply interested," I said.

Lord Assche explained.

"When Rowles—Sebastian Rowles, that is, our ex-butler—when he got my letter, he came to see me at once. He said he couldn't understand it, as of course he had been present at my brother's accident, and in fact he had felt himself to blame for it. But he suggested that this impersonation might have been connected with a visit paid by his younger brother Henry to the mental institution where my half-brother was being cared for."

"So he really had a brother called Henry," I said thoughtfully.

"Yes," said Lord Assche, "a younger brother who was by way of being a complete ne'er-do-well. This young man had already given his widowed mother—a respectable boarding-house keeper in Portsmouth—considerable trouble: there had been thefts, trouble with the police and so on. The young man had been spoilt—patronised by some relative or acquaintance, a woman, I believe, who had a little money. In fact, our man Rowles—Sebastian, the elder brother—had had difficulty in extracting him from various scrapes; and at this time a position as ship's steward had been found for him, to get him out of the country and give him a new start in life."

He gave me another of his keen looks, and I said:

"I understand."

Lord Assche continued:

"The young man went to visit his elder brother Sebastian in Cumberland before sailing—Rowles thought, to ask him for his forgiveness and promise a reform. But unfortunately Henry Rowles remained true to type, as they usually do: stole a quantity of things, so our man Rowles says, articles of jewellery and so on, from the patients' rooms. So it's natural to suppose he used the opportunity to steal my brother's papers, and then made use of them when he reached South Africa. I have no doubt that the money deposited at Johannesburg represents the proceeds of these thefts, and I should say that as it's in my brother's name, legally it belongs to *me*."

I let this pass.

"And is it your lordship's view," I said, "that this man who was recently murdered was actually Henry Rowles? Surely even after forty years he would still be identifiable—by his brother Sebastian if by nobody else."

"Quite so, quite so," Lord Assche conceded. "No, that is *not* my contention. As a matter of fact, as soon as I read the report of this man's murder I wrote again to Sebastian Rowles pointing out the name and address, and I told him he ought to get in touch at once with the police and ask to see the body. Very distressing for the poor fellow if his brother has turned up again after all these years. The Rowles family thought he had died years ago."

"Perhaps," I said quietly, "he had."

Lord Assche gave me a blank stare.

"Eh?" Then he thought he understood. "Oh yes, quite so. It is to be hoped so, at any rate. Very respectable family. Rowles was a very good servant. You don't get his sort nowadays."

In the next room the telephone bell rang. The secretary entered by the communicating door.

"Your lordship," he said, "if I might interrupt you for a moment: Rowles is on the telephone. He would like a word with your lordship *personally*, if he may be allowed."

Lord Assche looked annoyed.

"Eh? Couldn't he give you a message?" Then, convinced by something he read in the secretary's face that the matter was important, he said testily: "Very well, very well: put him through."

The secretary retired, and Lord Assche took up a telephone receiver on the desk. A metallic voice came through, but the words were indistinguishable. Lord Assche at intervals said "Yes. No doubt. Of course," and once "Ha!"

He replaced the receiver.

"Just as I thought," he said to me with a nod.

"I beg your pardon?" I said.

"This fellow," he said triumphantly, "the murdered man, wasn't Sebastian Rowles's brother either!"

"Indeed?" was all I could think of to say. But there was no need for me to say anything. Lord Assche was preoccupied with what he regarded as the confirmation of his own theory, and had ceased to notice my reactions.

"It was a man Rowles had never seen," he assured me. "On receiving my letter Rowles took my advice and got in touch with the police immediately. He has just returned to his home after having made the journey down to your part of the world, to view the body of the murdered man."

"And he failed to identify him?" I said.

"Of course! Never saw him before in his life, he says. It's the body of an unknown man of about sixty—which is the age his brother Henry would be if he were alive. But it's not the body of Henry Rowles. It's not at all like him, he says."

"How does he account for the fact that the murdered man was using the same name?" I inquired. "Does he suggest that it's a coincidence?"

"He suggests," said Lord Assche, "that this fellow—the murdered man—met his brother Henry Rowles somewhere abroad and stole all his papers, among them the papers stolen by Henry Rowles from my half-brother. I hope I've made his explanation quite clear? It seems very feasible to me."

"It's very *clear*," I said.

He rose, with a cough that indicated his determination to be rid of me.

"Well, I don't think there's anything more I can do for you. I trust you now see that nothing is to be gained by pursuing this false trail any further."

I also had risen.

"And Pollicott?" I said.

Lord Assche made a slight gesture of dismissal.

"Well, so far as I can see," he said, "your client's guilty. Of course you'll have to do your best for him, but it doesn't pay to be too quixotic, you know. Obviously the old fellow was imposed upon—believed he was looking after a rich man and would get his reward. The trouble was, he was a little too impatient over it!" He laughed, and rang the bell. "Pewsey will get you a taxi. And I say!" he called out to me as Pewsey appeared at the door. "If you hear any more about this money deposited in Johannesburg, I shall be obliged if you'll communicate with my solicitors. But please see to it *my* name doesn't appear in the matter at all. Good day."

I went away.

7

That evening after I had got home and had dined, I rang up Lomax and asked him to come over. He listened with interest to the story of my two interviews and their results.

"And now, what's the next step?" he said when we had discussed their implications.

"Another journey," I said.

"You're going to see Lord Assche's solicitors?"

"No, no, not I!" I said. "*They* won't give me any help, you may be sure of that. They'll be entirely concerned to protect his lordship from any annoyance. By the way, would you have thought it possible that a man of his immense wealth should trouble to tell me—or even think it—that he might be able to claim this money deposited at Johannesburg in the name of Harry Clairvaux?"

Lomax shook his head.

"No," I continued, "I shan't waste my time visiting Lord Assche's legal advisers. I shall be taking a trip to Portsmouth."

"Portsmouth?" said Lomax. "You're not thinking of visiting this Sebastian Rowles?"

"No, not yet," I said. "I gather he has been here?"

"That's what I was waiting to tell you," said Lomax, "when I'd heard your story. He rang up the police here, said he had had a brother named Henry, presumed to have died abroad, and asked to see the body. Fadden told him to come immediately, as the funeral was taking place today."

I nodded.

"And Sebastian said he'd never seen the man before," I said.

Lomax looked surprised.

"That's right. How did you know?"

"From Sebastian Rowles's own mouth," I said, enjoying Lomax's mystification.

"You've seen him?" he said.

"No," I said, "but I've heard him—over the 'phone." I explained how this had come about, and added: "So he didn't recognise the body?"

"Well," said Lomax doubtfully. "I suppose a man could be mistaken after forty years."

"Not in his own brother," I said, "nor in his old master, I should think. However, don't let's waste time surmising. How's Pollicott?"

Lomax looked grave.

"Pretty bad: sunk again into a lethargy. I took Clipper to see him yesterday, and that cheered him up a bit—but not for long. He soon sank back into his torpor. His whole faith is pinned on *you*."

"I know, I know," I said. "Tell him to hold on a little longer. Tomorrow I'm going to Portsmouth, to call on a firm of solicitors called Bodger and Danton. You may remember there were some letters among Rowles's papers, addressed to him from the offices of this firm. I hope I shall be able to find them. The address is twenty years old, and a lot has happened to Portsmouth since then, I fancy. I haven't been there since I was a boy. I've always wanted to go back."

8

Portsmouth has pleasant associations for me: not merely the town but even the name. It reminds me of a song my father used to sing, while my mother accompanied him on the piano. I don't know who wrote the words or the music, and the song-book in which it was included has long since disappeared, but I do remember one or two of the verses.

The melody and some of the words were running in my head next day as I walked along one of the main streets of Portsmouth. It was a pleasant surprise to me, therefore, to hear the strains of that very same song. As I approached, I saw three men standing on the kerb, one with a concertina, one with a placard round his neck asking for help for three disabled seamen, and the third holding out a box to the passers-by. All were singing lustily and in excellent harmony:

> "There were three pretty girls in merry Portsmouth town,
> And each was like a posy on a tree.
> There was black-eyed Margaret and trim-set Sal,
> And sweet Kitty from the north countree..."

My glance in their direction instantly caused one of them to thrust the box under my nose with:

"Spare a copper, sir! Disabled seamen..."

I dropped a coin into the box and asked him to direct me to Spalding Street.

"Spalding Street, sir?" he said. "There's precious little left of that now, sir. 'Twas bombed to bits in one of them big air-raids. But if you walk along to the end of this street and turn left and then right..."

He gave me the usual complicated instructions, and I made the usual ineffectual effort to remember them. I thanked him and walked on to the strains of the concertina and another verse:

> "Then up spoke those jolly sailor boys,
> All arm in arm so jolly for to see,
> 'There are girls across the water from Jamaica to Gibraltar
> Who can dance right merrily as ye'..."

After a few turns to right and left, I had not succeeded in finding Spalding Street, nor had I any idea what to do next. I stopped a likely-looking passer-by and said:

"Excuse me: can you tell me if this is where Spalding Street used to be?" But of course he answered:

"Sorry—I'm a stranger here myself."

I walked on until I saw a policeman. There were many gaps here among the buildings, and I was beginning to wonder if Spalding Street was merely a memory. In response to my enquiry, the policeman said grimly:

"This is it, sir."

"Dear me!" I said, looking round. "You got it pretty badly here."

"That we did, sir," he said. "Hardly one stone left on another in some places. You're a stranger here?" His accent was more cockney than a Londoner's, and mine must have seemed equally odd to him.

"Yes," I said. "I was looking for the offices of Messrs. Bodger and Danton, solicitors. But I'm afraid the only address I have is twenty years old. Could you tell me if the firm still exists, and if so, where they've gone?"

"Bodger and Danton," he said. "Let's see." He took out a pocket directory and thumbed the pages. "Ah yes: they moved from here in 1942—luckily for them. They'd had some damage before that at their offices here in Spalding Street, and afterwards they and several other firms moved elsewhere—Bodger and Danton: yes, here we are. They're now at 110 Liddell Square; that's behind the Town Hall. Take the first to the right, then cross Dime Square, and then second on your left and third to your right. That takes you straight into Liddell Square. You can't miss it."

Overwhelmed with fresh instructions, I thanked him and walked on, and at last came to 110 Liddell Square. The offices of Bodger and Danton were on the third floor. I rang for the lift and ascended.

9

After a brief wait I was shown into one of the offices. A youngish man rose to greet me, and held out his hand.

"Ah yes, Mr. Vaughan," he said affably. "We got your letter. How do you do? Sit down, won't you?"

"Mr. Bodger?" I enquired.

"No, no," he said. "My name's Danton. I'm a great-nephew of the original Danton, and the junior partner. The Bodger family died out a quarter of a century ago." He laughed as if there were something funny about this, and then checked himself. "You've come a long way to see us."

"Yes," I said, as I sat down. "And I shall ask you to come quite a long way back with me—in time."

He smiled, and looked at me with interest.

"You said in your letter you were acting for the accused in the Sea Wall murder case."

"I am," I said.

He leaned back in his swivel chair.

"Curious business," he said, "those two old bachelors living together in such a lonely spot—and then, one of them coming to a violent end." His manner suggested that he did not envy the task of the defence.

I said firmly:

"I'm convinced, Mr. Danton, Pollicott had no part in it. Otherwise I shouldn't have come out of my retirement. To the police, of course, the matter is straightforward: one old man makes a will in another's favour—and the testator signs his own death-warrant. But it's not really as simple as that."

"You think not?" said Danton sceptically.

"I do," I said. "I've been pursuing a separate line of investigation.

I've come to the conclusion that the dead man may not have been what he seemed, namely, an obscure person named Henry Rowles who left home forty years ago and returned destitute some twenty years later. I have reason to believe that he may have been of much more exalted rank."

"Indeed?" said Danton, already bored. I could see he had already decided that he was dealing with a crank. "Oh yes, I remember reading in the papers that he had claimed some connection with Lord Assche, the head of Silk and Synthetic Fabric Industries. But these claims always turn out to be fairy tales—impersonation, whether deliberate or merely crazy."

I had no wish to attempt the impossible. I said merely:

"Well, that's as may be. What I came to ask you about was a much smaller point, but nevertheless one of the pieces in my puzzle."

Danton jerked himself up.

"I'm all attention."

"I don't suppose you're aware," I said, "that twenty years ago your firm handled a matter concerning this same Henry Rowles—or at any rate, a man of the same name?"

He laughed.

"It's before my time, I'm afraid." A way of escape presented itself. "But my senior, Mr. Chools, might remember. He has a prodigious memory. I'll call him." He reached out for the house-telephone and turned the handle.

"Thank you," I said, "though I hardly think it's likely he'd *remember* such a very small matter. If you would look it up in your files—"

Danton spoke into the telephone:

"Ask Mr. Chools if he's disengaged and can see myself and another gentleman for a moment."

Almost instantly the telephone buzzed back.

"Thank you," said Danton, and to me: "Come this way, Mr. Vaughan."

10

We walked to the next office, where a much smaller, elderly man sat at a larger desk in a larger room.

"This is Mr. Vaughan," said Danton. "Mr. Chools, my senior partner. He has come to make some enquiries in the Sea Wall murder case."

"Come in, Mr. Vaughan," said Chools. "Please be seated. Now what can we do for you?" His manner was drier than his partner's, and he did not offer me his hand. Danton officiously explained:

"Mr. Vaughan was asking about a matter we acted in, apparently, about twenty years ago. I said you might remember."

"Possibly," said Chools without enthusiasm.

"The matter is this, Mr. Chools," I said. "It so happens that among the dead man's papers—which happened to come into my possession just before he was murdered—there are three rather curious letters, all of them on the writing paper of the firm of Bodger and Danton, Spalding Street, Portsmouth."

Chools gave a small dry cough.

"Those offices," he said, "were destroyed in an air raid in 1943."

"So I gather," I said. "The letters, however, are dated 1928 and were written at intervals of a fortnight."

I opened my brief case and took out the three letters. "They are addressed to Henry Rowles, otherwise known as J.H.V.P.D. Clairvaux. The first is addressed to him care of the *Kalamata Castle*, Southampton." I drew the letter out of its envelope. "It runs as follows:

"'Dear Sir,

"'We have to inform you that there is a sum of money standing to your credit under the will of Mrs. Adelina Baker, deceased, and to request that you will kindly call at these offices to collect this sum, which will be paid to you on proof of identity.

"'YOURS FAITHFULLY,
"'BODGER AND DANTON.'"

Danton, leaning over the back of my chair, said:

"A pleasant surprise for a man landing in this country!"

"So one would imagine," I said, folding up the letter and putting it away. "But the odd thing is, *this* man *refused* to collect his legacy. The next letter"—I drew it out—"is addressed to him Poste Restante, Gloucester, and is evidently written in answer to one of his. It says that in spite of the fact that he denies that this legacy in any way concerns him, nevertheless Messrs. Bodger and Danton are *satisfied* that he is entitled to a sum of money from this estate. If he will kindly come and collect it, they will be glad to send him a couple of pounds for his railway fare." I looked up. "You see, gentlemen, there was eagerness on somebody's part to see this man face to face, and"—I paused—"great determination on his part not to show himself."

Danton said incredulously:

"Surely the legacy drew him?"

"That's the curious thing," I said. "It did not. Here is a third letter"—I picked it up—"addressed to Henry Rowles, Poste Restante, Gloucester, which shows by its wording that the second one remained unanswered. This third and last letter *pleads* with him to come and collect his legacy, saying that otherwise it will be paid into the Law Courts Branch, Chancery Division, of the Bank of England. Now, gentlemen," I said, putting the letter away, "it seems to me that there's only one reason why a man would refuse to collect a legacy, and that is—overpowering fear. He was *afraid* to display himself."

"Because he wasn't Henry Rowles, you mean?" said Danton.

"More than that," I said. "Because he *was* somebody else—somebody whose existence was inconvenient, perhaps even dangerous, to certain other persons."

"Then why did he answer the first letter?" said Danton.

"Perhaps he thought that if he denied all interest in the legacy no attempts would be made to trace him. Instead of turning up at the offices of Messrs. Bodger and Danton in Spalding Street, he put as great a distance between him and them as he could. He went to earth, as it were—and ever since then he had lived in hiding, in the hut of Pollicott, who is now accused of his murder."

There was a pause. Danton said:

"Deuced odd!"

Chools said slowly:

"And what do you expect *us* to do about it, Mr. Vaughan?" I thought his tone implied a determination to do exactly nothing. I therefore spoke more sharply.

"There's nothing either you or I can *do* about it, Mr. Chools. The man is dead. But what I ask myself," I went on thoughtfully, "is, why was he so much afraid to show himself if he was Henry Rowles? And if he wasn't, who was he? Why was he so reluctant to claim his legacy? Who gave Messrs. Bodger and Danton the information that Rowles would be disembarking at Southampton from the *Kalamata Castle*? In short"—I looked Chools straight in the eyes—"will you examine the file relating to this legacy to Henry Rowles from the estate of Mrs. Adelina Baker, and see if there is anything—any correspondence or note of an interview—that might throw light on this curious affair?"

Chools said without change of expression:

"What year did you say this occurred in?"

"In the year 1928," I said. "I have not had time to confirm the arrival of the *Kalamata Castle* in Southampton—but the months were May and June. The letters are dated May 24th, June 7th and June 30th."

"One moment," said Chools, rising. "I shall enquire." He went out, rather quickly, I thought.

Danton sat on the edge of the desk.

"That's funny," he said. "He usually remembers." He ran on: "It's astonishing what a memory that man has. It's a prodigy. I've never known anything like it. It's almost a burden to him, I believe. Most of us can't remember things: *he* can't forget." He laughed. "His mind's like a photographic plate. Oh, here he is!"

Chools came in. His hands were empty. He took up his position behind the desk again and said without sitting down:

"I very much regret to tell you, Mr. Vaughan, that all our papers for the year 1928 were destroyed when our offices in Spalding Street were struck in 1943."

Danton got down off the desk.

"Oh, but," he said in tones of astonishment, "I thought we'd already moved all our stuff to a safe place before then!"

Chools, ignoring him, went on with growing emphasis:

"Unfortunately the files for *1928* were left behind by mistake. *Everything* was destroyed in the fire that followed. I am sorry, but we are not able to supply you with *any* information *whatsoever*."

He spoke with a finality that forbade further inquiry. I said, "Good day," and left immediately.

VI

Investigation: Last Steps

MR. VAUGHAN'S STORY CONTINUED

I

When I reached home that evening I sent messages to Lomax and Superintendent Fadden, asking them to come over next morning. Lomax arrived first.

"Did you find out anything, Mr. Vaughan?" he said anxiously. "In Portsmouth, I mean."

I made him sit down, and mixed him a whisky and soda.

"The trail came to a dead end," I said cheerfully. "I was—curiously enough—denied *any* information *whatsoever.*" I gave a laugh as I remembered Chools's definite tones.

Lomax looked startled, and then extremely disappointed.

"What?" he said. "That's bad, Mr. Vaughan. Old Pollicott's in a poor enough state already. I don't know how he'll take your news. He's off his food again. He's had nothing, it seems, for the last twenty-four hours. He just sits staring into space. Today he wouldn't even rouse himself to speak to Clipper. If Pollicott doesn't get released soon, there'll be no need to hang him: he'll just die of his own accord."

His concern was obvious. I hastened to reassure him.

"Don't be so gloomy, Lomax!" I said. "I've not given up, you know! I only said I'd been denied information. Don't you *see* how very significant that is?"

"I'm afraid I don't," said Lomax glumly.

"Well, now," I said, filling my own glass, "shall I just correlate the results of my three journeys? What do we find?" I counted them off on my fingers: "At the mental institution, my first call, I found that the place had changed hands, and by a *coincidence* the records relating to the period I am enquiring about don't appear to exist. At the home of the present Lord Assche, my second call—Lord Assche who succeeded to the title on the death of his half-brother forty years ago—I found a monumental indifference to anything but his lordship's comfort, and, I suspect, behind that, an iron determination *not to permit any enquiry whatsoever* into the circumstances of his half-brother's death."

"Ah!" said Lomax, alert again.

"Last of my three calls," I continued, "I went to the offices of Messrs. Bodger and Danton—"

"Who?" said Lomax.

"Oh, I forgot," I said. "You don't yet know about them, or do you? They are the firm of solicitors who handled the matter of a legacy left to Henry Rowles by a certain Miss Adelina Baker, twenty years ago. You may remember that there were *three* letters among his papers referring to an *unclaimed* legacy."

"Ye-es," reflected Lomax. "Now you mention it, I do remember glancing at them, and I must say I thought it odd, to put it mildly, that he didn't go and get the money, as he was so hard up—especially as, if I remember rightly, they even offered to pay his fare."

"Precisely!" I said.

"And yet here he was," Lomax went on, "going to all this trouble trying to get hold of money he'd left behind in Johannesburg. Funny he didn't even pick up this money waiting for him so much nearer home."

I laughed quietly.

"As you say, Lomax—as you say. Well, when I called on Bodger and Danton, again there was a curious coincidence: the files for 1928, including the one relating to this legacy, were missing!" Lomax looked at me, puzzled.

"I don't know how it is," he said, "but I get the impression you're feeling a good deal more cheerful about this than *I* am. In fact, I don't think I've seen you cheerful at all until now. And that's funny too, because you began by saying that the trail had come to a dead end."

"Yes," I said, "but I didn't say there was nothing at the end of the trail."

"What?" said Lomax, baffled. "I don't think I understand." He glanced up at me with renewed hope. "D'you mean you *have* found out something after all?"

"More than that, Lomax," I said. "I know *exactly* what happened. All we have to do now is to prove it, or rather, that part of it which still matters—the part of it that will set Pollicott free. Much must lie buried with certain dry bones in the family vault at Ashenford."

"Good lord!" said Lomax, round-eyed. "You really mean to say you know who killed Henry Rowles—or whatever we're to call him?"

"Certainly," I said quietly. "Why? Don't you? It's perfectly obvious. That's not the problem. The problem, as I say, is to get proof."

"Well!" Lomax studied me, prepared to admire but still incredulous. "And how are you going to do *that*?"

"I don't know—" I began.

"You don't *know*?" Lomax was impatient. "And yet you're so cheerful?"

"But," I went on calmly, "I think we can manage it—together."

"Together?" he echoed. "Who? Who's 'we'?"

"You," I said, "and I—and Superintendent Fadden: that is, if he'll agree. I've asked him to drive over here this morning too. I said I had something interesting to communicate. He should be here quite soon."

2

At that moment I heard a car arriving. Mac barked. A minute later Mrs. Williams showed Fadden into the room. He looked quickly from me to Lomax and back again, as if he suspected conspiracy. I gave him a glass of whisky.

"Thanks," he said. "Oh, by the way: the handwriting expert confirms that those signatures of witnesses to the will are both by the same hand, rather clumsily disguised." His complacency was apparent: "I fancy you had some doubt on that point."

I had long ceased to care whether the signatures were by the same hand or two different hands: my conclusions had made the question of little importance. I murmured, however, half to myself:

"Only one of them must have done it, then."

Fadden overheard.

"Eh?" he said. "Oh, you're still thinking of those men who called at the hut while you were there on Saturday night."

I gave him a sharp look.

"Your handwriting expert hasn't proved that the signatures are in *Pollicott's* hand," I reminded him.

"All in good time, Mr. Vaughan," he said, stiffly.

"No, Superintendent," I said bluntly, "because Pollicott never wrote them." Before he could argue, I asked him: "Have you traced those two men?"

"Not yet," said Fadden, a trifle less smugly. "But I have information that there *were* a couple of fellows who used to come regularly and comb the foreshore for dabs and winkles at low tide—"

"Dabs and winkles!" I said, laughing quietly at the recollection of those two honest fishermen, Jack Dodds of Cornwall, and Dan Moore of Cork.

Fadden ignored my interruption.

"They had a small boat with an auxiliary engine," he continued. "They'd stay a few days in each place, dispose of their catch, and move along elsewhere. There's good reason to believe they came from somewhere down Channel, or perhaps across the Irish Sea. In the latter case it'll be difficult to get hold of them. Rather shady characters, no doubt, and we've had our eye on them for some time past, though we've nothing definite against them so far. But you can put them right out of your calculations, Mr. Vaughan, as far as this case is concerned. They didn't kill Henry Rowles."

"Really?" I said. "You sound very definite on that point."

"That's because there's definite proof," he said. "Those two men left here *before* high tide. They were almost certainly the two men who put ashore at Lynmouth later that night and asked for petrol. They got it—and since then nothing's been heard of them." Satisfied with his reasoning he added: "Very likely they don't want to be involved." He gave me a somewhat pitying look.

I said:

"I agree that those two men had no part in this murder."

"You *agree*?" said Fadden, completely taken aback.

"Yes," I said. "I've known for some time that *they* were not the men who added the signatures as witnesses to the will and murdered the so-called Henry Rowles."

"Well!" said Fadden. "You surprise me, Mr. Vaughan. Then, according to you," he challenged me, "who *did* commit this murder? Not Pollicott's gypsies, surely?" he said with a laugh.

"Maybe," I said.

He laughed again and said kindly:

"Ah, so you won't be drawn! You amateur detectives like to try to pull a rabbit out of the hat! Another point: I took up the matter of the red handkerchief found on the floor of the hut." This did interest me.

"Yes?" I said.

"We found," said Fadden, "it was one of the products of Silk and Synthetic Fabric Industries—"

I took up the story:

"The firm in which Lord Assche holds a controlling interest. How his name keeps cropping up, doesn't it?"

Lomax, who had retired to an armchair in the corner and had so far listened without speaking, now said meaningly:

"A-ah!"

Fadden said stiffly:

"Is that so?" Then, continuing: "But the really curious thing is, the handkerchief had never been used. We sent it to the laboratories of S.S.F.I. for expert examination, and they said that it represented one of their early experiments in the use of a particular red dye—a dye which was discarded because although from the laundering point of view it was a fast colour, it was too sensitive to light to be any good commercially. I can show you the S.S.F.I. chemist's report if you're interested. It proves quite conclusively that this particular handkerchief must have been kept away from the light, and so, as I say, never used."

I turned this over in my mind for a moment. Then I said:

"Did they say in what year or years this experimental red dye was being tried?"

"Yes," said Fadden. "It so happened that they could date it accurately. It was tried and discarded in the year 1908."

Lomax from his corner commented:

"1908? I say!"

"And what conclusion are we to draw from that, Superintendent?" I inquired.

Fadden answered confidently:

"It seems pretty certain that this handkerchief was dropped by the man who called himself Henry Rowles as he sat at the table writing his will. It could of course have fallen from his hand when Pollicott struck him from behind."

"But," I said, "where did this man, this so-called Henry Rowles, obtain a handkerchief which had not been in use for forty years?"

"That's easy," said Fadden kindly. "Oh, but of course I forgot you weren't here when we got this particular bit of information. You know, I suppose, that we had a visit from a man called Sebastian Rowles, who asked to see the body."

I nodded.

"Lomax told me—yes."

"Well," said Fadden, "this man's evidence cast considerable doubt on the right of the murdered man to call himself Henry Rowles, either. He was probably no more Henry Rowles than he was Henry Clairvaux. He was a professional impersonator, as you might say. Sebastian Rowles said he had had a brother called Henry, who had left England many years ago and not been heard of since."

"I know, I know," I said pleasantly. "I've heard all that from the present Lord Assche—the horse's mouth, as it were."

Fadden looked astonished.

"You've been to see *Lord Assche*?" he said, almost with awe. "Well! I must give you amateurs credit for enthusiasm and hard work—even if it *is* a bit misplaced sometimes. I didn't intend to trouble Lord Assche myself unless it became absolutely necessary. We're in touch with his solicitors, of course."

I could see that in spite of his assured manner, my visit to Lord Assche had shaken him.

"Tell me some more about your interview with Sebastian Rowles," I said.

"Ah yes," said Fadden, recovering. "We showed the red handkerchief to him, and he recognised it after a moment or two. He said he believed it was one of those that must have been stolen by his brother Henry, during one of his visits, from the ninth Lord Assche—the real Henry Clairvaux—together with other effects, papers and so on. Sebastian Rowles didn't try to cover up his brother Henry's light-fingeredness: he said that's why Henry Rowles had to leave the country. He thought that this other chap—the dead man—must have got all these things from Henry Rowles when he assumed his name."

"Ingenious—very," I commented when he stopped.

"But you don't agree?" he said sharply.

I said mildly:

"No."

Fadden was exasperated.

"Then what *is* your theory?" he said. "It seems to me it's time *you* did a bit of talking for a change. If you know something different, let's have it. It's easy to cast doubt on other people's theories—not so easy to prove your own."

I smiled.

"If I undertake to try to substantiate *my* theory, will you give me a little of your time?—unofficially, of course."

"Substantiate?" Fadden was suspicious. "That's big talk. How much of my time would you want?"

I said boldly:

"A day."

"A whole day?" said Fadden, as I had known he would. "Good lord, no! I couldn't spare a day!"

"Not for the sake of finding out the truth?" I said quietly.

"Ah," said Fadden, "if it *were* the truth—"

"And you, Lomax," I said, turning to him, "would you be unwilling to take a day off, too?" I knew also what *his* response would be.

"No," he said. "You can count me in. I'd do a good deal more than that to get to the bottom of this." He cast Fadden a challenging glance.

"All I ask," I said, "is your company, both of you, on a little trip—to Portsmouth."

"Portsmouth?" said Fadden, surprised.

"And perhaps," I said persuasively, "we could use one of your cars, as it's police work. But you might care to communicate with the Chief Constable of that area, in case it's necessary to make an arrest."

Fadden studied me thoughtfully, rubbing his chin. He was weakening, I could see—or rather, the idea appealed to him.

"It's some time since I visited Portsmouth," he said. Then, making up his mind to take a chance: "Yes: I'll do it. But if it's a wild-goose chase, Mr. Vaughan, you'll do well to go into retirement again as quickly as possible"—he laughed drily—"and as far as possible from here."

"Good!" I said, undaunted. "You won't regret it. First thing in the morning, then. You won't mind if I bring Mac with me in the car?"

Mac, who was lying with his muzzle on Fadden's foot, wagged his tail at the mention of his name.

"Of course not," said Fadden, "so long as he's not car-sick—though I don't see much fun in it for him."

"Mac won't be coming just for fun," I said. "He'll be coming to see what's at the end of the trail. One thing more: before we go on this—I hope—last excursion, I'd like to have a word with Pollicott—just a brief word."

"Certainly," said Fadden. Now that he had agreed to come, he was all amiability. "I'll drive you in."

3

When we reached the gaol I asked to be taken straight to Pollicott's cell.

"No, don't get him out," I said to the warder. "I don't want to disturb him more than's necessary. Just leave me with him for a few minutes and stand outside."

Pollicott was lying on his bed; his face was turned to the wall. The cell smelt of soap and disinfectant, as did the whole gaol. I could imagine how a man like Pollicott, used to the open air and the sea breezes, could die quite soon in an atmosphere like this. Hygiene isn't everything: there is such a thing as being robbed of one's vital nourishment, and that may be the sight of green fields and the smell of fresh air.

"Pollicott!" I called him gently. "Pollicott, it's I—Mr. Vaughan." He rolled over, and sat up, dazed. "Do you know me?" I said.

Pollicott said hoarsely:

"The legal gentleman—Mr. Vaughan, sir—"

I was shocked at his appearance.

"Pollicott," I reproached him, "you promised me you'd look after yourself. What have you been doing with yourself while I've been away?"

Pollicott shook his head.

"I done my best, sir. But I couldn't. The food did seem to choke me, sir. I couldn't get it down nohow." His breath came fast and hard.

"All right, all right," I soothed him. "Don't upset yourself. I came to tell you: hold out for just another twenty-four hours. That's not long. Can you? When next I come back, I hope it will be with an order for your release."

He looked up at me, his red-rimmed eyes full of appeal.

"You ain't deceiving me, sir? Begging your pardon—but you're a kind gentleman, and you maybe says it just to cheer me up, like—"

"No, Pollicott, no!" I assured him with all the emphasis I could put into my words. "*I have discovered who killed your friend Henry. I'm going off on one more journey to prove to Superintendent Fadden himself what I know to be the truth. It won't be easy—but it shall be done.*" I smiled at him. "And Mr. Lomax is coming, too."

Pollicott brightened.

"Mr. Lomax!" he said. "Ah, he's another kind gentleman, he is. He do bring Clipper to see me when he comes—but I don't seem able to rouse myself even for Clipper—though indeed it do seem as if that dog was a-trying to tell me summat." His eyes clouded for a moment, then he said: "Mr. Lomax he do think I be ungrateful, but I ain't. It's just that I can't rouse myself, like—"

"I know," I said. I could see that his strength was going, and that I must get to my point quickly. "But there's one more thing. I want you to pull yourself together and answer me a couple of questions, Pollicott. Then you must go to sleep and forget everything till I come back." His chin had sunk on to his chest and I was afraid his attention had already left me. "Are you listening?" I said. "Can you understand?"

His voice was very low, but he said:

"Yes, sir—I be listening."

I spoke slowly and clearly.

"When Henry was telling you his story," I said, "do you remember his saying that he had fallen off his horse once, and broken his leg? When he was a boy, wasn't it? Think now! Take your time."

"Broke his leg... broke his leg," repeated Pollicott vaguely. Then with sudden animation he said: "Yes, sir, I remembers. Henry he were a-telling me about how he played with his little sister—he were that lonely, he says—and she were a-playing in front of the house, and he goes to her and they was having a game together, and the little one she give him a kick on the shin—not so as to hurt, she were too little for that, but playful like. They was playing picky-back, you see, and she says to him, she says she do want to ride on a big horse, and will he take her? And he do tell her she's too small, and he do say to her,' If you had a big horse, you might fall off like me and break your leg,' and he do show her the place, which was where she'd kicked him." Pollicott gave a feeble chuckle. "She must-a been a rare one! Henry he used to laugh when he come to that bit—though he weren't one to laugh as a general rule."

"Thank you, Pollicott, thank you!" I said, overjoyed at the confirmation. "Now one question more—only one. About those gypsies—"

Pollicott gave a start, and his thin cheeks flushed.

"Gypsies!" he muttered angrily. "They *was* gypsies! I see'd 'em!"

"Yes, Pollicott," I said. "I *know* you saw them. Tell me, though: how did you recognise that they were gypsies? They had ear-rings on, you said: you saw the ear-rings in the light of your charcoal fire. Anything else?"

"Gypsies," he muttered again, though less angrily, "of *course* they was gypsies. Their faces was dark brown, and they had them bright handkerchers round their necks, too."

"Oh, did they?" I said, controlling my eagerness.

"Yes, handkerchers," he said emphatically, "them coloured handkerchers they do wear—they be *that* fond of a bit of colour."

"Did you notice *what* colour?"

Pollicott's answer came slowly:

"One were a yellow handkercher with big spots—I see'd it plain—and the other were red. They all likes red, the men as well as the girls."

"You're *sure*?" I said.

"Ay, sir, I'm sure," said Pollicott. "But nobody don't believe me—except you."

"Never mind, Pollicott," I said, impatient, now, to be away. "They'll all believe us *both*, quite soon now. Now try to sleep—and forget about everything till you see me again."

4

We reached Portsmouth—Fadden, Lomax, Mac and I—by midday, and went straight to an hotel for luncheon. While the others were ordering lunch I made a telephone call.

When I got back to the table there was a smile on my face that the others must have noticed, but they had entered into the spirit of the adventure and asked no questions. Nor did they make any objection when, after consulting a map of Portsmouth, I ordered a taxi and asked the driver to put us down at the corner of a certain street.

"Now," I said, "we shall take a little walk."

They continued to fall in with my wishes. Lomax walked beside me with Mac on a lead. Fadden followed behind.

"This town always reminds me of 'The Three Jolly Sailor Boys,'" I said. "I don't know whether you know the tune." It was running in my head at the time.

"Nothing very jolly about this quarter," remarked Lomax. "Nothing but boarding-houses. I prefer the bombed area myself. At least the sun can get in *there* sometimes."

We came to another road at right-angles. I looked up at the name.

"This is it," I said. The street was even drearier than the one we were leaving. How much better to live in Pollicott's hut than in one of a row of houses like these, in spite of the water and gas laid on! They certainly did some dreadful things in the Victorian era.

But the time had now come to deploy my forces. They awaited my orders.

"Now, Superintendent," I said, "if you don't mind, I'd like you to stay on this corner—always in your unofficial capacity, of course—for, say, about fifteen minutes. Then walk slowly along this street and take your stand opposite the house you'll see us enter—number forty-three."

"Won't that look rather obvious?" demurred Fadden.

"That's exactly what I want," I said. "I want you to look like a detective. That's all I ask of you."

Fadden laughed.

"That's easy. We're usually asked to do the exact opposite. It's a remarkable way of spending a day off. I hope you know what you're up to. Still—I'm under your orders, just for today. I'll do it."

"If you would, it would be a great help," I said. "And would you look after Mac? Lomax will relieve you of him after we've paid our call."

"What am *I* supposed to do?" said Lomax.

"Hand Mac over to Fadden and come with me. Now, Mac," I enjoined on him, "stay with the Superintendent until you're told. And no barking, mind: not a sound till you see me again."

The highly intelligent Mac wagged his short tail and lay down on the pavement beside Fadden's feet. His brown eyes watched us longingly as we moved away, and his tongue lolled out, but he did not move.

"Where are we going?" said Lomax.

"We're going to visit a certain Madame Elfrida Cann, palmiste and clairvoyante," I said.

"What on earth for?" protested Lomax.

"You, my dear fellow," I said, "are going to have your fortune told."

Lomax stopped dead.

"Oh no, I'm not! What do you take me for? I'm a farmer, not a silly woman with nothing better to do. *My* fortune's in the meteorological reports."

"Nevertheless, you are going," I said, taking his arm and moving him forward. "I've made an appointment for you to consult this excellent lady about your future." He walked on, though reluctantly at first. "Crops don't come into it," I said. "You're a trainer. You have a racing-stables. Can you remember that? I have to give you an outdoor *rôle:* you aren't pale enough for a professional man."

Lomax, beginning to grasp what was afoot, laughed loudly.

"Hush!" I admonished him. "You have a sorrow—a great sorrow. Your wife has left you and run away with another man."

Lomax laughed again.

"Ho, ho! Molly? I wish she could hear you!"

"I'm glad she can't," I said. "Now I want you to realise that you are suffering terribly about this—and you naturally want to know where your wife has gone. The eloping pair are in hiding somewhere, you understand—so you want this gifted lady to look into her crystal and tell you what she sees. Think yourself into the past, Lomax: you can leave the talking to *me.*"

"I'll be glad to," said Lomax.

"Then, at a certain point, I shall give you your signal to go. I want you to go outside, collect Mac from Fadden, come back, and wait outside the door where you can hear what I'm saying. Hold Mac in your arms and see to it he doesn't make a sound. He mustn't bark. I don't think he will if you tell him not to, but hold his muzzle if necessary. *You* are to make the only sound there is."

"Me?"

"Yes, you. Listen for your cue in what I shall say while I'm talking to this Madame Cann, and when you hear it, I want you to imitate Clipper whining. Can you do that? *Clipper*, you understand—not Mac."

Lomax would have stopped again, but I moved him forward.

"Heavens, Mr. Vaughan!" he said, "I wouldn't have come if I'd known! I'm no actor."

"Haven't I seen you once on the stage at the Women's Institute?" I said.

He groaned.

"Molly persuaded me—and I said at the time, 'Never again!' But this is much worse!"

I cut short his protestations.

"Here we are."

Outside number forty-three there was a large and dingy-looking brass-plate, bearing the words:

MADAME ELFRIDA CANN, M.I.C.P.
FIRST FLOOR.

"Member of the Institute of Clairvoyants and Palmists, I suppose," I murmured. "Now, Lomax, act up for all you're worth. The matter's dead serious for Pollicott, I assure you."

We climbed the narrow stairs—the front door was unlatched—and came to a dark door leading into the first-floor front room. A wheezy female voice from inside called "Come in!"

5

We entered. There was a mingled smell of dust, stale food, tobacco and spirits in the room which made me pause for a moment on the threshold. The light was excluded by heavy black velvet curtains, and there were similar hangings across the back of the room at right-angles to the windows. The electric light was dim. On the walls hung charts of heads and hands divided into numbered sections. Against the black hangings was a green baize table carrying a crystal, and at the table sat the prophetess.

"Madame Cann, I presume?" I said with assumed timidity, making room for Lomax also to enter. I took in her appearance with interest: she was enormously stout, with a relatively small head and sharp black eyes. But there were other details about her appearance that interested me even more...

"That's right," she said curtly. "Come in, both, and sit down." There was a pause while she studied us. "Is it you or your friend wants to consult me?" she asked me.

"Well, actually," I said, "it's my friend here—Mr.—Mr. Loam. He's had a blow—a very great blow—and I wondered if you could help him—perhaps tell him what's likely to happen—that's right, Loam, isn't it?" I prompted him.

Lomax said in a suitably earthy voice:

"'Sright."

Madame Cann said, still curtly:

"Before I begin, you've got to understand I don't tell fortunes—only people's characters."

"Of course," I said deferentially.

Madame Cann's voice developed a whine as she continued:

"Though sometimes—if it comes over me—I *may* see a little more than's in the crystal. It means going into a trance, which takes it out of me." She rolled her eyes upward: "That's a couple of guineas extra."

I whispered audibly to Lomax:

"What do you say, Loam? I think we should make the fullest use of Madame Cann's powers, don't you?"

"Sure," was all Lomax could manage to get out, and even that nearly let out his violently suppressed mirth as well.

Madame Cann whined:

"If my spirit guide comes through, *he* may say more than I could."

"I've heard you had a spirit control," I said respectfully. "That's why I've brought my poor friend. We want to hear *all* you and your control can tell us."

Madame Cann's tone changed completely.

"Right!" she said, briskly and loudly: then, after a brief wait, she gave a half-glance over her shoulder to the dark hangings behind her and shouted "Right!"

Music started, a soporific melody through which one could hear the whining of a gramophone and the scratching of the needle. Madame Cann folded her fat hands on her stomach and gently rocked a little with closed eyes.

"Yes... yes," she said with a sigh. Then she opened her eyes, keeping them fixed high up on the wall behind us. "Is that you, Red Feather? We are waiting for you. Speak—speak! What's that you say?" She gave a fat chuckle. "Now, now, we mustn't be naughty! We want to help *every*body, don't we? And here's a poor gentleman wants to know about"—she paused—"about something very dear to his heart."

Lomax whispered loudly to me:

"Ask—ask if she'll ever come back!"

"Hush, Loam!" I admonished him. "You mustn't disturb the lady. Can't you see she's in a trance?"

Lomax half rose.

"I want to know where she is now," he said violently, "and that scoundrel!"

"S-sh!" I said, pulling him down. "She'll tell you if there's anything to tell."

Madame Cann said dreamily:

"All right, Red Feather, all right. Don't hurry me! I shall come back into the past with you, but not too fast—not too fast..." In a lower, more urgent voice she went on: "Yes, there she is—a veiled figure—a woman—carrying an attaché case—leaving a house in the country. As she gets to the gate she looks over her shoulder—"

"Oh, she does, does she?" said Lomax aggressively. "And is there anybody with her, eh?"

"Quiet, Loam!" I whispered. "You *must* have patience. The lady can only tell you what her spirit control shows her." Madame Cann droned on:

"She is going towards a crowd near a big house—no—a railway station. She is alone. She is walking along the train, looking into carriage after carriage. She stops by one near the engine and gets in..."

"She's forgotten her ticket!" said Lomax anxiously.

There was a trace of irritation in Madame Cann's voice, though she still droned on:

"The train leaves. I see her arriving—at a big station. Somebody is coming towards her—a man. He raises his hat—takes her case from her—they go off together."

Lomax leapt to his feet, overturning his chair.

"The scoundrel! I'll thrash him to within an inch of his life! But where am I to find them?" He looked round wildly, and I was afraid he was so carried away by his part that he might really make a rush at the dark hangings, which did not suit my purpose—yet.

"Control yourself, Loam!" I said sternly. "Now see what you've done! She's coming out of her trance!"

Madame Cann rolled her head from side to side and groaned:

"Where am I? That's queer: I thought I was at a big railway station." She turned on Lomax viperishly: "You shouldn't have done that. You shouldn't have shouted. Don't you know it's very dangerous for me to be wakened so suddenly? It might have cost me my life."

"I'm sorry," said Lomax with mock contrition. He took a step towards her. "You said 'a big station.' Where was it, do you know? Ask Red Feather if I could catch them."

Madame Cann had had enough of Lomax.

"I don't know *what* I said," she told him bluntly. "I never know what I say when I'm in a trance, because it's not me, it's my guide speaking."

I said brightly:

"The station sounded like Paddington." The right time had now elapsed, I thought, so I continued: "You're too overwrought, Loam; you'd better go. But, Madame Cann," I said, turning to her politely, "if you can spare *me* a few minutes, I wish very much to consult you about *myself—in private*." I nodded with a meaning look at Lomax.

"All right," he said sulkily. "Shall I wait outside?"

"Yes, please do," I said.

6

Lomax went. Madam Cann said pettishly:

"I'm not sure if I feel strong enough to go on today. That friend of yours has properly upset me. I don't think I can get Red Feather back again." Her hand went to her hair, which was tied up in a head-scarf. "Red Feather hates noise," she declared. "He had too much of it when he was alive, he tells me."

I said softly:

"Oh, I don't think we shall need a spirit guide." I drew up my chair to the baize table. "If I may just sit opposite you and look into this crystal, *I* might be able to tell *you* what I see there. I too am supposed to have psychic powers."

Madame Cann was puzzled and a little suspicious.

"I don't usually let clients look into the crystal," she said. "It's a waste of time. They never see anything."

"Never mind," I said. "Perhaps I shall do better. At any rate, I'd like to try. Five guineas, shall we say?"

"Well, if you really want to," said Madame Cann bluntly. "But don't say I didn't warn you. And don't be too long. I've got another client coming."

I could see that she thought I was an elderly crackpot who must be made to pay for his follies; but she also longed for me to go. I would have to work quickly. At any moment she might decide to get rid of me. At that moment I heard a faint sound outside the door: to my relief Lomax had returned, and presumably Mac was with him.

Madame Cann also heard them. She said with a jerk of her head towards the door:

"Are you paying for him too? Three guineas."

"Yes," I said. "I'll pay you—in full." I drew up my chair closer to the table. "Can I begin?"

"If you like," she said indifferently. "We'd better have some music. It may help you." She shouted. "Right!" and the music, which had stopped during her trance, began again.

"May I bring the crystal a little nearer me?" I said, doing so. "Thank you. *I'm* not favoured as you are. *I* have no spirit guide. But I have just a little private intuition—a hunch, as our American cousins call it, I believe." I stared into the crystal and laughed quietly to myself. "Yes—yes. I *do* see something—something moving. I *can* see—yes," I went on more slowly, "it's in the country—a lonely spot near the sea." I started back. "And what's this? A little building of some sort—a wooden shack—a *hut*, I suppose you'd call it." I raised my voice. "The door opens. An old man comes out. He has a *dog* with him"—I again raised my voice—"a *whippet*. I can even hear it whining—"

From Lomax's side of the door came the sound of a dog whining, a very good imitation of Clipper. Even in my preoccupation I found time to wonder what Mac was making of this and whether Lomax was holding his muzzle.

Madame Cann broke in roughly:

"Here, you! what d'you think you're up to? Are you cracked?"

"Hush! Hush!" I said, holding up my hand. "It's dangerous to interfere with crystal-gazing, too. You know that. Let me see what there is to see." I could hear her heavy breathing and feel her impatience as I began again in a low monotonous voice: "Ah! Now the door's opening again. I can see into the hut. I can see the inside. What do I see? An elderly man, bowed over a table. He is writing—writing. What is he writing, I wonder?" I sank my voice to a whisper. "Can it be he's writing his *will?*"

Madame Cann spoke a good deal more roughly.

"Look here, if you don't stop it and get out, I'll call the police. You're making it all up. You can't see anything."

"Sssh!" I said reproachfully. I returned to the crystal.

"The old fellow—it is an old fellow, as I said—about sixty, I should say—he goes on writing. Now he's come to the signature. But he's hesitating. He looks up. He's got nobody to witness his signature. Ah!" I said loudly. "What's this I see now?" I crouched over the crystal. "Two men—two men dressed as gypsies, creeping up to the hut through the mist and the darkness... They're going in. At first the man at the table seems to expect them. Without turning round he calls to them to come in—to come closer. He signs the will. As he finishes doing so, one of the men, who has come up close behind him"—I paused—"strikes him on the back of the head with something heavy. Oh no!" I said, as if unable to bear what I saw, and covered my eyes for a moment. Then I looked again. "He falls—he falls to the floor. The other man begins searching. The man near the table looks more closely at the paper covered with writing—then he too writes something at the bottom. Then both men pick up the body—"

Madame Cann let out a shattering scream.

"He's daft!" she yelled. "For God's sake!" She screamed again. "Father! Louis! Get the police! This chap's looney! He's escaped from somewhere." She wriggled in a vain attempt to get out, but the table pinned her down in her chair.

7

The curtain parted behind her. A heavily-built man stepped into the room.

"What the devil's going on here?" he said. He advanced on me. "What do you mean by coming in here and frightening my daughter? Who *are* you, anyway?"

I had risen and retreated.

"Mr. Sebastian Rowles, I believe," I said blandly. "I'm so sorry if I've alarmed this good lady—but I can't help it if *I* have psychic powers too." I peeped past him to where Madame Cann still sat helplessly in her chair. "I was just looking into her crystal—and it was all so extraordinary what I saw there." I looked round me and upwards and said dreamily: "And now—this room: it too *is full* of spirits. Can't you see them?" I stepped back a pace and pointed. "Good gracious, there's one standing right behind your chair, Madame Cann!"

She gave a scream as she half-turned in her seat.

"Where? Where?"

Sebastian Rowles said sharply:

"Don't be a fool, Frida. This man's up to something." He stepped up to me and seized me by the coat lapels with both his powerful hands. "What's your game, eh?" He began shaking me.

I gasped out:

"Madame Cann—you must warn your father—a great danger is approaching him. That young man standing behind your chair says he's your long-lost uncle, Henry Rowles. But you wouldn't recognise him, because he died before you were born—and anyway, he's got no face! *His* face is blown away!"

"Damn you!" said Sebastian Rowles. "Shut up, will you, or I'll break your neck!"

He shook me so violently that I managed to get free. Standing with my back to the door, I said firmly in an ordinary tone:

"You'd commit a third murder, Sebastian Rowles? You can't go through life killing *all* the people who stand in your way!"

From the other side of the door there came a whining like Clipper's, and I thought I heard a suppressed bark.

"Don't you dare say that word!" said Sebastian. "It's not wise." He stood where he was, threatening but uncertain. At that moment there was a sound of someone running up the linoleum-covered stairs. The door burst open. A younger man entered, followed by Lomax with Mac under his left arm. Mac was now barking to his heart's content. Sebastian stared at him with starting eyes.

"That's not the dog!" I heard him say: then realising he had betrayed himself, he turned white. I cast a look of triumph at Lomax as the young man shouted:

"Look out, Seb! Beat it—down the back stairs! There's a dick outside in the street watching the window!"

"Louis!" screamed Madame Cann.

Sebastian strode to the window.

"Where?" he said, looking out through an opening in the curtains. "My God!" He drew the curtains together again. "It's that Superintendent Fadden!" He glared at me with head lowered like a bull about to charge. "*You* brought him here! Crystal-gazing!" He came towards me purposefully.

Lomax, still holding Mac under one arm, stopped Sebastian with a well-planted blow.

"You'd best deal with *me* first," he said.

8

Pandemonium broke out. Lomax dropped Mac and turned to deal with Louis Cann, who was about to hit him with a chair. Madame Cann screamed. Lomax hit Sebastian again, and this time sent him crashing against the table with the crystal, where Mac bit him on the leg. I picked up the crystal and threw it at the window, but by the time I got there myself and looked out Fadden had disappeared. A moment later he threw open the door.

"Now then, you fellows," he said. To me: "Are you all right?

Why the deuce are those curtains drawn?" He strode over and pulled them back with a rattle of curtain rings.

"I'm all right, Superintendent," I said, still rather short of breath, "thanks to Lomax. He's quicker with his fists than with his tongue." I pointed. "*There* are Pollicott's gypsies!"

Sebastian was still lying on the floor, with blood running from the corner of his mouth. He raised himself on one elbow, but it was his son-in-law who faced up to Fadden.

"You've got nothing on me!" He turned furiously on Rowles. "Seb, you fool, what did you want to go off the deep end for?"

Sebastian said gloomily:

"You heard what he said. He said he saw *Hal* there." His eyes were wide with fear. "And then I thought I heard that blasted whippet whining—like it did then—whining and whining—but it wasn't the whippet after all—"

"I don't know what you're talking about!" said Cann. "You're drunk!" His face, too, was white. He was the type nowadays known as a "spiv," I believe, with sleek black hair, black moustache and "sideboards." He came aggressively to me, but this time I did not retreat. I had picked up Mac, who growled and bared his small teeth, longing for another bite.

"Listen, you," said Cann, keeping his distance, "whoever you are—you can't pin anything on *me*. I've got nothing to do with it. My wife and I run an honest business here—"

Madame Cann's voice rose in a wail:

"I've got nothing to do with *anything* but spirits. I swear to you I don't know anything about anything!" She rolled her eyes up at Fadden.

"Don't explain yourself to *me*, Madam," said Fadden. "I'm just another visitor. Keep your explanations for the Portsmouth police. Mr. Vaughan will ring them up at once."

But Madame Cann was not listening. This time she really did seem to have left the world of consciousness. Lomax watched her sagging and said to me:

"The lady seems to have passed out."

"She's all right," I said unfeelingly. An idea struck me. "I wonder, Fadden," I said, "if we were to take of those ear-rings of hers? I'm sure she'll be better without them—and they'll interest Pollicott. And that yellow head-scarf with the black spots that she's wearing—shall we impound that too, for Pollicott?"

Fadden did not object. I crossed over and took the handkerchief from her head and the ear-rings from her ears.

"I think we can assume that the lady will come out of *this* trance quite safely," I said. "I wonder if it would help if someone were to hold a red feather under her nose?"

No one resisted me. Madame Cann, having fainted, was unaware of my activities, and probably would not have known their full significance. The two criminals, who certainly did, could do nothing.

VII

The Enquiry Ends

MR. VAUGHAN'S STORY CONTINUED

I

We were back again in my sitting-room: Lomax, Fadden and I. Rowles and his son-in-law were safely in custody, and Pollicott was free.

Fadden leaned against the mantelpiece, his elbow near my grandmother's clock.

"Well, Mr. Vaughan," he said, "you must be given your due. I did certainly think we had a cast-iron case against Pollicott. But you did have one advantage we didn't have—an unfair advantage, if I may say so."

"And what is that, Superintendent?" I said mildly.

"You saw the dead man's papers," he said. "I *could* get tough with you for keeping them to yourself for so long. But in view of all that's happened, I won't." He laughed magnanimously.

"Those papers," I reminded him, "refer to a legacy twenty years old—and there's a copy of a will forty years old. By all means take them away with you."

Lomax broke in.

"Poor old Pollicott!" he said. "You should have seen him when he and Clipper met. I believe he thinks as much of that dog as he did of his friend Henry, even."

"*I* think," I said with a sly glance at Fadden, "the thing that gave him the greatest satisfaction was the vindication of his story of the 'gypsies'. Do you remember, Lomax, how he used to rise every time they were mentioned?"

"Don't I!" said Lomax with a laugh. He imitated Pollicott. "'They *was* gypsies. I see'd 'em.'"

Fadden looked at Lomax in surprise and amusement. I said to him:

"You didn't know, did you, Lomax was such a good mimic? Pollicott or Clipper: it's all one to him. His wife should enlist him for the next village concert: 'Lomax and his animal impersonations.' It could be followed by Pollicott and his guitar."

"If I may ask," said Fadden, "what made you believe in that story of the gypsies, Mr. Vaughan? I must say I thought it was a tall story."

"I did too," said Lomax, "ridiculous, in fact."

"Well," I said reflectively, "the first thing I go on, naturally, is character. Pollicott so obviously isn't an accomplished liar. I don't think he's capable of that degree of invention. So when I realised that it was common knowledge that the gypsies who had been recently camping here had moved on a week or so earlier—and when Pollicott insisted that he had seen two gypsies on the night of the murder—I told myself that he must indeed have seen two men he really *mistook* for gypsies."

"Ah!" said Lomax.

"Then I found out," I went on, "that he had taken them for gypsies solely because they wore ear-rings and brightly-coloured scarves, and were apparently dark-complexioned. I couldn't help noticing, moreover, that they had gone to a lot of trouble to attract his attention, with their 'good nights' and their question about the time. And I said to myself, 'Pollicott was *meant* to mention them as his only and quite improbable alibi.' As easily as *that* these two men arranged for him to be discredited and to plant suspicion on *himself*."

Fadden stroked his chin.

"It's cunning and simple."

"It is indeed," I said. "And then, when Mrs. Lomax found that red handkerchief lying where it couldn't be missed as soon as the room was examined, I thought: 'Yes—the handkerchief's been planted too. We're meant to think that Pollicott has put it there to substantiate his unlikely story that the callers had been gypsies. Actually they were, as we now know, Sebastian Rowles and his son-in-law, Louis Cann."

"Well," said Fadden, finishing his whisky, "they're safely in the bag, and we shan't have much difficulty now in proving their guilt to twelve good men and true. I must be getting off. There's a good deal to do. Good night, Mr. Vaughan. Sorry your brief return to active service has lasted such a short while."

We shook hands and he left.

2

As his car drove away Lomax said from his corner:

"I notice you don't strain Fadden's patience too far."

I glanced at him shrewdly.

"You mean, about the identity of the murdered man? No, Lomax, I propose to leave him to find that out for himself, if it's necessary and if he can."

Lomax pulled at his pipe for a moment or two. Then he said abruptly:

"Aren't *you* convinced that this man who called himself Henry Rowles was who he claimed to be: Henry Clairvaux, ninth Lord Assche of Ashenford?"

I too reflected before speaking. Then I said:

"Yes, Lomax, I think I *am*. At any rate, I could prove it one way or the other if I chose. For instance, I could prove it if the body in the family vault were *not* that of Harry Clairvaux."

"After forty years?" said Lomax.

"Certainly. A broken shin-bone will heal, and quickly—but the broken bone will always retain the mark of the fracture. An X-ray would reveal it still—or else, would reveal its *absence*. An X-ray would also reveal it, if it exists, on the shin-bone of Pollicott's murdered friend."

Lomax blew several smoke-rings.

"It certainly opens up—possibilities," he said.

"It does, Lomax, it does," I agreed.

I took a cigar, and we smoked for a time in silence.

"And his mother?" said Lomax suddenly, expressing my own thought.

"Lady Assche?" I said. "Ah, yes. What of her? Sebastian Rowles was *her* choice as a butler also. Was it a reward for past services—since Harry Clairvaux died whilst in his charge? Well, she's gone to join poor Harry now."

"Strange that she, a delicately-bred woman, should have brought herself to go and identify those ghastly remains," said Lomax.

"Stranger still," I said, "that she didn't notice if the dead man had the hands of—a worker. Harry Clairvaux's hands must have been those of a man who had never done a day's manual work in his life."

We smoked in silence again for a while, and the room grew cloudy with the mingled smoke of his pipe and my cigar.

"But this Sebastian Rowles," said Lomax. "What reason could he have had for wanting to get rid of his younger brother—if he did?"

"Something to do with a woman, I'd surmise," I said. "Most probably the woman who patronised Hal Rowles and spoilt him and left him a legacy—that mysterious unclaimed legacy."

"Ah yes, the legacy," said Lomax, "which was the bait for the trap when Clairvaux returned."

"Exactly," I said. "Somebody must have informed Sebastian Rowles—possibly in all innocence, or perhaps he had his spies—that there was a Henry Rowles sailing on the *Kalamata Castle*. Sebastian Rowles then got those Portsmouth lawyers, Bodger and Danton, to act for him: a fact that Bodger and Danton would now prefer to forget!"

There was another pause for reflection. Then Lomax began again.

"So I suppose what started the hunt again this time was when Lord Assche got Henry's letter asking for an annuity, and forwarded a copy of it to Sebastian Rowles."

I nodded.

"Yes, of course. The Assche family have quite a way of getting other people to do their work for them without actually asking in so many words."

Another pause.

"What was the name of that woman who left the legacy?" said Lomax. "Baker, was it?"

"Yes, Mrs. Adelina Baker," I said. "Why?"

"Oh nothing," said Lomax. "But I was just wondering what happened to *her*."

"Too late to go into that now," I said. "We've got enough on our hands already."

"True, but I was just thinking she died very conveniently..."

"Your imagination's getting very active, Lomax," I said drily.

Lomax laughed.

"Perhaps we'd better stick to the present, as you say. What do you suppose those chaps were looking for in the hut—if that mess-up wasn't a fake, as Fadden thought it was?"

"I think it *was* partly a fake," I said, "and partly genuine. I think to begin with they were looking for the letters they'd written to Henry—or perhaps for any papers proving his identity. Then afterwards they turned the whole place upside down. Their object throughout was to throw suspicion on Pollicott, of course; that's why Sebastian signed the will. The police were meant to say: an obvious forgery; a faked search; a red handkerchief planted to support a concocted story of gypsies. And so they did. And so we might have done, too, if you hadn't fortunately let Pollicott give you those papers and handed them to me. If it hadn't been for those I should never have heard, through Pollicott, the strangest story that's ever come my way—and a lawyer hears some very strange stories..."

I thought how Pollicott had told me of Henry's words, that he had never been happy before in his life, and how his earliest recollection was of a conversation with his stepmother, linked up with her playing the piano.

"Poor Henry!" I said. "Poor Harry Clairvaux!"